At the HEART of CHRISTMAS

JILL MONROE

At the Heart of Christmas

Print: 978-1-947892-33-0
eBook: 978-1-947892-32-3

Hallmark PUBLISHING

www.hallmarkpublishing.com

Table of Contents

Prologue

"Quinn! Don't run up ahead too far."

His young granddaughter gave a dramatic heavy sigh and her shoulders slumped. Then, with a smile, she took several backward skipping steps until she stood closer to him.

Quinn tucked her hand into his, giving him a light squeeze. "What's that, Grandpa?"

She shot away from him once more before he could answer her question. With an indulgent chuckle, he shook his head, keeping an eye on her as she raced toward a large building. She hopped from one foot to the other, waiting for him to catch up.

This dear girl put a spring in his step.

He lightly ran his palm down the pitted and rough wood of the old scarred door. He still remembered the solemn day when his own father had shuttered the Hardwick Ornament Company for the last time. Decades later, the melancholy still lingered. His family only came out to the old farmhouse a few times a year.

Other than to do a quick checkup, rarely did anyone step inside the building where the once-thriving family business began.

Something tight unwrapped in his chest as he glanced down at his curious, mischief-making dreamer of a granddaughter. "This is the very first Hardwick Ornament Company workshop. Want to peek inside? I think I have a key."

Quinn gave him a solemn nod, as if understanding, even at seven years old, how important this old building once was to him. To them all.

He dug around in his pocket and tugged out the set of keys he carried when he inspected the old farm and works. He unlocked the padlock and flipped the hasp. He guessed the old, rusty doorknob was the original from the late 1900s. The door's lock no longer functioned, but he'd never been able to bring himself to replace the mechanism. The added padlock kept the place secure just fine.

Quinn reached up her tiny hand and clasped the knob, but it only spun around against her palm.

"There's a trick." He leaned his weight against the door and pushed slightly toward the hinges. "Now give it a try."

Quinn tried the knob again, and this time the mechanism clicked and the catch released. The ancient wood creaked as he pushed open the door.

Light streamed inside, and Quinn was brave enough to step past the entrance.

"Hello," she called.

She frowned when only a muted echo returned her call. In the silo, her voice had boomed until she'd giggled.

"This place makes me want to sneeze," she said as she twirled around.

The earthen scent of dirt and stale air tickled both their noses. "No one's been here for a long time," he explained.

Their footfalls tapped on the old fieldstone flooring as they explored inside. Sunlight streamed through the yellowed glass of a single window and dust danced in the afternoon rays. "I'll be boarding up that window again this week," he told her. He kicked a broken slat of wood out of the way. "This one didn't do its job very well."

"I can help, Grandpa. I'm good with a hammer."

He chuckled at her offer.

Nothing much remained from the old workshop. The furnace and kilns and glass blowing tools had been sold or given to retiring employees long ago. But the long table where crafters created and shaped the cooling glass endured.

"You made the Christmas ornaments here?"

Quinn's question dragged him from his thoughts. "Well, my grandfather began with making jelly jars."

"But also Christmas ornaments."

"Then he added vases and dishes."

She fisted her hands against her hips. "And Christmas ornaments?"

He laughed and tapped the end of her nose. "And

Christmas ornaments. There used to be a time when a Christmas tree wasn't a Christmas tree without a Hardwick ornament hanging from the branches." He rapped the tabletop with his knuckles. "I'd watch my dad, your great-grandpa, for hours. Blow the glass, shape and reheat and work a molten blob until it became something beautiful."

"Why don't we make Christmas ornaments anymore, Grandpa?"

He smiled down at her upturned face. "Now that's a very good question. To run a place as special as the Hardwick Ornament Company, the dream has to live inside you. I wanted to be a doctor. I'm good at treating sore throats and broken bones."

"Just like my daddy."

"Exactly." His gaze traveled the room. "Right after he was born, we shuttered this place up for good."

She slipped her hand into his again. "Don't be sad, Grandpa."

He crouched down before her, face to face. "Thank you, sweetie. Grandpa's not sad, just…wistful."

"I'm wishful too," she told him, her sweet voice earnest and solemn.

"That you are."

"Am I a dreamer, Grandpa?"

"You betcha, and what's more, you're a doer. That's the best kind of dreamer. Little Quinn, you may be the one to bring life back to this old building."

Chapter One

Quinn Hardwick fought back tears as she clutched the documents in her hands. When her grandmother had asked for Quinn's help checking on the old farmhouse, she'd never expected to be reading through paperwork. The deed to the family farmland. Another for the house. And finally, a copy of her beloved grandfather's will, listing her as the new owner of the Hardwick Ornament Company.

"I'm a travel agent. What do I know about running an ornament company?" Quinn dropped the papers on the picnic table her grandfather had built himself while she had helped with the very important task of fetching nails. She breathed deep and wished she'd brought a coat. The air was growing chillier as fall changed to winter and the sun set earlier each night.

Gram took Quinn's hand in hers, her hazel eyes warm. "That's the great thing about learning. You can always begin. When you quit is when the trouble starts."

Quinn glanced from the old mint-painted farmhouse, a color no one in the family had dared to change, to the red and white barn, and finally to the workshop she'd first explored with her grandfather when she was a little girl. "Gram, I'm not sure I can take this."

"You're the only one of your generation who's ever shown any interest in this place. Why not you?" she asked with a shrug, sending her large red and orange leaf-shaped earrings swaying. "Because you think your brother and sister will want to do it? Landon is married to the law and Emmaline is enjoying college. Maybe too much. She won't want to bear this responsibility. And don't worry about your cousins. Chloe is in Boston being the reporter she's meant to be. Alara isn't going to shack up here in Bethany Springs unless that man of hers proposes. Silas is probably on a baseball diamond even as we speak."

Quinn's gaze strayed from the dear, familiar scrawl that only a doctor could get away with, the paperwork representing her grandfather's last wish of gifting her with the Hardwick Ornament Company. His passing four weeks ago had left her devastated. After the funeral she couldn't bear to attend the reading of his will. Her heart ached at his loss, but she was also blown away that her grandfather had believed in her so much. She took a deep breath and tried to focus on anything other than the tremendous gift she'd been given.

"So you think Derrick's going to propose, too?"

The older woman wrinkled her nose and tucked a strand of her gray hair behind her ear. She picked a piece of lint off the cuff of her black and brown patchwork sweater. At some point, she'd appliqued leaves and bright red cranberries to the pullover, a staple of Gram's fall wardrobe.

"Honestly, I don't know what's taking that boy so long. She's perfect for him."

Alara might be her goofy cousin, but Gram was right. Derrick wouldn't find anyone better.

Gram cupped Quinn's cheek. "And you stop trying to change the direction of this conversation." Her grandmother's hands dropped, and she gathered the documents into a pile and stuffed them into the large manila envelope where she'd retrieved them earlier.

"It's so much easier to worry about someone else's problems than your own," Quinn pointed out.

"Don't I know it," Gram said. "I can fill an entire day with just my six grandkids alone." She tucked the envelope back into her oversized purse and tugged the strap over her shoulder. "Walk with me," she invited as she looped Quinn's arm through hers.

Quinn smiled as they walked side by side, the fallen leaves crunching beneath her boots. Even though the farm was right outside of Bethany Springs, Massachusetts, visiting here had always been a special treat, reserved for splashing in the creek in the summer and sipping hot chocolate around the fire when it grew cool. She always felt lighter here. Carefree and creative.

"I do love it here," Quinn said with a sigh as they walked along the wooden fence line, eyeing the rolling mountains of the Berkshires in the distance.

"Your grandfather wanted you to have this land and the workshop. I know you have ideas."

Quinn gave a hesitant nod. She *did* have ideas. But none she'd ever shared. Gram's eyes narrowed, and she practically vibrated with expectation. Quinn's parents had instilled pragmatism and solid skills, like typing and paying bills on time…but her grandparents? They'd gifted all their grandchildren with the permission to dream.

Quinn fought off the melancholy threatening to take over. "Seeing all this unused land and the old workshop makes me think about how much of the past we've lost. Not that I'm against progress."

"That phone that's rarely out of your hand clued me in," Gram said with a wink.

"I would like to bring back the Hardwick Ornament Company."

Gram wrapped her arms around Quinn in a tight hug. "Your grandpa would be so proud. Now tell me your plans."

Her mind raced with the many ideas she'd considered over the years when she daydreamed. "First I'll have to modernize the workshop and bring it up to code. If I sell my condo in town, I could move out here and live in the farmhouse. That should give me enough startup money."

"Good idea." Gram's face turned thoughtful as she

studied one of the outbuildings, its roof caved in and a side listing. "It's too bad the old storefront is falling down."

Quinn pointed to another building, its paint peeling, but with a far sounder foundation. "What about using one of the bunk rooms in the old Berry House? I thought maybe we could repurpose a bedroom to set up an area for memorabilia, showcasing old designs and catalogues. You still have all that stuff, right?"

Gram made a scoffing sound. "Like I'd get rid of any of that. You'd pore over those collections for hours as a kid. I had to practically drag you out of the attic to play in the backyard with your cousins."

"Not that Landon or Emmaline would ever tell you this, but our cousins could kind of be pains back in the day. Although they're pretty cool now," she said, nudging her grandmother's arm.

Gram's shoulders began to shake, and her earrings rocked back and forth as she laughed. "It would probably surprise you to learn they felt the same about you guys."

Quinn gasped. "No way. We were way too cool for them," she defended, although a small part of her suspected her Gram was right about their cousins. Those three had probably tried to ditch them as much as she and Landon and Em had tried to find the best place to hide.

"My attic is open to you any time. No one's moved anything since you've been up there. I like the idea of a mini-museum. It'll be nice for others to enjoy the history."

Quinn's thoughts ran wild, and she allowed herself to dream for a moment, as her grandpa always encouraged her to do. "Once we're up and running, we can give tours of the workshop, demonstrate the old techniques of glass blowing. Maybe even offer classes."

Gram rubbed her hands together and grinned. "Now tell me about the ornaments. You adored those as a little girl, so I know you have plans there, too."

Quinn's gaze focused on the horizon. The sinking sun set the sky ablaze with color. "That's the harder part. Lots of dreams and ideas, but I can't draw or design. Well, I can, they're just…not that great. I'll have to hire someone who can take my scattered concepts and design them into a workable glass mold."

Gram wrapped her arm around Quinn and stared at the glowing reds and yellows and oranges in the sky. Her voice lowered. "Well, between you and me, the Hardwicks always worked better in sales and planning than the artistic side of the business."

"That's what I was afraid of. No matter how many how-to videos I watch on the internet, I'm missing the creator gene." Her head dropped forward. "Where do I find a person who's an expert glass blower, *and* who's willing to relocate and design for next to nothing?"

Chapter Two

Nolan Vesser jerked awake, adrenaline rushing through his body. What was that? The loud wail pulsed with a blast of sound.

The fire alarm.

He rolled to the floor from his bed, rubbing his eyes to clear his vision. A thin layer of smoke already trailed into his bedroom. *Have to get out of here.* Nolan slid into the jeans and shirt he'd worn earlier, grabbed a discarded T-shirt off the chair near his bedroom door to cover his nose and mouth, and raced out of his apartment. He owned nothing in the place worth risking his life for.

More smoke filled the hallway, pouring from the air vents, but he felt no heat. Yet. He glanced toward the two other apartments. *Please be safe.*

What if something in his shop below had caused the fire? Had he closed the hatch? Checked the flue? His stomach pitched. He had to make sure everyone escaped before the smoke fully engulfed the floor. He pounded on the door of the Kent family. It swung open from the force of his fist and slammed against the stop.

"Hey!" he yelled into their living room, but heard nothing. With the door ajar, the family must have already fled. One more apartment to go.

He swung his fist against the last door, but this one didn't budge. "Jake! Joshua!" he called and pounded again. No answer. The two teens must be safe too. Their mom worked second shift, and the boys spent most of their evenings alone, but the two teens trusted him and would've let him in if they were inside. The smoke wasn't so thick yet that they would've been overcome, but still, he tried the handle. Locked tight. If he'd been responsible for this fire...

The smoke turned darker and more acrid. With his eyes watering, he mashed the T-shirt harder to his mouth and nose and raced down the stairwell and into the sweet night air. His shirt fell from his fingers as he braced his hands on his knees and gulped in deep, long breaths.

"Oh, thank goodness." Lucy Kent gripped his forearm and patted him on the back. She shoved a bottle of water at him. "Drink that. Grant was about to go back up since you weren't down here yet."

Nolan ignored the bottle. "The boys okay?" he asked between gasps for air.

Lucy pointed to where Grant huddled with Jake and Josh. "They're fine. Now drink." She pushed the bottle toward him to emphasize her words.

"I'm glad you got the boys out first before worrying about me. They're more important." After all, he'd been taking care of himself since the age of seventeen.

"Why are you still not drinking?" Lucy asked, intent on fretting about him anyway.

He brought the bottle to his mouth. The water soothed his aching throat, but worry still jabbed him. Was he to blame for the fire? His father had trained him to be careful. Nolan always followed a precise order of securing the furnaces and locking the kiln. Accidents happened when caution took a break, or so his father had always said. It took only one unmindful moment to set destruction in motion. Had he been careless tonight?

The roar of glass breaking and crashing to the ground forced their attention to the building that housed both his workshop and home. Flames poured out from the gaping hole where once a picturesque window had displayed the glass art he created. His muscles clenched, ready to spring into action. Everything in his studio—all his tools, his current projects, everything he'd worked for—could be gone in minutes.

Next to his studio, plumes of smoke rushed from the ground floor restaurant Lucy and Grant Kent owned. Flames licked at almost every surface inside the eatery. The fire must have originated there. The Kents stood silent, watching their livelihood burn. Where were the firefighters? The flames grew fiercer with each tick of the clock. Soon everything would burn away.

He bit back a cough. Was that the shrill cry of a siren? The faint honk of a horn sounded from an approaching fire truck and Nolan's knees almost buckled in relief. With help on the way, maybe they wouldn't lose it all.

"Biscuit!" Joshua yelled, then flung off Grant's restraining arms.

The boys had rescued Biscuit last year. They'd found her in the alley behind their apartment, filling her belly with discarded scraps from the restaurant.

Nolan blocked Joshua from flying up the steps. "You can't go up there."

"I can't leave Biscuit inside. Her barking woke us up. I thought she was right behind us." Desperation laced Joshua's voice, his gaze determined.

"Your front door was shut when I passed by," Nolan hated to say.

Now both boys made for the stairwell. "She'll be scared," Jake said, still more boy than teen, his voice heavy with fear and unshed tears.

"We can't leave her there," Josh said again, and tried to sidestep Nolan.

No. They couldn't. Nolan eyed the destruction in front of him. Flames fully engulfed the restaurant now. His workshop and storefront were in better shape, but there only appeared to be smoke in the nail salon under the boys' apartment. From the sound of the sirens, it would still be a few minutes before the fire trucks finally arrived. Minutes Biscuit might not have. If Nolan hurried, she might just make it.

"I'll go." Nolan retrieved the shirt from where he'd tossed it on the ground. He poured what remained of his water on the cloth.

"Nolan, you can't go up there," Grant said. "You're still coughing. I'll go."

"You got a wife who loves you to think about."

Lucy gasped.

"Don't worry," he assured her. "I won't do anything stupid." *Too stupid.* He turned to the anxious boys. "Your door was locked earlier."

"I have a key," Josh said, digging it out of his front pocket.

"Thank you, Nolan." Jake's whisper was frightened, his eyes straying over and over to his bedroom window. "She'll probably be under the bed. That's where she goes when she's scared."

With a nod, Nolan raced back to the stairwell that led to the apartments, took a deep breath, then climbed the stairs two at a time. The smoke lay heavy and thicker in the hallway than before, but the kids' apartment was the first one near the stairs, so he could still see. He checked the door and knob for heat as he'd been taught in some long-ago safety lecture. Satisfied, he fumbled for a moment with the lock, then the door swung open. The air in the living room wasn't as smoky and he released the breath he'd been holding, and then drew in several deep breaths through the wet T-shirt. "Biscuit," he called, but he doubted the dog would be able to hear him over the blaring of the fire alarm.

Nolan rushed to the boys' room and crouched on all fours to search under the bunk beds. Biscuit's dark eyes met his, and her little brown body shook in fear. For a moment, Nolan wondered if the frightened dog would slink against the wall.

"It's okay, Biscuit," he said, his voice soothing despite the smoke drying his throat. He moved the T-shirt to the side of his face in hopes the dog would recognize him.

Biscuit scrambled out from under the bed and launched herself against Nolan's chest. "Good girl." The lights flickered overhead. Once. Twice. Then went out completely. "Let's go."

Nolan tucked Biscuit's squirmy body under his arm and headed for the exit. He made it outside the same moment the firefighters poured out of their red truck. Jake and Joshua caught up to him, and Biscuit leaped toward the boys. *Ingrate.*

Deep, racking coughs attacked him, and he had to brace his hands against his knees.

"Biscuit's not breathing right," Joshua's panicked voice called to the firefighters as they rushed to extinguish the flames. "Please, you gotta save her. If she hadn't barked—"

"Bring her over here," a paramedic said. "We have breathing masks perfect for pups just like this one."

A different paramedic drew Nolan near the

ambulance that had arrived right after the fire truck. "I'm all right," Nolan said.

She shoved a mask against his face. "You let me be the judge of that."

Nolan dragged in a deep breath only to wind up pushing the mask away to cough.

"See? So you saved that dog, huh?" the paramedic asked, popping the mask over his nose and mouth again, so Nolan could only nod.

"That was pretty brave. And dumb."

Nolan couldn't help but chuckle. Brave and dumb, yeah, that described him.

The brutal inferno continued to destroy. The families could only stare as the support beams of what used to be their homes and businesses cracked and buckled. The sizzle and pop of water connecting with flame hissed in the air as the firefighters battled the fire.

"You've got quite a few burns on your arms. They're superficial, but one of the docs at the hospital needs to look you over."

"They don't hurt," he told the paramedic even though the mask distorted his words. Nolan scrutinized the wound like it belonged to someone else.

"That's the adrenaline, buddy. In a couple of hours, you'll be thanking yourself for taking my advice."

"Nolan. Hey, Nolan."

His sister Kaylee's voice sounded worn and far

away. And that's the way he wanted it. He settled deeper into his pillow.

"It's time to wake up." Kaylee grew more insistent, and he knew from experience he'd be waking up whether he wanted to or not, so he might as well follow through on her demands.

"Hey, sis." Nolan blinked and fought against the sleep fog. His drained body had finally succumbed to a deep unconsciousness once his sister brought him to her apartment.

After the paramedics had patched him up, he'd spent eight long hours in the emergency room. The ER doc worried about the burn on Nolan's arm and had insisted on an overnight stay as a precaution. Nolan had a fitful night's sleep on the bustling hospital floor.

Of course, waking up to the very anxious face of his sister beat a fire alarm, but he hated to see the apprehension in her blue eyes. The color always reminded him of the waters of the Pacific; sometimes a peaceful blue, other times a chaotic gray. Right now they were a murky slate, tinted by worry. *Power through the pain.* He was supposed to take care of her. *Power through the pain.*

"Good afternoon, evening, and now back to morning, sleepyhead. The doctor said you'd sleep, but it's been over sixteen hours."

"Hard to believe. Your couch is so lumpy," he croaked. His throat felt like the desert. Nolan rubbed his eyes and swung his legs to the hardwood floor. It still felt weird to breathe, so he kept his inhalations shallow. The morning sun shone brightly through the large window that had sold Kaylee on this one-bedroom apartment after she graduated college. That, and the easy access to stores and restaurants in the bustling neighborhood not far from Old Pasadena.

Kaylee's lips twisted. "I did offer you the bed. After all, you're a hero."

Nolan stretched to his full six feet and headed in the direction of his sister's small kitchen. He needed water, whatever meds Kaylee would force on him to ease the sting of the burn on his arm, and then another few hours of sleep.

"I'm no hero," he said, lifting a glass from the wooden drying rack sitting on the tile-covered countertop near the sink.

"Not according to the paper." Kaylee barely hid her smile. She held up the local newspaper.

Centered above the fold was his soot-streaked face. He cradled a squirming Biscuit against his chest, surrounded by smoke and flames. As an artist, Nolan could appreciate the work of the photographer. In all the commotion, he'd never noticed media, just two frightened boys anxious about their dog. The person who'd snapped the picture had managed to capture a moment of danger and raw emotion… Too bad it was *his* raw emotion. Worry, pain and primal terror were etched in the lines of his face. If he closed his eyes, Nolan knew he'd hear the whoosh of the fire sucking the oxygen from the building to feed the flames.

Don't close your eyes.

"Local Artist Saves Furry Friend," Kaylee read the headline out loud. "You hungry?" she asked, striding toward the ancient gas range.

"Still doesn't make me a hero," he said, using his left hand to twist the faucet to fill the glass. Doc wanted him to lay off straining his right side for a day or two. "I don't think I can eat yet."

"Rescuing a dog definitely ranks in hero territory. Don't give another thought about that article. Most of it is about Biscuit."

He lifted a brow.

"Sorry, dude, dog's cuter than you are." Her smile faded, and she gripped his fingers. "I could have lost you."

His instinct was to say something flippant, like then she'd inherit all he had left, which, sorry, was nothing. There'd only been the two of them since a car accident took their parents a few days before he'd turned eighteen. Kaylee had been only fourteen, but they'd somehow made it work by not dwelling too much on the past or worrying about the future.

Day by day.

Lines creased Kaylee's forehead, and her eyes brightened with tears. Somehow the emotion made the scattered freckles across her nose and cheeks stand out. Now wasn't the time to be glib. He gave her hand a squeeze and tucked a strand of her curly golden hair behind her ear. "But you didn't."

She gave him a tight nod and blinked back her tears. Neither one of them needed long explanations or drawn out reflections of their feelings. When it came to emotion, lock and contain proved more their style.

"The investigator at the fire department called while you slept. He cautions that his findings are preliminary, but it appears the fire started due to some faulty wiring in the restaurant's kitchen. A problem long before you ever signed a lease."

Nolan's shoulders sagged. "That's a relief."

"Were you afraid you'd caused the fire? That's so like you, even with a restaurant and a nail shop filled with chemicals on the bottom floor. Besides, you're a nitpick about safety."

"From years of Dad's warnings–"

"Accidents happen when caution takes a break," they both said together.

"It's nice to know I'm not responsible for bringing the building down. The furnace fires up at over two thousand degrees, so the concern is always there." His breath came out in a heavy sigh. "Never saw the downside of living over the place I worked until now."

Kaylee reached for a sack. "I'd put these away to give to you for Christmas, but I figured you'll need them now."

Nolan tugged out a pair of jeans and a flannel shirt. "Thanks, Kaylee. I'm ready to get out of these smoky clothes."

"I should have brought these up to you at the hospital so you could change into something new when they finally let you out of that gown." Kaylee sucked in her bottom lip. "All I could think about was getting up to the emergency room to see you. They didn't tell me anything over the phone."

He gave her shoulder a gentle squeeze. "Don't give it another thought. Is there any point in going back to my apartment?"

Kaylee shook her head. "It's all gone."

She would have said more, but he quickly nodded. He knew what she'd say next. How sorry she felt. His workshop. His art. His home. Things could be replaced, of course, but he'd lost more than a couch or kitchen table. Every picture and memento was now reduced to little more than ash. He'd never been a sentimental guy, yet it hurt to think that other than the few things Kaylee had kept, every last remnant of his parents no longer existed. In less than an hour, the flames had destroyed everything he'd ever built.

But he and the boys, Biscuit, and the Kents were alive. He could start over. It wasn't like he hadn't done it once before.

"I want you to have this." Kaylee tugged a thin gold chain from her pocket. A simple gold wedding band acted as a pendant.

He shook his head, already pushing the necklace toward her with his left hand. "That's Dad's wedding ring. I wanted you to have that."

"I still have Mom's." Kaylee crossed her arms against her chest. "I won't take no for an answer."

After three years of law school, Kaylee knew how to win any debate. No sense trying to talk her out of her plan, and besides, with nothing left, it would be nice to have something of his dad's. Nolan answered with a nod, and she reached up to slide the chain around his neck, the weight of their father's band heavy against his chest.

"And also, your Jeep's okay," she told him with forced perkiness.

Nolan couldn't help but chuckle. "There's a start. Now I just need to find a place to live, somewhere to set up shop and the money to buy a kiln and a furnace and–"

His sister lifted her hands. "First things first. We're off to the bank. Well, a shower for you first, and then the bank. Unfortunately, you have a lot of paperwork to file. If you're up to it."

"I am. I'd rather be doing something with my arm in a bandage than cooped up with my arm in a bandage," he told her, keeping his voice light.

She brushed her hands together. "Since you took my now incredibly high-priced legal advice, you've saved yourself the time of searching for all your important documents by storing them in the safety deposit box."

"Can't wait," Nolan replied.

An hour later, Nolan and his sister walked along Colorado Boulevard in Old Pasadena. The differing types of architecture always caught his eye. His mom and dad would've loved to see how the historic district had revitalized; it now bustled with people and restaurants and businesses. Their bank was housed in a Spanish Revival building, lovingly preserved. Even in his surly teen years, Nolan had always tagged along with his mom to this place. Something about the red-tiled roof and the carved stone frieze made him itch to create and leave something generations in the future would still enjoy.

Can't create when you have nothing.

Nolan tamped down the feelings of defeat trying to batter him. He could rebuild; things were replaceable.

Most things. Losing his book of design drawings had been a punch in the gut. And, more importantly, his dad's design book, now nothing but ash. He'd never again flip through his father's sketches and diagrams for inspiration. Or just because the action made him closer to the father he'd lost at seventeen.

"When does it rain inside a bank?" Kaylee asked as they stepped inside, her heels tapping on the tile floor.

"What?" he asked, his voice echoing around the high ceiling.

"I asked, when does it rain inside a bank? Wait for it… When there's change in the weather."

Nolan groaned and shook his head, but smiled. His sister could always be counted on for a bad joke to lighten the mood.

Kaylee would have to keep the jokes coming, then. Right now, he owned two changes of clothes, a Jeep not of this decade, and his sense of humor. See? He hadn't lost it all.

"How can I help you?" the receptionist asked.

"We need to get into our safety deposit box," he said.

The woman wiggled her mouse to wake up the computer. "Okay, I'll need your box number and a form of ID."

"128," Nolan said, reaching for his wallet. Lucky for him, he'd left the billfold in his jeans the night before. If he hadn't, a trip to the DMV and several calls to his credit card company would be on his to-do list, too.

"Oh, this is one of our older accounts," she said peering at the screen.

"It was our parents'," Kaylee informed her.

"Ah. Okay, I'll need you to sign on the screenpad." After comparing his signature to the one on his ID, she grabbed a round ring of keys and stood. "Follow me."

Kaylee chatted with the receptionist as she ushered them to the vault where the metal safety deposit boxes lined the walls in rows. The sound in the small room was muted and industrial and lacked the warmth of the rest of the bank. Nolan rarely spent much time inside the cage when he visited. Usually he'd toss the latest documents on top of the pile and return the box to the safe.

He slid his key into the lock and after their escort inserted hers, the box popped open. "There's a table for your use. I'll step outside to give you some privacy."

Kaylee took over, tugging the box out and placing it on the table so he'd avoid using his arm. "Oh no, it's worse in here than I thought. You have an apartment lease in here from seven years ago. That's like three apartments ago."

"Where should I keep it?"

"The shredder. Okay, found your renter's insurance paperwork. Since we're here, I'm going to sort through this mess. Why are you keeping the mortgage to mom and dad's old house?" she asked.

Nolan shrugged. "It must be from when they put it in the box."

"Okay. Hmm, what's this?"

His sister held a manila folder, aged and worn on the edges. He slid his finger under the edge of the flap. The glue was practically an antique and quickly gave way. He tugged out several pages printed on heavy bond paper. "Must be important. It's been notarized."

Kaylee ran her finger down the side as she scanned the forms. "This looks like some kind of a deed." Then she gasped.

"What?" he asked.

She pointed to a line of typewritten text. "Apparently you're the proud owner of the Hardwick Ornament Company."

"That place Granddad worked? And wouldn't that be *we* own a company?" He made a scoffing noise. "A lot of good the deed will do us. That company hasn't been around since before we were born."

"Still, it's probably something I should check out." She slid the papers back into the folder and then stuffed it and his insurance paperwork into her purse. "This is all we need. Ready to go?"

"Thought you wanted to sort through the rest of the box," he reminded her.

"Not when I have cool mysterious paperwork to research," she said, patting the side of her bag. "C'mon. One of those sidewalk bistros is calling my name."

Minutes later they were strolling along the tree-lined sidewalk. "What do you remember of those stories Dad told about the Hardwick Ornament Company?" Kaylee asked.

Nolan shook his head, careful to avoid brushing his injured arm against the wall of a building. "Not much. I know it's somewhere in New England, uh, Massachusetts maybe. Two generations of Vessers were the principal glass blowers for the company, but our grandparents moved out here before Dad was even born."

"Yeah, I remember him saying something about the business closing down in the Sixties, so I guess that's why no one ever did anything with the deed. Still, it's weird. Why would we even own a part of it? It was a family company. The Hardwicks'."

"I have no idea."

"Maybe due to a gambling debt. Or a secret romance, or–"

"It certainly wasn't for money," he said.

Kaylee laughed. "That's true. Oh, this is the place."

They paused in front of a host stand outside the restaurant. Wooden tables and chairs shaded by colorful umbrellas lined the sidewalk. Boxed planters filled with flowers added a fragrant scent. He breathed in the delicious savory smells of Italian food, and his mouth began to water. The last time he'd eaten was off some unappetizing plate in the hospital.

The greeter seated them quickly, and Nolan stretched his long legs under the table. The light breeze felt good on his face, and he closed his eyes. His sister had the right idea about this outdoor café. The sun on his face and good food on the way eased him somehow.

"You look like you're feeling better."

"I am," he said with a smile toward his sister.

"I knew it. Must have been the bank joke," she said with a wink.

"I think it was seeing that old deed."

Surprise flickered in the blue-gray of her eyes. "Really? The more I think about it, I realize it's probably nothing. Dad never did anything with it."

"No, it's not that. It made me realize businesses come and go. A long time ago, the Hardwick Ornament Company meant everything to our family, and now it's only a memory. But the Hardwicks and Vessers are still around. I keep telling myself that things can be replaced, but I don't think I really meant it until I saw that deed."

She gave his hand a squeeze. "That *and* the corny bank jokes."

"Absolutely."

The waiter brought them water, so Nolan could take his pain pill, and then took their order. Afterwards Kaylee tapped something into her phone. "Whoa, look at this." She whipped her phone in his direction so he could see the website she'd pulled up on the screen. "'The Hardwick Ornament Company Coming Soon.' I just wanted to see some pictures of the old place, and this popped up."

"Wow. We...we own a company," he said, dropping his injured arm onto the table and wincing. Nolan scrubbed a hand down his face. With his aching arm, losing his livelihood, and finding a deed to a whole new life, he fully felt the weight of the last forty-eight hours.

She crossed her arms against her chest. "Correction. *You* own a company. After putting me through college and law school, it's only right this one is all yours."

"But what exactly do we own? The brand name? A percentage of the profits of any future company? The property?"

Kaylee's brows drew together. "I'm not really sure. Real estate law isn't my specialty, so I'll have to do some research. Check out the notary. It's over seventy years old. I bet nothing will be on any kind of online database. This will take some time. You should drive out there and check it out."

"So, what, I show up and say, 'Hey, I'm the new boss.' That should go over well with the wealthy Hardwicks. What do I know about running an ornament company?"

"After taking over Dad's glass blowing business and making it something special and unique, I think you know plenty about how to run a company," Kaylee said, her smile encouraging.

Nolan shrugged. "That's different. We grew up in his workshop." Still, the idea intrigued him. What would it be like to run a company? He'd operated his business as a one-man shop, but the Hardwick Ornament Company used to mass-produce their creations. If he followed the original formula, the new company would be a much bigger operation than his studio, with employees and automation and distribution. Challenging, yes, but it could also be very rewarding. Not to mention lucrative. He'd done well with Vesser GlassArts—put a roof over both their heads and Kaylee through college—but owning something like the Hardwick Ornament Company held so much more potential for him financially. He could finally replace the Jeep and help Kaylee set up her law practice.

"Go there and check it out. If you don't like it, you can always sell them your ownership of the business. It shouldn't be hard for the Hardwicks to buy you out. Since you were seventeen, you've been stuck taking care of me." She rubbed the back of his hand, careful not to disturb the bandage further up his arm. "You did that. It's official, I can take care of myself. You took over the family business to support us, but you never got the chance to be carefree or figure out what you want to do. Now you can. Get out there. Explore. Maybe the Hardwick Ornament Company isn't the right option, but selling it will give you the money to figure out what is. How many times in life do you get to start all over?"

Chapter Three

Outside Gram's house, Quinn shifted her weight from her left foot to her right, not-so-patiently waiting to share her good news. Thankfully, the large overhanging roof protected her from the falling snow. Before she had to ring the bell a second time, she spotted Gram through the large picture window.

"Come in, come in," Gram greeted her with a widening smile. Today's earrings were tiny pinecones that appeared to be made of oxidized brass. "I just put the kettle on for tea."

Quinn stomped the snow off her shoes and followed her grandmother inside her 1930s Colonial Revival home. "I thought Dad bought you one of those instant hot water machines," she said, unwinding her scarf and shaking out of her coat.

Gram wrinkled her nose. "He did, and I use it for coffee, but I like the whistle of the kettle. Doesn't feel like tea without it."

There was no arguing with that logic, and really,

Quinn preferred the whistle over the gurgle of the machine herself. Besides, no one in the family had ever won an argument against Gram. They went into the kitchen and Quinn sighed with pleasure. No place on earth stood as cozy as Gram's sweet yellow kitchen. Here, Quinn had learned to roll out dough for gingerbread cookies, how to sew on a button that wouldn't come off, and how to snap the ends off green beans. They'd also shared mugs and mugs of tea.

Gram scanned the canisters on her cabinet. A few years ago, she'd ditched the hammered copper set she'd used since her wedding for ones she'd made in a pottery class at the senior center. A bit misshapen, but Quinn adored how Gram had finished them off with a pale blue glaze. "Chamomile or the hard stuff?"

Quinn's lips twisted. "What's the hard stuff?"

"Ginseng."

"Then bring it on," she said with a laugh.

Gram spooned the dried herbs into the strainer and then motioned for Quinn to sit at the table. "I can tell you're just about bustin' at the seams to tell me something."

Even though Gram had lived in New England most of her life, she'd been born in Texas, and every now and then a word like *bustin'* came through. One of the million and ten reasons Quinn loved her grandmother so much.

"Did the bank approve your business loan application?" Gram asked.

"Not yet, but I'm sure they will after they hear

about this. Guess who contacted me about the possibility of a job in the future ornament workshop?" She held up her hand. "Never mind, don't even try to guess, 'cause you never will, and I can't wait to tell you. Nolan Vesser."

Gram's gray brows lifted. "Vesser, as in former designers for the Hardwick Ornament Company? That kind of Vesser?"

"Yes. He's Milos's great-great-grandson. And get this—he designs and blows glass. I looked up his stuff online, and he's amazing. He does these beautiful installations for museums and libraries."

"It's a shame we didn't keep in contact with the Vessers after the company closed down. It will be nice to meet him. Our families used to be so close. Hardwicks and Vessers worked side by side for two generations. I know the third hoped to make a go of it, but…"

"Well, here's our chance, because he's on his way. It's actually kind of sad. A fire destroyed his workshop and where he lived all on the same night, so I think he's about as excited to help with HOC as I am to have him here. I could even offer him the use of the workshop once I've ordered the furnace and kiln. He'd mentioned orders he won't be able to complete due to the fire. If he gets used to it here, maybe he'll want to stay and make a go of the HOC with me."

"When a door closes…"

"Exactly. And it's all thanks to your website." Gram had been playing around with website design in a computer class she took at the senior center. She'd gotten a kick out of putting what she'd learned in class into practice on the web.

"It's just the basics," Gram said, with a wave of her hand.

"That's all I needed. We talked today for over an hour. He suffered some smoke inhalation and a second degree burn on a small part of his arm."

Gram's hand fluttered to her throat. "That's terrible."

"I know, but he assured me he felt fine. I asked Dad about it, and he said the burns should heal completely in about two to three weeks. Since Nolan has this forced time off, he's going to take this chance to visit the workshop where his family once worked. Kind of have a look around and talk business. He's never designed ornaments, but once he creates one… I'm going to do everything I can to convince him to stay. With his name attached to the company, things could really happen. Finally." Quinn didn't want to say more, as if voicing her hopes out loud might dash them before they'd even begun to find roots. Better to not get too excited only to be disappointed.

Gram laughed and gave her hand a squeeze. "It's good to see you dream again. My little pragmatic Quinn."

"Well, it was *very* pragmatic to ask the man if he wanted to design for me," she said, running her finger along the handle of her tea mug. "He doesn't have a job. I happen to need a designer. He doesn't have a place to live. With the Berry House, there's a whole empty bunkhouse on the farm. He's spending Thanksgiving with his sister, and then driving out here from California the Monday after."

Gram tilted her head. "Sounds like you're trying to convince yourself. You know, one way you could get the ball rolling is legally accepting your inheritance. Landon's just waiting for you in that law office of his."

"He's so busy getting established in that new office, I sincerely doubt he's waiting on me, but I'll get on it soon. I promise." Quinn tried to shake the jitters from her hands, but her nerves refused to go away. She felt like anxiety had grafted to her bones. She pushed away from the table and began to pace around the kitchen. "Oh, Gram, I'm so nervous. What if when he arrives, he looks around and gets right back in his car? Not that I would blame him, because he's a world-famous designer, and I'm just a ramshackle–"

"Enough. You're Quinn Hardwick, and you're making something special. If he runs away to his car, then you kick the bumper to help him on his way."

Quinn laughed at the image. Gram for sure would be chasing after the man's taillights, her earrings swinging.

Gram patted the seat beside her and Quinn sunk down on the chair.

"Have you ever thought he'll take one look around and be intrigued by the challenge? You always invent problems where there aren't any," she said, smoothing away a lock of Quinn's brown hair from her cheek.

"It's called being prepared for anything."

"No, it's called borrowing trouble," Gram corrected. "To borrow worry is to own doubt. The best way to chase away doubt is to be excited. So this calls for a toast."

"A toast? With our tea?"

"We toast with anything nearby." Gram held up her mug. "To the Hardwick Ornament Company. First steps."

Quinn clinked her tea mug against Gram's. "To the Hardwick Ornament Company."

Quinn brushed Lulubelle's flank with a brush. The horse sidestepped the attention, turning the nightly routine into her horsey version of a game. "You're supposed to be docile, you know."

The vet assured her the older horses, Lulubelle and her sister Maribelle, loved nothing better than eating their oats, getting brushed and looking picturesque. That was why she'd agreed to adopt them a year earlier than her plan called for. The grand ladies had grown a little too old for the daily carriage rides downtown, but the vet believed the pair would be perfect for the occasional evening hayrides and horse-drawn sleigh rides she hoped to hold at the Hardwick farm.

"Horses need a purpose," he'd assured when she'd asked if the pair would rather enjoy their well-earned retirement.

It seemed that Lulubelle's purpose was to thwart

Quinn whenever she could. The horse had already discovered two escape points in the fence. With a sigh, Quinn put the brush away. "Even though it's the weekend and we like to get a little wild around here, you've probably already had enough. I'll get you two a little more hay and then it's night-night."

She'd grown into the habit of talking to the girls in the two months she'd lived out here alone. "Oh, look, ladies. It's snowing. I hope that doesn't slow down our guest."

Nolan Vesser had left California on Monday, stopping at motels along the way when he grew tired of the drive, so neither of them knew when he'd actually arrive. She kind of envied him the adventure of it. Still, with it now being Friday, he shouldn't be too much longer, and she'd stocked the Berry House with milk and eggs. "I hope he doesn't arrive too late to use them, or I'll be forced to make a breakfast casserole out of the supplies."

Large flakes floated in the late afternoon sun. With a whinny, Lulubelle took off at a trot to prance around in the yard as the snow fell on her face. "That will teach me to not shut the barn door," Quinn said to Maribelle. The other horse looked like she was laughing at her. With a sigh, Quinn secured the stall and took off after Lulubelle.

She whistled. "C'mon, girl."

The roar of an engine startled them both and Lulubelle broke free in a run.

"It's only a Jeep," she called in some vain attempt to

lure the horse back. Quinn didn't often have visitors to the farm. Probably someone who got turned around.

With a heavy sigh, Quinn followed after the horse. "You're not fooling anyone, horse. I know you're using that noise as an excuse to run." But the boots she used for her chores around the barn weren't the best for snow, and she found herself sliding, only managing to stop herself from landing backside down in the snow by grabbing onto the front bumper of the stranger's Jeep.

A whicker followed her antics and Quinn knew Lulubelle delighted in laughing at her, too.

The driver of the Jeep rolled down his window and stuck out his head. The man wore his sandy blond hair short, with streaks that came from the sun. With his tan at the end of November, this guy definitely came from warmer climes. His brown eyes were tired but filled with humor.

"What are you doing?" he asked, in a smooth baritone.

"I'm, uh…" Admit it? Might as well. "I'm chasing after my horse."

"Didn't realize horses played chase. Does it fetch too?"

"Just trouble." She rubbed the muddy snow off her jeans and straightened. Using his bumper as a brace, she worked her way to the window to give the directions this lost driver needed so she could be alone with her embarrassment. "How can I help you?"

"I'm Nolan Vesser."

"Of course you are," she said dryly. She'd hoped to be impressive when they'd first met, not looking like someone barely holding her dreams together. Why couldn't this guy be asking directions into town or something and she could be mud-free when she met Nolan? Her eyes narrowed as she glanced his way. "I wasn't expecting—"

He lifted a brow, his expression full of curious interest. "What?"

Someone so handsome. So sunny. So… "Young. I wasn't expecting someone so young."

"Yeah, we're probably about the same age."

Last year in the twenties. She plastered the brightest smile she could manage on her face. "Welcome to the Hardwick Ornament Company. I'm Quinn Hardwick." Why hadn't he put his picture on his website? Probably because no one would look at the art, only him.

Nolan's smile faded and the warmth in his eyes dimmed. Had she done something wrong? His back stiffened ramrod straight. Was his reaction because she'd riled him or just a stretch because he'd driven cross-country in only a few days to arrive in Bethany Springs?

She pointed to the building near the workshop. "I've made a room for you in the Berry House."

"Berry House?" he asked, his tone wary.

"It's where we used to wash and prepare the cranberries after harvest." Like the rest of the farm, the Berry House hadn't been in use for years. Now, seeing the beloved red clapboard building through a stranger's eyes, Quinn spotted its flaws. The combination fruit storage and bunkhouse had certainly seen better days. The peeling white paint on the corner boards remained a bit of an eyesore, she'd admit, but the steps to the porch were solid, only sagging a bit. She should offer to set him up in the Bed and Breakfast in Bethany Springs. But with what money?

Lulubelle's whinny drew their attention and Quinn sighed. "I'll be back after I convince her to go back into the barn."

"Will that take a while?"

"I have a secret weapon. I don't like to bring it out, 'cause it seems like I'm rewarding naughty behavior, but I'm ready to get out of the snow." Quinn dug around inside her coat pocket until her fingers wrapped around the object no horse would turn down. "She can't resist carrots."

Quinn veered away from Nolan's vehicle and traipsed through the snow toward Lulubelle. Not the kind of first impression Quinn had wanted to make, boots caked in muddy snow and chasing after a mischievous horse. She extended the carrot in Lulubelle's direction. "C'mon, girl. Help me out here. We're both cold and there's no way I'm going to convince Mr. Dreamy Glass Blower over there to work here for questionable room and board if I look so incompetent."

"Need some help?" he called.

Her breath hitched at the sound of his raspy voice. Had Nolan heard her describe him as dreamy? She swallowed the nervous lump in her throat and opted for a breezy tone. "Oh, no. We're fine here. Feel free to get settled inside."

"Where would you like me to park?" he asked. Snow crunched under his footsteps as he approached.

Quinn squeezed her eyes tight for a moment. *Grrrrr.* Lulubelle's nose twitched as Nolan neared. Yeah, he did smell kind of nice. Like sunshine, fresh and warm and kind of welcome during these cold days of fall turning to winter.

Nope. Stop right there. The sun has no smell.

"Don't you want to be in your nice, dry barn?" His voice resonated low and soothing, and darn if that horse didn't take a step toward him. The man hadn't even offered up the carrot. "There you go. Keep going."

She watched as Nolan pivoted and aimed toward the red barn, without waiting to see if the horse followed. Lulubelle trotted past her, not even bothering to sniff out the carrot Quinn still held in her hand. She blinked back her astonishment.

The barn matched the construction of the Berry House, but she'd managed to get the red clapboard painted before it had gotten too cold. She hadn't yet had a chance to touch up the white trim of the corner boards and fascia, but a few summers ago, her grandparents had replaced the gambrel roof, a nod to the Dutch influence in the area. The horse's hooves clicked on the fieldstone foundation.

"Last stall," she called, closing the large barn doors against the frigid winter air. Maribelle whickered to her sister like the two horses shared some kind of joke. Quinn had half a mind to shove the carrot back into her pocket. Instead she broke it in two, giving the larger piece to the horse who hadn't made her take off at a run.

After the horses were secured, Quinn flicked off the lights. "Thanks for your help. I'm sure you're ready to relax after all that driving. How long did it take you?"

"About four days." He flashed her a rueful grin, and a tiny flutter tingled in her stomach. "Got to visit a few states I'd never seen before, but now I feel like I could sleep for hours."

"I'll give you the full tour of the place tomorrow, then. Your workshop is to the north." She paused. "Oh, sorry, I'm getting ahead of myself. I guess it's still just *the* workshop. I know you haven't officially agreed to design yet."

"One building housed the whole Hardwick Ornament Company?" he asked, his interest more clinical than friendly.

She shook her head. "Only at first. Glass blowing used to be a practical chore for life on a farm. Milk bottles, jars for the cranberry jams and jellies, that kind of stuff. Once they went into full production, they had a factory in town. But this is where it began, and where they always designed. It seems fitting that we restart it right here."

They stomped the snow from their shoes before stepping onto the porch of the Berry House. The old boards creaked a little under their weight. "I promise you it's sturdy." Although replacing the steps would definitely be a summer project. She unlocked the former bunkhouse, and then paused so both of them could slip off their shoes in the mudroom. "Here," she said, handing him a key.

She flipped on the lights, revealing a large central room now fully swept and dusted and scented with pine cleaner. With money tight, she'd only been able to furnish it with a secondhand couch, kitchen table and a few chairs, but each piece was solid and comfortable. A bunkhouse kitchen with fridge, oven and stove, and a long countertop waited in the corner. She had added several colorful magnets with a few emergency numbers, the one place in Bethany Springs that delivered pizza all the way out to the farm, and the location of the fuse box.

"I'll start a fire if you want to get the rest of your stuff," she said.

Nolan tossed his duffel bag at the end of the couch. "That's it."

"I can show you the way into town when you're ready," she offered, eyeing his one lonely bag. She crouched in front of the fireplace and added a bit of kindling to the top of the logs already on the grate.

"Don't worry about a fire," he said, his voice tight.

She glanced up at him, confused. "You sure? There's no central heat in this place. This is the only way you'll get warm. Oh, but there's a space heater in your bedroom."

Nolan shuddered. "I've had enough fire and flames for a while. No worries, I'll be all right."

"I'll bring by a few extra blankets if you need them." She dusted off her hands and stood, sensing he wasn't the kind of guy who'd want to dwell or make a fuss about his problems.

Oh, I'd almost forgotten. Quinn stooped again and plugged in the string of twinkle lights she'd strung along the carved wooden mantle.

"Nice touch. Kind of gives it a dreamy quality," he said in a way that made her wonder if he'd turn them off the moment she left.

Her head jerked in his direction. *Dreamy?* He *had* heard her, hadn't he? To hide her embarrassment, she crossed to the corner where she'd assembled a rickety fake tree probably older than the both of them. Combined. "I also found this up in the loft."

"That tree has definitely seen…" his words trailed off.

"Better days, I know. But I thought it could help with inspiration."

He reached out and touched one of the needles. "I can't remember the last time I had a Christmas tree."

"Don't let my grandmother hear you say that. You'll leave here with a truck full of lights and tinsel and ornaments. She may even rope you into making something out of your handprint. Think tempera paint, watered-down glue and glitter."

He chuckled. "Your family big on Christmas, then?"

Now it became her turn to laugh. "At the Hardwick

Ornament Company, Christmas doesn't just come once a year. It's a way of life."

His forehead scrunched. "But the ornament company hasn't been around for decades."

"But traditions stick around. When you got a pint of milk, like in your school cafeteria, what was the first thing you did?"

He blinked as he thought about her question. "I don't know, open it?"

"No. Most people shake the carton. Have you and I ever lived in a time where we didn't have homogenized milk? Have our parents?"

His gaze turned interested. Thoughtful. "Huh. I guess not."

"But we shake the carton, because our parents shook their carton, because their parents and grandparents had to shake theirs. That's how traditions are. They live on, even if we don't know why or how they even began. The Hardwick Ornament Company meant something to people a long time ago. I want to bring that back to life."

His lips tightened and his gaze fell away from hers. Quinn felt the heat of a flush warm her cheeks. Had she said too much? She took a step away from the tree. "Here I've gotten carried away, and you probably only want to kick back and relax after your trip. Down that hall are the bedrooms." She brushed past him.

He followed her, pausing only long enough to lift his duffel bag and tug the strap over one of his broad shoulders. The bedrooms, two on the left and two on the right, were traditional bunkrooms, and slept four each. With her brother's help, they'd removed the second set of built-in bunk beds from the room she'd chosen for Nolan. They'd also detached the top bunk so he wouldn't feel like he'd returned to summer camp.

At least Quinn had splurged on one of those memory foam mattresses. She wouldn't be able to provide him a palace, but he could sleep like a king. Even if the bed in question was a twin.

She'd found a nice bedside nightstand and matching chest of drawers in the farmhouse, which she had dragged out here with the help of her brother. Gram had donated one of her handmade quilts, and the small room radiated an old-fashioned homey feel. The whole room was a testament to Hardwick cooperation.

The one thing she hadn't counted on… A twin bed might not be the most comfortable size for a man as big as the one currently eyeing the single so warily.

"You said this was a bunkhouse? So there are other rooms?"

"Well, you have your choice of three others, but this is the only one that's clean."

His chuckle was rueful. "Guess I'll be taking this one, then."

"I left you a few things in the kitchen I thought you might need. Bread and eggs."

"Milk?"

She nodded, although she couldn't tell if he was teasing her or not. He wasn't the easiest guy to read. A bit closed off. "And I promise you don't have to shake it."

Say good-bye and get out. She backed out of the kitchen and toward the front door, her escape almost complete. "So, you should have my phone number. I hope you'll be happy here. I'll see you in the morning."

Her socked feet flew across the hardwood floor. A few more steps and she'd be out of there. She reached for the knob, began to turn and–

"And Quinn?"

Her shoulders slumped. She plastered on a smile and spun on her sock to face him. "Yes?"

"Sweet dreams."

"Uh, you too." She paused only long enough to slip into her boots, and then raced across the clearing so she could escape into the farmhouse.

She had learned two things about the man. His hearing definitely proved to be a hundred percent. He knew she found him easy on the eyes, and he didn't mind teasing her about it.

Also, tonight would be the last time she ever talked to the horses.

Chapter Four

Nolan managed not to fall out of the narrow bed in middle of the night, thanks to his utter exhaustion. When he'd first spotted the bed, he'd given it a wary eye, but it turned out to be more comfortable than he'd expected. With the time changes and all the driving, he'd expected to sleep well past noon. But his stomach had other ideas.

He stretched, closed his eyes again, and willed himself back to sleep. But nothing. With a sigh, he slid out of bed, and then tugged the sheet and quilt up to the wooden headboard in a lazy attempt at making it. Last night he'd been too tired to take in the small room. A festive red poinsettia rested on the nightstand where he'd tossed his phone and watch the night before. Quinn's Christmas spirit struck again. Even the quilt had subtle touches of red and green. He fingered the edge, realizing someone had taken the time to make this by hand.

The fact that he lived here, on the site of the

Hardwick Ornament Company, sleeping in a...fruit building would take some getting used to. The reality of the place no way resembled what he'd first imagined with assembly lines and automation. But Quinn's sound plan of starting small and relaunching from the original workshop made sense.

He and Kaylee had grown up listening to their father's stories about this place, passed down from *his* father. Their dad would show them black-and-white photos of their great-grandfather supervising the glass blowing at the old company, as well as his sketches of heart ornaments. Luckily, his sister kept the scrapbook in her apartment. Otherwise it would've gone up in flames, like their dad's design book. She'd offered the scrapbook to him the day he left California, but he'd snapped a few pictures with his phone instead. Kaylee could always mail it if he decided to stay.

The Hardwick Ornament Company. All this time, the Vessers had owned it.

Excitement had him surging down the hall, ready to begin the day. He tried a few doors until he found a shower room that reminded him of the locker rooms from high school. A row of three showerheads on one side, and a row of sinks on the other, and colder than any place he'd ever been. But the water was warm and it felt good to stand beneath the spray and wash away the travel grime. He would've lingered, but his stomach growled again.

After dressing in a T-shirt and pair of jeans, he surveyed the contents of the fridge, pulling out a carton of milk, a jug of juice and some eggs. He shivered and eyed the fireplace. Nope, he could easily carry the space heater from room to room. For now he'd scramble something up quickly, then begin surveying his new business. The one Quinn thought she owned.

Nolan slammed the refrigerator door harder than he'd meant to. Quinn had been so welcoming last night, anxious to make him happy here. He'd expected a rich heir, bored, reopening the company on a lark. In fact, he'd first thought the woman chasing after the horse worked here as a farmhand. The down-to-earth woman who talked to horses and greeted him with her friendly smiles and welcoming brown eyes appeared to be the opposite of bored and rich. How would she take his news?

He pushed away thoughts of her disappointment and refused to let himself think about the copy of the deed to the Hardwick Ornament Company burning a hole in the pocket of his duffel bag. He tamped down the hint of guilt that never seemed too far away and nudged him to do…what? He didn't know. This week would be about connecting with his family's past. He would learn everything he could regarding the business. Things people might not admit to the new owner. Then he would break the news.

Coffee. That was what he needed. He'd been living on cheap gas station brew as he crossed the country. Nolan tugged open a few of the cabinets in search of some elusive grounds, but no luck. He scanned the countertops. No coffee maker to be found.

The sound of a heavy door closing drew his attention to the window. He pushed aside a frilly white curtain to spot Quinn standing on the porch of a simple two-story farmhouse in desperate need of a touch-up to its… Wait, was her home green? Like the color of mint ice cream?

Her cheeks were pink from the cold, her long dark hair a soft wave around her shoulders. Quinn's quick smiles and kindness were a distraction he didn't really need right now. He'd come here to kick-start a business, not get sidetracked by a beautiful woman.

As if he'd ever been distracted before. Right after his parents died, there weren't a lot of women interested in dating a man raising his fourteen-year-old sister. Truthfully, there'd never been time to share his life with someone special. His sole focus had been to keep Vesser GlassArts from going under, getting Kaylee through high school, and later, college.

As his sister kept reminding him, she'd grown up, and Vesser GlassArts only existed on insurance paperwork. Fire had torched all his old responsibilities. Zero obligations. *How many times in life do you get to start all over?* For the first time he was free.

Then why did he feel so aimless?

His gaze fell on Quinn's upturned face as she stood on her porch. Her eyes closed as she soaked up the wintry morning sun. No, he felt…alone. Then he spotted the mug she cradled in her mittened hands. Nah, he wasn't lonely. He was decaffeinated. And Quinn held the answer. Nolan grabbed his jacket off the hook by the entry, and rushed down the warped steps to blessed caffeine. His boots crunched in the snow as he advanced toward her farmhouse.

Quinn straightened when she spotted him, her smile hesitant for a moment, then she shook her head and her grin widened. "'Morning," she called, then her eyes narrowed as her gaze fell to his lightweight jacket. "You must be cold."

"I'll need a heavier coat. Not a lot of snow in Pasadena."

"Never had a white Christmas?" she asked.

He rubbed his chin. "Hmmm, not sure I ever have."

Quinn made a sweeping motion with her hand toward the inches of snow. "Well, you won't miss it this year."

He was more concerned with what rested in her hand than the landscape. "If that's coffee, I'd love a cup. I couldn't find any in the kitchen."

Her grin faded. "Oh, Nolan. I'm so sorry. I don't drink coffee myself, so I forget other people do. I've got plenty of tea. You want a cup?"

He beat back a shudder at the very thought of replacing the nectar of life with something like tea, but he didn't want to seem rude. Eyeing the flowered ceramic mug in her hands, he asked, "How much caffeine is in that?"

She flashed him a sympathetic look. "It's oolong, so a bit, but probably not what you're used to. I can pop into town later this afternoon and buy some coffee.

Do you like those single cup machines or a regular coffee maker?"

He stuffed his hands in the pockets of his jeans, hating that she continued to be so nice. "Whatever's easiest for you."

"C'mon inside. There's still some warm water in the kettle. It won't take long for a cup of tea to steep."

"I didn't realize you were living out here too," he said, following her inside.

"Sold my condo and moved out here a few months ago to save money." Quinn motioned to the peeling paint on the frame and bare plywood standing in for a missing pane of glass. "As you can see, the place needs a lot of work. Still, I thought I'd really miss the bustle of the city, but I've gotten used to the country calm."

She'd sold her condo to save money. Guilt slammed into him. Was he really going to take her business?

The door opened with a squeak. The low ceilings and creaking hardwood beneath his boots divulged the home's age.

"Is this the original house?" he asked.

She shook her head and indicated the hooks by the front door where he could leave his jacket.

"No, but pretty close. It was built in 1840 in the Greek Revival style that was so popular at the time. My favorite thing is how the house seems to come alive with the day. The kitchen is on the east, so it catches the first rays of sunshine, and there's a western porch to watch the sunset at the end of the day. The living room faces the south, so with one peek out the window I can see the horses as they graze, and then when it's growing season, the cranberry bogs."

"You love it here." Realization blasted him. He had it in his power to take away the life she'd created out here. Suddenly he wasn't sure he could swallow, even if she'd had coffee.

"Yeah, I really do."

She turned, and he followed her through a comfortable-looking living room and into the kitchen. Quinn opened a white painted cabinet to retrieve a tin box. A fresh, slightly floral scent filled the room as she scooped dried tea leaves into a strainer and placed it on top of a mug. She didn't spill a drop as she poured the hot water before returning the kettle to the stovetop, an ancient turquoise built-in. He quickly took in the kitchen with its booth seating and rounded knick-knack shelving that reminded him of something he'd seen in black-and-white movies. A laminate he could only describe as cracked ice covered the countertops, all edged in shiny metal.

"It won't hurt my feelings if you stare. This kitchen pays homage to the early 1960s. Not quite vintage yet, but if I just hang on long enough..." She crossed her fingers and smiled.

Nolan liked that she could make light of her situation and surroundings. She motioned him to the built-in booth seating, a contraption much better suited to children. He folded his long legs beneath the table and worked to get comfortable.

She toyed with the handle on her mug. "What's

wild is that I had no idea how much I'd like being out here. The plan was to save money, but so much needs to be updated including a new coat of paint, so that'll have to wait. Barn first. Your workshop and then the storefront."

"You going to keep the green on the house?"

Quinn's hand paused on the handle. "Hold up now. That's not just green. It's mint."

"Well, when you put it like that…" Nolan twisted in his seat, again trying to find a comfortable position.

"Rumor has it great-grandpa adamantly opposed the color, too. He said with the red barns and the green house it would always be like Christmas wherever he looked. And that's when the idea of making Christmas ornaments originated. No one has ever changed the color scheme since."

"Ahh. Can't buck tradition. Why don't you show me around?" he suggested, because he couldn't straighten his legs under the table.

"Sure."

"Your tea should be steeped now," she said. After he'd taken a sip, she asked, "How is it?"

"It's not coffee," he replied, and she laughed. They grabbed their mugs and retraced their steps down the hall and outside to the porch.

She swept her arm like a game show hostess. "This used to be acres and acres of Hardwick farmland."

"What did they grow?" Although he lived right outside of L.A., he loved driving up and down the

Pacific Coast Highway. Ocean on one side and rows and rows of green farmland on the other.

"Mainly cabbage." She made a face, and Nolan laughed. "That was the major cash crop around here until some long-ago Hardwick realized the acidity of the soil grew cranberries perfectly. In fact, you barely missed the famous Bethany Springs Cranberry Fall Festival."

"Sorry I missed that," he said, tugging the collar of his jacket up to shield his neck from the cold.

She laughed. "No worries, you won't have to wait long for the next one. If there's something Bethany Springs never misses out on, it's a funfest. It's not only the Cranberry Festival; there's the Longest Night of Light celebration, Mayfest, Art in the Park. You name it, we celebrate it."

Their pace slowed as they neared a fence. She pointed to the land, in perfect game-show-hostess-fashion again. "Over the generations, we've sold off parts and leased the rest long-term. I only have to worry about ten acres now. See that area to the north? I've been toying with the idea of planting pumpkins and maybe even corn. This town needs a good corn maze in the fall."

Quinn grew silent, leaned her arms against the fence and rested her chin on the backs of her hands. She seemed like she wanted to say more but held herself back. "Why just toying with the idea?" he asked.

"Well, dreams…pipe dreams aren't very practical, and I don't have any experience in most of the stuff I want to do."

"Tell me what you envision for this place," he invited. She grinned, and something zinged through his chest as her face grew more animated. Anticipation rolled off her in waves, and he hated the idea of her quashing her own dreams without sharing them, at least.

"Well, you already know about starting with the ornaments… *An* ornament. I'd also like to host tours of the glass workshop. I'd love to have a Christmas-themed sled ride in the winter, and midway we'd take a break and have hot chocolate and I'd share the legend behind the very first Hardwick ornament. That's why Maribelle and Lulubelle came out here to live with me."

"What's stopping you?"

Quinn stuffed her hands in her pockets. "Oh, everything. No one really remembers how the old HOC operated from day to day, so I'm kind of making up everything as I go along."

"I can help with that," he said. After all, he owned the place.

The smile she flashed him forced his guilt to resurface. She thought he offered to be supportive, not because he owned the company. "I have a truck I've learned how to fix by watching videos on the internet. Buildings I'm refurbishing, one room at a time. I have my eye on an eight-passenger sled the girls can pull. It's a beautiful green, and trimmed in gold. Soft beige cushions and covered in rope lights, but I could buy a new car for the amount of that sled."

"Dreams don't cost a thing."

"Free is something I can afford," she agreed with a laugh.

"Show me the workshop," he urged, sensing it was time to change the subject. He followed her to the long, rectangular building.

The workshop stood a distance away from the rest of the buildings. He appreciated how the builder had constructed the shop out of brick with a copper roof instead of a red-painted wooden structure like the rest of the buildings dotting the farm. The windows were boarded and he could only imagine what kind of electrical and exhaust system he'd find inside. Quinn had mentioned the first ornament here had premiered sometime in the late 1920s, so he doubted anything had been updated to code.

A silver hasp minus a padlock suggested someone had been inside recently. She waved him on to open the door. "Go ahead, it's yours now."

His. Her word made him pause. Quinn meant the workshop would be his domain, but he knew he actually owned everything. He turned the knob, but the door wouldn't budge.

"Oh, wait. There's a trick," she said.

Something fluttered across her soft features. A memory perhaps? Then she leaned her shoulder against the door and pushed slightly toward the hinges. "Turn the knob now."

The change in weight shifted and the lock released. The door opened wide.

"Guess I should fix that. I just haven't had the heart to. It's the way Grandpa left it."

"We can think of it as another layer of security."

Her soft and musical laugh lifted his spirits temporarily. "I like the way you think. There are also some easy access exits in case of emergency, if you were wondering."

Yeah, determining the quickest way out of a place had become a way of life for him. She flipped a switch and the heavy ballasts overhead stirred up with a hum. The stale workshop smelled of dust, old wood smoke, and time.

"I opened the building up last week to get a little air in here and sweep, but it's going to be a little sneezy until we get the boards off the windows and give the place a thorough wash down. But the old workshop has good bones." Determination steeled her words. "I'll get it into shape."

He rotated slowly, taking in the space and breathing in the air. The building stretched long like a small assembly plant, perfect for constructing the ornaments in an orderly fashion. There was plenty of space for a furnace to melt the glass, a reheater to keep the glass hot enough for the finer detail work, and a kiln so projects could cool without the glass breaking.

Of course he could use the furnace to reheat the glass, but he'd always preferred two separate pieces of equipment in his own small shop, and eventually if his plans progressed, there would be several artisans working in here, and they couldn't all be crowding around the same furnace. Besides, his father had always had a reheater, and Nolan liked knowing he followed his dad's example.

Warmth began to spread through him all the way to his fingers and toes. *This* was where his great-great-grandfather created art and taught a young son how to blow glass. Who'd trained his son, who trained his, and finally, Nolan. He swallowed past the lump in his throat.

Soon Nolan would sweat, design, and craft in here like generations before him. A bond lined the past to the present through him. Under this roof, they'd all created, with both disappointment in a failed design and pride when that oh-so-elusive quest for art finally appeared. Quinn's link to Hardwick was strong, but so was his.

The woman beside him beamed. "Kind of wild, huh? You don't expect it to hit you. Another person's dreams. That connection."

He could only shake his head. "How'd you know?"

"You had that 'knocked in the gut by the past' look on your face. Let me show you something. This will really blow you over." Quinn led him to a corner and pointed to a wooden beam. At first he thought it was just a scarred slat, but no, someone had carved their initials. MV and the year 1927. "I bet your great-great-grandfather carved this. His name was Milos, right?"

"Yeah." He rubbed his finger along the etched letters and numbers in the wood. *Yes.* A sense of rightness fortified him. He belonged here. Sometime in the past, the Hardwicks had wanted his family to own this company. His unease faded.

Quinn turned away from the wall, a strand of her dark brown hair falling from its clip. "So, as you can see, there's not much here. The floor is fieldstone in case of fire, and the—"

Quinn continued to speak but something seized in his gut, tight and raw. His mouth dried and a ringing in his ears blocked her words. For a moment, he wasn't in a rundown workshop in the middle of Massachusetts; he stood on the second story of an apartment engulfed in smoke and the heat of fire. He no longer stood on fieldstone, but on a tiled hallway as he rushed to rescue a tiny dog. Flames licked at his arms, his lungs burning as he gasped for breath.

"Nolan?"

He straightened and scrubbed a hand over the back of his neck. *Get it together.* "What?"

Her brown eyes narrowed and she gave him an understanding nod. Quinn's lips parted and while he'd known her for barely hours, he realized she was searching for something comforting to say. Because everyone rushed to offer compassion. "I don't mean to pry, and you barely know me, but I want you to know we can hold off until tomorrow. Or even the next day."

He cleared his throat and swallowed carefully, even though his vocal cords no longer ached from breathing in smoke. "I'm good."

"Your arm must still be hurting, and I don't want to rush you."

"No need to worry about me." Nolan didn't want her sympathy or her pity. He'd tackled far worse in his life and handled every challenge all on his own just fine.

"So what do we need to turn this into a workshop you can use?" she asked.

He appreciated how she respected his request to move forward. Nolan shook his head to clear the memory of the shrill sound of a fire alarm. *Be present. You're not in California.* He made an effort to examine the room, his eyes drawn to the ceiling. "Smoke alarm and sprinkler system. We'll need to rework the ventilation. The furnace should go there," he said, pointing to the various spots around the shop, "the reheater over by that wall and the kiln near that window."

"So you'll stay?" Quinn bit the corner of her lip.

Was that caution he heard in her voice, because she wanted to keep herself from getting too excited? A lot was stacked up against them and most new businesses failed.

This is your chance. Tell her about the deed. His lips parted… But he couldn't, not with his sister researching what exactly he owned. He had zero reason to feel ashamed for driving out here to claim the Hardwick Ornament Company. "Yeah. I'll stay."

"Woo hoo! Oh, Nolan, you won't regret it. Actually, you'll probably regret it every day, but thank you," she said, her voice teasing.

"You don't really know how the hard sell works,

do you?" he asked, crossing to the center of the room where a long wooden worktable stood.

"Probably not. But as my grandma always says, 'Regret is just another way to say trust.'"

He ran his hand along the top of the old scarred wood of the tabletop, tested the sturdiness of its legs, but paused as her words sunk in. "Huh?"

A frown formed between her brows. "Hmmm, now that I think about it, that's not one of her better ones. It sort of made sense at the time."

She smiled up at him, and his breath caught in his chest. He hadn't expected all this… emotion here. His plan had been simple. Go to Bethany Springs. Check out the Hardwick Ornament Company. Decide if he wanted to keep it or sell his ownership back to the Hardwicks. Personal involvement couldn't be part of his plans. Or admiring the woman in front of him.

He stepped backwards. *Running away?* He grasped the corner of the table instead.

"I can get rid of that," she offered, nodding toward his white-knuckled grip on the table.

Nolan shook his head. "No, don't. It's not a good surface for glass blowing, but it's perfect for my tools and for spreading out designs. I like the idea of having something from the past hanging around."

"Think you can give me a list of the equipment you'll need tomorrow morning?" Resolve strengthened her voice. Quinn Hardwick appeared ready to get things moving along.

"So early?"

Her shoulder lifted in a sigh. "The sooner we get to work, the sooner we get to pay off the bills. Hopefully." She eyed his empty tea mug. "So, for tea, how'd it taste?"

"Not bad."

"Don't worry. I'll pop into town this afternoon and get coffee. Anything else you need?"

He shook his head and handed her the mug. "Thanks for the tour."

"Thanks for taking a chance with me, Nolan. I know this isn't what you're used to at all, and..." Her words trailed off on a wave of emotion.

Her gratefulness and hope left him dazed. He hadn't expected to feel this way. Guilty. Drawn to the past. Admiring Quinn Hardwick. Not for only her pretty smile and deep brown eyes, but her enthusiasm. Her excitement to risk everything on her dream.

To take a risk on him.

He gave her a tight nod and turned.

Quinn watched Nolan race out of the workshop. Had she embarrassed him with her show of emotion? Good to know. Okay, from now on, she would keep it light between them. She could handle that. After her grandpa died, she'd been overwhelmed with a sense of sadness and responsibility, so she understood if he needed to be alone in this space where the past seemed to beckon.

But now she had a plan. With Nolan here and his

agreement to help, parts of her strategy were falling into place. As they'd stood together in the workshop, she'd been almost overwhelmed. Quinn would always be grateful to him for taking a chance on her dream. This world-famous glass blower basically entrusted his own reputation in her very inexperienced hands. Reaching for the light switch, she envisioned what they'd accomplish in this building together, rather than the many things she still needed to do.

She savored that feeling; it hadn't come around often since she'd moved into the farmhouse. So excited, Quinn almost gave in to the urge to twirl in the old studio exactly the way she'd once done with her grandpa. One step closer to making the Hardwick Ornament Company a reality again.

Darkness surrounded her after she flipped the lights off, and as she checked the lock she made a vow. She would do whatever she could to help Nolan feel at home here in Bethany Springs. He may have lost everything, but he had so much to find here.

But first… She had plans with hay and a shovel, a.k.a. stall duty.

Chapter Five

After completing her morning chores, Quinn leaned the shovel against the wall and took off her heavy work gloves. A high-pitched creak echoed through the barn, and she whipped around with a shriek.

Nolan stood in the entryway, his handsome face concerned. Her hand fluttered to her chest as relief engulfed her. "Oh, you startled me."

He lifted his hands in a show of innocence. "Sorry."

She waved off his concern. "I must've gotten more used to being alone out here than I'd thought."

"Talking to horses doesn't count?"

Quinn propped her hand on her hip. "You know, a nice guy would forget he ever witnessed that. In fact, if it ever comes up, I *will* deny it."

"I'll remember that." He lifted his phone to the sky. "Is there a trick to getting a signal out here? I wanted to call my sister and look up some items online for the workshop."

She huffed in shared annoyance, ruffling the hair on her forehead for a moment. "It's so hit or miss out here. I usually drive into town when I need to use the internet. I'm heading out there now to pick up the coffee. You're welcome to come along."

"Could stand to get a heavier coat now, too."

"So you decided to take my advice, huh?" Quinn fought a smile and angled her head toward the passenger side of her truck. "Let's go."

Although the roads were slushy, the ride into town didn't take long. Neither mentioned the earlier emotion they'd shared, or almost shared, in the workshop. Instead they kept their conversation to easy chitchat and some of the interesting things he'd spotted on his cross-country trip. The roads grew clearer as they traveled closer to town, and she appreciated the fully plowed Main Street when she turned onto it.

She couldn't hold back a smile as she spotted the city workers and volunteers twining garland around light poles and bringing in crates full of the city's decorations.

"This town really goes all out," he said, as two men unrolled a long banner that would eventually grace Main Street.

"Yes, it takes them awhile to get everything set up. I suspect it's to draw out our anticipation. Bethany Springs rarely misses a chance to decorate and have a party." A touch of pride graced her words. Quinn flipped her blinker and pulled into a space in a parking lot behind a row of shops. She killed the engine and rotated in her seat to face him. "I should probably warn you about my town," she said, her voice more of a sigh.

"Ahh, now here it comes," he said, his tone dubious.

"Here what comes?"

"The secrets." Then his voice lowered, and he took on the swagger of a movie announcer. "Bethany Springs may look like a quaint New England town blanketed in snow, but beneath those gently falling flakes lies danger."

Quinn couldn't stop from giggling. "You've been watching way too many scary movies. If anything, Bethany Springs would be more like a cozy mystery where a statue is stolen."

"So what's the big secret?" he asked, unbuckling his seatbelt.

"This is going to be very anticlimactic," she told him with a shake of her head. "In fact, I don't think I'll warn you at all now. You'll just have to be worried, wondering when one of the townspeople is going to…"

"What? Pounce? Lure me to my doom?" He stared out the window. "Wait, no. They'll lure me to some kind of place that I'll have to decorate with garland."

"C'mon. I think your new exposure to this kind of cold must be making you light-headed. The GS is right down the street, and we should be able to find you a coat there."

He lifted a brow. "The GS?"

"It's short for the Bethany Springs General Store,

but that's a mouthful. We should be able to get your coffee there too."

They scrambled from the car and he followed her lead around the buildings and to the long sidewalk lined by streetlights that looked like throwbacks to an earlier time.

"Although it was built in the 1920s, we call this New Main Street," she told him. Small shops with large picture windows and brightly colored awnings stretched on either side of the block. They passed a hair salon, hardware shop, diner and dance studio until finally stopping in front of a red brick building with a bench on either side of the door.

The GS greeted them with the soapy scent of cleaning supplies and the starchy smell of new clothes still on the rack. A tiny bell tinkled as they entered, and the woman at the counter displaying magazines, breath mints and gum welcomed them with a smile. Then she performed the kind of double take usually reserved for TV sitcoms. "Oh, hi, Quinn."

"Hi, Mrs. Jennings."

The older woman laughed. "Quinn, you're an adult now. You can call me Kay." She glanced over to Nolan, her gaze full of scrutiny as she gave him the once-over. "Your mom hadn't mentioned you were bringing, uh, someone here for the holidays."

Quinn gripped the handle of her purse. She should have had formed some kind of plan before venturing one inch into the GS. Head down. Eyes focused.

Anything other than casually strolling inside the central hub of gossip in Bethany Springs.

"This is Nolan Vesser. He's here to help with the reopening of the Hardwick Ornament Company," she said, already angling her body toward the small selection of coats and other winter outerwear.

"Your mom and dad are so excited about you reviving the old company. Although they're a little concerned about you living out there all alone. Well, except for the horses. You made Dr. Burton's year when you could take them both in." She cut her eyes over to Nolan, her lips pursed. For someone who ran a general store, she could be suspicious of strangers.

"Nolan's great-great-grandfather helped with the HOC back in the day," Quinn informed her.

Kay's features softened, and her smile grew friendlier. "Well, then… Welcome back to Bethany Springs."

With a tug at his elbow, she led him to the rack of coats before Mrs. Jennings could mention how long it'd been since Quinn had been on a date. Or how nice she'd been to take in Nolan, like she had with Maribelle and Lulubelle.

"It's like she knew your life story," he said as soon as they were out of earshot.

"It's a small town. Kind of goes with the territory."

"When you said you'd miss the bustle of the city, I thought you were referring to the people and cars," he said.

"Ah, I see what you mean. No, Bethany Springs

is about as different from L.A. as two cities could be. But, you have to admit there's a lot more bustle here than at the farm."

He bobbed his head. "You do have a point."

The GS had three racks of coats, one each for men, women and children. "If you're wanting a bigger selection, we'll have to go to Danvers or may–"

"This one looks good." Nolan grabbed a coat, glanced at the sizing on the tag, and then popped it off the hanger.

"What? You make a decision just like that?" She watched as he folded it over the crook of his arm. "You didn't even try it on or take a selfie in it."

With a good-natured sigh, Nolan slipped his arms through the holes; his broad shoulders filled the hooded gray puffer coat. Quinn's mouth dried. Yeah, the man knew how to pull off the outdoorsy style.

Gaga over a coat, Quinn? Seriously? The thing is basically a big, bulky sack.

And the man did amazing things with big, bulky sacks, what could she say?

"It fits," she finally managed to say. She'd chalk that comment up in the inane column. "C'mon. Coffee and stuff is over there."

Quinn introduced Nolan to two neighbors as they selected a maker and grounds, and another as they waited in line to pay. Mrs. Jennings cut the tag off the coat so he could wear it outside, but once on the sidewalk he paused. "You hungry?"

She had worked up an appetite. Usually she ate

a quick sandwich over the kitchen sink, so she could easily be tempted. Besides, she could almost hear her favorite restaurant in town calling her name. "Absolutely."

After stowing the supplies in her truck, he opened the driver's door for her.

"Oh, that's okay, we can walk."

"Really?" He closed the heavy door after she nodded.

"One of the nice things about living in a town built before cars—most everything we want is nearby." She led him in the opposite direction of Main Street, the sidewalk bricked instead of poured concrete. "This is Town Square or just the Square, the Main Street of two centuries ago. That's the Green." She pointed to a large grassy area with a beautiful rounded gazebo, the architecture not too fancy, simple columns, but with a two-tiered cupola and metal weather vane.

"Quinn, hey." The breathless voice behind them could only belong to her cousin Chloe. "I thought that was you."

Quinn spun around to give her a hug. "It's so good to see you. We missed you at Thanksgiving."

"Had to cover the festivities in Plymouth for the paper." Her cousin pulled away and focused her hazel-eyed attention on Nolan. "Who's this?" she asked without preamble, her usual guarded smile back in place as she sized up the man sitting across from them.

"This is Nolan. He's going to work with me at HOC. Nolan, this is my cousin Chloe. She's a reporter in Boston, so be expecting questions that come out of nowhere."

He flinched and his friendly smile faded.

"I'll give you a day before I start the full interrogation," Chloe assured him, pushing back a strand of her dark hair.

His brow arched. "A full day?"

Chloe pretended to examine her nails. "My real investigating is done mostly online."

Nolan's face paled.

"Don't worry," Quinn assured him. "She's kidding." There wouldn't be much to find, as she'd run his name through several search engines before she offered him a job and a place to stay. The most recent story was behind a paid firewall, and she assumed it covered the fire. "I didn't think you were going to be back until closer to Longest Night."

"I'm only here for the weekend. Mom said she wanted me to help get Christmas decorations out of the attic, but I think she really wants me to help set the stage."

"For what?" Quinn asked.

"This is the first time Derrick and Alara will both be back in town at the same time. She's convinced he's going to propose."

Quinn explained to Nolan. "Alara is another cousin, Chloe's sister. Derrick is her boyfriend, but he's a pilot in the Air Force and rarely gets back here." She returned her attention to Chloe. "You think he will?"

Chloe shrugged. "Mom's rarely wrong when she has a hunch."

Wow. Married. The first one out of their generation of Hardwicks.

Chloe shivered. "Brrr, it's getting cold out here. I'm going to run to my car and turn the heat up full blast. It was nice to meet you, Nolan."

"Nice to meet you too," he called, then faced Quinn. "How many relatives do you have in this town?"

"A lot," she told him with a laugh. "My grandma, then my parents and aunt and uncle. That doesn't include my brother and sister and my cousins. You?"

"Just the sister."

Her family could certainly be in her personal business, but having only one person to share childhood jokes with, keep secrets for, and tease to coax a smile on a dreary day was hard to imagine. She flashed him a sympathetic smile, but he didn't seem torn up about missing out on a nosy extended family. In fact, his gaze tracked from one building to the next, his artist's eye for detail drinking in the old homes and buildings.

She said, "These houses and businesses that face The Green date all the way back to when they first founded the town."

"Pretty different from home," he said, rubbing his chin.

Her eyelids fluttered closed. "I'm envisioning palm

trees, bungalow homes, and outside dining even in January."

"Palm trees can leave a lot of trash on your car."

She held up a hand to stop his words. "No. Don't ruin it for me."

His smile widened. "Wouldn't dream of it. I'll even toss in the Rose Bowl Parade."

"Sounds amazing." But the spell broke apart. She remained in her beloved snowy Massachusetts. In fact, she'd gotten so lost in their conversation they almost passed the restaurant. "We're here."

Nolan stared up at the two-story building, painted a deep steel blue. "This looks like someone's home."

"It was," she said, as they stepped inside the foyer. "This is the Giddings House, built around 1750. The council is really strict about renovations and new builds in this area. Everything has to stay in the First Period architecture. The owners really ran with that, so you could be eating in the drawing room or the parlor. One of the rooms upstairs used to be the playroom, and they've decorated it with toys and a small table for coloring, which makes this place really popular for families with little kids."

"Welcome to the Giddings House," their hostess greeted, then some of her formality faded. "Oh, hi, Quinn."

"Hey, Beth. How's it going?"

"Two more weeks of working the floor, and then I'm in the kitchen." The other woman crossed her fingers. Many aspiring chefs worked through the program at

The Giddings House, but the owners required the students to work as a dining room host and wait staff before rotating through the various stations in the kitchen. Their philosophy held that a great chef must first understand the workings of the entire restaurant. "The dining room is full, but I have plenty of tables in the library."

"Sounds perfect."

Beth grabbed two menus then led them through first one room, then another, both packed with guests. Several people waved to Quinn as they passed. Their hostess indicated a carved wooden two-person table near a large, picturesque window. Although this room wasn't as crowded, Nolan still attracted several curious glances.

"I figured out what you wanted to warn me about. It's everyone looking at me," he said after Beth left them alone with their menus.

"Nailed it in one," she said.

He shrugged out of his new coat. "I'm not used to being the center of gossip."

"Welcome to life in a small town. Although we don't call it gossip. It's disguised as news and information. Helpful, actually," she deadpanned.

"There's like fifteen different kinds of toast on here," he said after scanning the menu.

"It's what the place is known for. I really recommend the pumpkin."

"I see there's also cranberry," he said and laughed after she wrinkled her nose.

"Giddings House also has good WiFi. Should help you create your shopping list."

"Ah, now I see your game. Ready for me to work." But he whipped out his phone anyway.

"You're the one who mentioned food," she reminded him.

A few minutes later, their waitress took their order. Relief swamped her as she caught Nolan scrolling through his phone, hopefully compiling his shopping list and not bargain hunting for flights out of this place. Then she heard a familiar voice.

She flattened her hands on the table and leaned toward Nolan. "You know that part about small towns and gossip and feeling like people are staring at you?"

He nodded.

"Buckle up. It's about to ratchet up a notch."

"Hello, dear."

"Gram," she said as she stood to give the older woman a hug. Gram's short gray hair sported a discreet green strand for the holidays. She'd gone for a subtler glitter eye make-up today, but her earrings, as always, remained big and reflected the current season.

"I see you've already added the vests."

Gram glanced down at her half sweater, complete with a Christmas bow-wearing kitten playing with gold curling ribbon.

"I pulled these out from the back of the closet the day after Thanksgiving." She turned her kind eyes toward the tall man sitting at the table. "Don't tell me this is Richard's grandson."

Nolan pushed his chair back, ready to greet their new guest. She waved him back onto the seat, but he stood anyway. "Nolan Vesser."

She clasped his hand in both of hers. "I'm so glad you're here. I knew your grandfather in the last century," she said, laughing at her own joke.

"This is my Gram Hardwick, Nolan. She made the website you found."

He lifted an eyebrow. "Really?"

"You gotta stay up with all the new tech. Except pictures. I still like to sift through my pictures by hand."

Nolan's face lit in the way that suggested he found Gram charming. Like everyone else.

"Sit, sit. I won't keep you two. Just wanted to pop over and say hi when I heard you were in here." But Gram made no move to leave. "How's the ornament designing going?"

"Gram, Nolan arrived yesterday. In fact, the only reason we're even in town is to get him a coat."

Her gray brows shot up. "Did you forget some gloves?" She turned toward Nolan. "Quinn here is always forgetting gloves."

Nolan began to chuckle. "As a matter of fact, we did."

"Don't you worry about them. The Hardwicks will get you covered. So, you've been here a day, huh. Has Quinn already showed you all those notebooks of her ideas?"

"We're concentrating on getting the workshop set

up first. In fact, that's why we're here. Needed the WiFi."

"You're always welcome to use that at my house, too." Her tone turned conspiratorial as she included Nolan. "I've found that a dual-band router, high speed and lots of RAM keeps the grandkids popping by the house. And cookies.

"Hey," she continued, "we set the date for Reindeer Ruckus–the twenty-second. With Alara and Derrick both back in town, it's going to be a full house. Nolan, we'd love for you to join us." She tapped her chin. "Now that I'm thinking of it, the party will be the perfect time for Derrick to propose. Everyone will be there."

Quinn steepled her fingers on the tabletop. "Gram, I can almost guarantee you a hundred percent, proposing in front of our huge family would be the last thing any man would want to do."

Gram glanced at Nolan as if to get the male perspective. He wisely only shrugged and glanced down at his phone as if to confirm a price.

Gram's lips screwed into a frown. "You may have a point there. I'll have to rethink my bet." She snapped her fingers. "I just thought of something. Wouldn't it be great to debut the first Hardwick Ornament Company product at the auction?"

A rush of excitement darted through Quinn. The auction would be perfect, but then she pictured a calendar in her mind and tamped down her enthusiasm. The evening of Christmas Eve loomed too soon. "Gram, the auction is only a few weeks away. We'd never be ready in time."

The older woman leaned down and kissed her cheek. "Just a thought. Okay, I'm really going now." With a quick wave, she left.

Nolan slumped against the back of his seat. "She's like a whirlwind."

"Tell me about it. She's a retired engineer, and she loves to tinker with electronics. A lot of my friends joke about setting up the internet for their older relatives. Not Gram. You can never be off your game around her."

"Reindeer Ruckus?" he asked.

"It's when our family gets together to celebrate Christmas. You're invited, of course, but I'd planned to ease you into the idea. A house full of Hardwicks is something you have to prepare for."

After lunch, Quinn popped over to the post office, but Nolan strolled over to the gazebo in the Green to take advantage of the stronger cell service in town and call his sister.

"Hey, I was getting worried," she said in lieu of a greeting. "Thought I'd hear from you last night."

Remorse stirred inside him at hearing the relief in his sister's voice. He was so used to taking care of her, he could forget to check in to ease *her* peace of mind. "Sorry. The reception out on the farm is terrible. I had to wait until I drove into town to make the call."

"I hate for you to be someplace so isolated. What if there's an emergency?"

"Sis. It's okay. I've had one brush with bad luck, but I'm good. People have survived out in the middle of nowhere for centuries."

"No, they didn't. They moved. They invented things like 911. And cell towers."

Nolan forced himself to stifle a laugh. Chuckling would only encourage her.

"How's your burn?" she asked.

"It's fine," he told her, stretching his arm out and feeling only a small twinge. "I'm not even taking the pain meds anymore."

"Of course you're not." Disapproval laced her words.

"As they say out here, I'll have a wicked cool scar." Teasing could usually lighten his sister's mood.

"Gnarly."

"I don't think anyone says gnarly anymore. Like in decades."

"They do ironically," she said, her tone straight-up-lawyer-pushing-a-point. "Well, once you show them the deed and take ownership, you can move into a hotel or something. I know it's an inconvenience, but it's really to your advantage to stay on the farm until title is established."

He rubbed the back of his neck. "Yeah, about that. The owner..."

"Oh no."

"What?"

"I can hear it in your voice. The fact that you haven't flashed the deed yet. It can only mean one thing," she said. "The owner of the Hardwick Ornament Company is a woman. And she's pretty."

"It's not just that. She has plans, and I didn't understand..."

"Understand what?" Her hesitant one-word question hovered between them.

"That by realizing my own dream, I'd be taking away someone else's." And that had been nagging him since hightailing it out of the workshop this morning. The feeling had only grown worse as Quinn had introduced him to her family. Her Gram had mentioned drawings. Quinn had been working on the HOC for a while now.

Yet the HOC also waited as his birthright. No, it meant more than that. Fate had appointed him a caretaker to the legacy of the company. On the day they'd discovered the deed, he'd talked philosophically about businesses coming and going, but he no longer felt blasé about the Hardwick Ornament Company fading into the past and being forgotten. He felt passionate about this place. He knew every day here he'd grow to love it more. Maybe that was the very reason a Hardwick had passed ownership to the Vessers: trust. How could he turn his back on that kind of faith? Responsibility? Obligation?

"Nolan? Are you still there?"

"Yes."

"You were quiet for so long, I thought the

connection had cut out. I don't understand what the problem is. If the company meant so much to them, why haven't they reopened it long before now?"

"Quinn has already sunk a lot of money into this."

"They're a rich family. It's probably interest off a trust fund–"

"About that. Whatever money they once had, Quinn doesn't seem to have much now."

"That makes it even better." Kaylee's tone brightened. "That means she'll be even more eager to buy the property from you fair and square. Stick around, get a good idea of how much the buildings and business are worth. You can make an offer before Christmas."

Something flashed in the corner of his eye, and he saw Quinn turn the corner. Her dark brown hair trailed behind her, windblown and untamed. She grinned as she spotted him. Her quick smile filled him with fresh energy. She lifted her arm in a wave.

"And Nolan..." Kaylee said.

"Yes?" he asked, already returning Quinn's wave.

"Don't fall for her."

Chapter Six

Nolan tossed and turned in his tiny bed in the bunkhouse. By the time the elusive wintry sun peeked through the window, he had given up any attempt at sleeping. After dressing and shoving his feet into the snow boots he'd bought in town, he left to explore the area surrounding the Berry House. The snow crunched as he walked and the cold morning air bit into his cheeks, but he didn't mind. He needed time to think.

Don't fall for her.

His sister's warning eight days ago had acted more like a prediction. *Sure, I won't fall for Quinn… 'cause I'm already falling.*

He'd expected a rich woman who'd taken on the Hardwick Ornament Company as a lark. Someone who would take the money he offered and move on to her next project. Instead, he discovered a woman driven to succeed. Sentimental about the past—a trait Nolan never realized he'd find adorable. They both loved their families, although she definitely had a lot more relatives to love.

Her adventurous nature intrigued him. Quinn might be a bit obsessed with the past, but she also couldn't wait to try new things. She cared, and even though he'd only been on the farm for a short time, he'd been included in the long list of people Quinn blanketed in her kindness. She'd done what she could to make him comfortable in the Berry House, always on the lookout for ways to do more. Her compassion seemed limitless, whether directed at the almost-healed burn on his arm or his loss of every possession.

Don't fall for her.

He needed to slow things down and consider every option while Quinn wanted to move ahead at lightning speed. Yesterday some of the equipment she'd ordered for the workshop had arrived. He would pay her back for all of these things, of course, as soon as his insurance settlement came through. But why had he compiled that list so quickly? He could have dragged that whole thing out a lot longer.

Why? Because when he suggested a brand of furnace and the type of blowtorch that operated best, she flashed him a smile that made his heart pound. And he'd wondered if the glow in her eyes would brighten when the equipment actually got here...and he'd wanted to feel his heart pound again.

Don't fall for her.

He needed to make a decision about what to do with his ownership of the company. Keep the business or sell it back to the Hardwicks? He couldn't let guilt or his growing interest in Quinn affect his ultimate choice. To get a better feel for HOC, he must observe the place *as is*. Once he became emotionally involved in the progress and her improvements, his judgment would be clouded. That meant he had to make it his mission to block and delay Quinn's forward momentum…but only for a few days. Anything longer would be unfair to Quinn.

Only any time he'd thought he was close to making a decision, Quinn managed to change his mind. She'd whooped in excitement when the large truck delivered the furnace, and he'd wanted to share the joy of the moment with her. And yet… With the arrival of each new package, his hope and excitement dampened.

So he backed off. Two steps forward, three steps in reverse. He never visited the workshop. He'd avoided a location whenever he suspected Quinn would be there. Which proved tough, because Quinn worked everywhere, from the barn to the workshop to the farmhouse. He wondered when she slept.

Dodging her would be a lot easier if he weren't staying in the Berry House—too many opportunities to bump into each other. He'd even dialed the number to the Bed and Breakfast in town, but the poor reception prevented the call from going through. Probably a good thing, because Kaylee insisted that possession was nine-tenths of the law, and it would be easier for him to take ownership of the property if he was already living here. A wisp of guilt flared in his chest, but he tamped it down.

The clop of galloping hooves drew his attention. Lulubelle had escaped the paddock and was now headed straight toward him. She seemed to grin from ear to ear as she slowed to a stop beside him, and he gave the old girl a scratch behind her ears. He shifted so he could keep an eye on the barn, and sure enough, an exasperated Quinn marched out of the double doors.

She rolled her eyes after spotting the runaway prancing happily at his side. He leaned over to the horse and whispered. "C'mon, Lulubelle. You don't want to get in trouble." After what could be considered a nod, the horse began to follow him toward the barn.

"That horse," Quinn said as the pair of them approached.

"Don't worry. I'll get her set up in the barn."

Her eyes widened in surprise. "That would be great."

He may have heard a mumbled, "About time he's doing something" as she passed him, but he couldn't be sure. Quinn's patience must be nearing its end. He couldn't blame her. She'd brought him here to help build her business, and he'd come under the guise of doing so, but so far he'd only added chores to her plate.

Today she wore her dark hair piled high on her head, sported heavy work gloves, and carried a sledgehammer. Rather than her usual smile, her full lower lip stretched in a straight line as she stomped toward what used to be the old Hardwick Ornament Company storefront. The center of the roof drooped from the weight of the snow. The board covering the window had lost the fight long ago, hanging on by a single nail. The glass it protected was long gone. The whole thing reminded him of the houses he and his sister used to make out of playing cards on rare rainy Saturday afternoons, wobbly and ready to fall with the slightest movement.

Quinn lifted the sledgehammer over her head, and with a giant heave struck it against the side of the building. The head of the hammer sunk into the soft wood. With a thud, the plank shattered and fell to the ground. Her shoulders relaxed and a satisfied smile touched her mouth.

"Think she's mad?" he asked Lulubelle. Nolan gripped her halter and led her inside.

The vibration of his phone surprised him. He locked Lulubelle in her stall beside her sister and retrieved his cell out of his pocket. Kaylee's name popped up on his screen. He tensed. He could guess what she wanted to say, and he knew he'd hate it. "Hey, sis."

"Can you actually hear me?" she asked.

"Just a hint of static."

"Excellent. The planets must be aligning. The satellites all in motion. The sun not flaring."

He laughed at his sister's exaggeration. Although she may not be laying it on too thick. Nearly-clear calls were rare out here. Lulubelle stamped her front hoof for a carrot, proving her runaway tricks were a ruse to get her favorite treat.

"What's that noise?" Kaylee asked.

"It's Lulubelle."

"Don't tell me the Hardwick heir's name is Lulubelle."

He bit back a laugh, and showed both Belles his empty palms to prove he came to the barn without carrots. The girls lifted their noses and turned away. He no longer existed to them, and the realization made him chuckle. "No, it's her horse. She kind of follows me around. The horse, not the heir. I'm leading her back into her stall, and she thinks she deserves a reward."

"Hey, do me a favor. Put your phone in camera mode, pull it away from your ear and take a selfie of you with that horse. I really need to see that," his sister teased.

"Ha ha."

"Learned anything on your end about the company?" Kaylee asked.

Nolan leaned against the stall, Lulubelle sniffing along his arm. "They're definitely not the rich family we expected. To tell you the truth, I'm getting uncomfortable staying here knowing what I know. I've never seen someone work so hard as Quinn Hardwick. She's taking care of the farmhouse and this barn while trying to restart the business. And here I am just waltzing in and taking it away."

Kaylee cleared her throat, and he knew he'd soon

be on the receiving end of a dispassionate lawyer-type pep talk. "You're not taking it away. The Hardwick is yours to begin with. Repeat after me. It's not my fault they didn't know their great-great-grandfather gave the company away."

He massaged the back of his neck. "I'm not repeating that."

"Well, maybe this will ease your conscience. You won't be taking away as much as we'd first thought. Oh, great, now you've got me doing it. You're not taking rightful possession of as much property as we'd first thought. I've done some research into the deed, and it's only the name of the company, and two buildings that are yours free and clear."

"Which ones?"

He heard the sound of rustling papers followed by static. "Yes, here it is. The buildings are the ornament workshop and some kind of storefront."

The splintering crunch of a sledgehammer smashing into wood carried into the barn. "Yeah, I think that storefront's gone."

"What?" his sister asked. "You're cutting out."

"Guess the planets are no longer aligning."

"What about designing?"

"Never mind," he said, his tone grim. He ran a soothing hand along Lulubelle's powerful neck.

"Nolan, you need to make a decision about what you're going to do," his sister reminded him.

Why did *that* sentence have to come through loud and clear? "I'm still mulling things over."

"Well, can you mull things a little quicker? I leave for my Christmas vacation in Colorado in a few days. You know how nothing gets done that week between Christmas and New Year's. At this rate, it won't be until next year to make a move. We must take action now."

No way could he keep stalling.

"Nolan?"

"I'm still here," he reassured his sister.

"Thought maybe the call had dropped. Did you hear me earlier? It'd be great if you could tell me one way or another before the end of the week. That's the twentieth."

Lulubelle finally lost her patience and tried to root for the carrot herself. He backed away from the stall, his breathing turning shallow under the pressure of what he must do. "Yeah, I'll let you know."

"And maybe try to make that call from town."

"Goodbye, sis." He slid his phone into his pocket, and then glanced down to double-check that both horses had water. "I'll bring you carrots tonight." He lifted a warning finger. "Consider it a preemptive payment. No more escape attempts."

Maribelle made a small whinny.

"Yeah, you're not the horse I'm worried about," he said.

Lulubelle said nothing.

"Good plan, girl. No promises made, no promises to keep."

With a wave to the horses, he crossed the barn,

pulled the doors shut behind him and trekked through the muddy snow to Quinn. The storefront now lay splintered, with broken boards scattered on the ground. Quinn's cheeks were pink from the cold and her exertion. Her eyes were bright and charmingly pleased as she stood tall in the midst of her destruction. He'd expected rich; he hadn't anticipated stunning. With her bright red coat, she was a flash of shocking color on a cold winter's day.

"That took you no time," he said, admiring her handiwork.

She tugged off one of the heavy work gloves she wore. "I was motivated. How's the arm?"

Nolan extended his arm and rubbed where he'd been burned. "Good. Not even a twinge."

Her lips turned up in an enchanting grin. A smile just for him.

The air in his chest caught. He admired her and her determination. She had a dream, and instead of giving up after every obstacle thrown her way, she kept right on going. That old building had been no match for her. He might not be either.

"Wonderful." Quinn dove her ungloved hand into her pocket, and then produced a brand new pair of men's-sized work gloves.

He bit back a groan. Good play, Hardwick. She'd taken away all his excuses not to work. His fingers brushed hers as he took the gloves from her. Quinn's gaze lowered to the place where their fingers had touched. A line formed between her brows. In puzzlement. No…surprise.

He gripped the gloves tight in his hand as a warm rush of satisfaction zipped through him. Quinn felt that same flash of attraction too. Okay, this wasn't convenient. Certainly not well timed. But still reality.

How would he handle this? If he told her the truth, she'd want nothing to do with him. But if he didn't tell her the truth now, *could* he stay? Stay knowing he'd take away her dream? Stay, suspecting that their relationship could grow into something more than just professional? Eventually she'd learn the truth.

"What do you have in mind?" he asked, ready for a distraction from this awkward attraction.

"There have been a ton of deliveries for your workshop. I've been storing them in the cleaning room off the Berry House, but I think one of the large boxes today contained the new ventilation system and fire sprinklers. Now we can finally get the workshop ready for you to use."

No way could he miss the excitement in her voice. Now should be the time to boost his block and delay efforts. But instead he found himself staring into Quinn's animated brown eyes, getting lost in her enthusiasm. She wheeled around and he fell into step beside her, the snow crunching beneath their boots. He'd grown used to sand, marked by a dozen different footprints. Here the snow stretched before them like a vast palette of white, only broken by the path of a rolling leaf.

"Ever made snow angels?" he asked. Why? He had no idea.

"Sure, all the time. I mean, when I was little. It's not something I do after I get off work or anything. You? Did you make them in the sand?"

"Sure. Probably can do about the same things in the sand you can do in snow."

"Snow forts?" she asked.

"Sandcastles," he countered.

"Snow ice cream."

He could tell she thought she had him with this one. "Sand pudding."

She stuck her hands on her hips. "That's not even a real thing. Oh, wait. I think I've seen those in a magazine."

"Every beach party where there are kids, someone will bring sand pudding."

"Hmmm." She tapped her chin, lost in thought. Then stooped to tie her shoe. "But not snowballs."

Quinn rose with two premade snowballs. He'd fallen for her innocently tying her shoe ruse. "You planned this," he accused. It was so devious. So sneaky. So charming.

"Who? What? Where? Me? No way. These were waiting when I got here." She lifted her arm, snowball at the ready.

"You wouldn't dare," he said.

He'd practically challenged her to lob a snowball at him. With a laugh, she tossed the ball of snow in his direction, hitting him on the knee.

He stared down at the frost left behind on his pants. "You have terrible aim."

"That's a warning shot." Caution filled her voice, but trailed off into a delightful shriek as he began gathering snow.

But instead of running away, Quinn charged in his direction, and he fell backside first into a mound of fluffy snow. She stood over him, a grin spanning her face. "Amateur. You're in the perfect position for a face full of snow."

"California boy, what can I say?" He lifted his hands in defeat. He'd fallen right into her trap. Again. Of course she had the snow battle advantage growing up in Massachusetts and scuffling with a pile of cousins. Except he'd probably fall for her tricks again and again, if only to hear her laugh.

Heady off her win, Quinn offered a hand to help him up. His plan. With a gentle tug, Quinn fell off balance, joining him in the snow. "Yeah, yeah. I deserved that," she said, laughing. "Just like you deserve *this*."

And there came the promised snow in his face. Quinn scrambled away and took off running before he'd even wiped the snow from his eyes. He launched after her, his longer strides eating the distance between them. Her laughter floated across the air, and despite being wet and snow-covered, he hadn't felt this light and happy in…years.

For a few moments, Nolan enjoyed the day like a man without worries. Not about his sister. Or keeping his dad's business afloat so there'd always be food on the table or putting Kaylee through school. For now, he wouldn't waste a single moment thinking about all he'd lost in the fire or all he had to gain here in Bethany Springs. Thanks to the woman in front of him, he'd found a carefree soul inside him. A part of himself he'd lost since taking on the responsibility of caring for his sister. His hands anchored on her hips and he twirled her in the air. Who knew a smile could feed his soul?

Two quick bursts from a car horn shocked them both. They both turned their heads toward the intrusive sound, and he eased her slowly to the ground. A late model sedan parked a few feet away. Quinn stepped away from him as she gazed over at the man emerging from the car.

"Who's that?" he asked her.

She didn't appear too surprised. "My dad."

Nolan instantly straightened. Tried to make his step away from Quinn as nonchalant as possible. Mr. Hardwick's face proved unreadable, but he kept his brown eyes trained on Nolan. When had he last been sized up by a girl's father? Sixteen and going to prom? His back stiffened.

Quinn kissed the older man's cheek as he approached. "Hi, Daddy."

"Hello, honey," he said, giving her hand a gentle squeeze. "Miss seeing my Grinny Quinny."

Quinn took the silly nickname in stride, focusing her attention on Nolan. "Dad, I'd like to introduce you to Nolan Vesser. Nolan, this is my dad, Raymond Hardwick."

Nolan extended his hand. "Mr. Hardwick."

"Call me Ray," her father said, his tone even, his face still an indecipherable mask but his gaze direct.

Yeah, 'cause you were flirting with his daughter. The man couldn't have missed the snowball and chase thing you two had going. Or the way you leaned toward her or looked at her.

"Quinn tells me you burned your arm. She says you haven't been able to do much work. Since you're away from your regular doctor, I'm happy to take a look." No accusation lay in his tone, only kindly concern.

Quinn nudged his shoulder. "I was a bit worried about you."

"I'm feeling much better today," Nolan told him. He cut a glance toward Quinn, but she stared straight ahead at her father. Whether truly worried about his injury or trying to jumpstart him into action, calling her father the doctor was a good play on her part.

"And clearly able to lift objects over fifty pounds," Ray Hardwick said.

Yeah, the man hadn't missed Nolan spinning Quinn around. Nolan tried to gauge Ray's reaction, but he gave nothing away.

"Let's go into the farmhouse so I can take a look. I have my medical bag in the car."

Nolan hated to inconvenience the man. "I think I'm over the hump," he said, using his most reassuring voice.

Ray Hardwick lifted a brow. "Never turn away free medical care."

Nolan rubbed at his chin. "Can't argue with that."

"All part of the service." Ray headed for the car.

Nolan and Quinn followed him, and together they trod across the clearing to the farmhouse. Once inside, Ray turned to his daughter. "I'll examine him in the kitchen. Better lighting."

"Sure, I'll make some tea and–"

"Honey, I have to examine the man alone."

Her hands flew to her cheeks. "Of course, I'll be out in the cleaning room of the Berry House."

Inside the kitchen, Ray put on glasses and invited him to sit at the booth. "Haven't been in this kitchen in years. You can go ahead and roll up your sleeve."

"You were here a lot?" Nolan asked, following Ray's directions and unbuttoning his sleeve.

The older man peered around the room. "My grandparents owned this home, but we closed it up after they passed. My mom would come out a couple times a year to check on the place, and the neighbors kept an eye on it for us too. We should probably sell it, but none of us had the strength to let go."

Nolan's heart began to pound. He'd waited for this. Clues into the mystery of why the Hardwicks thought they still owned the ornament company. "So no one sold even a small part?" he asked, aiming for nonchalant.

"Oh, we let the small factory building in Bethany Springs go when demand went down. The place held no sentimental meaning to us. Not like out here. I'm going to remove the bandage now," Ray told him, in full doctor mode.

Quinn's father carefully pulled the sticky tape away and then positioned the suspended kitchen light so he could examine Nolan's burn more fully. The injury on his arm no longer appeared as red and irritated. The doctor gently probed around the wound. "How tender is this, and no being a tough guy. On a scale from one to ten."

"About a three."

Ray nodded his head. "Good, good. I see no signs of infection, and this is healing nicely. Although more than likely you'll have a scar. I can prescribe an ointment that will help, but it won't completely disappear."

Nolan angled his head to stare down at the backs of his hands. "I've worked around glass most of my life. An extra scar is nothing. Although it is itchy."

"That's to be expected. One of nature's ways of telling us we're healing. And your overall pain?"

"I'm good. Stopped taking the prescription stuff."

"Switching to the over the counter meds is perfectly fine too. You don't have to keep wearing a bandage unless you want an extra buffer when you're working. You'll want to avoid bumps. As your doctor, I'll be giving you the all clear to work now," he said.

The all clear. Grinny Quinny maneuvered more like Canny Quinny, cutting him off from using his burn as an excuse. His awe for her grew. She must be pretty disappointed in him. A wavy, sinking feeling dropped in his stomach. When had he started to care about disappointing her? He'd come here to assess the Hardwick Ornament Company. A company he, in fact, rightfully owned.

"Do you need some additional bandages?" Ray asked, opening his black medical bag.

"I have plenty from the hospital," he told the older man, still a little stunned how quickly his circumstances here on Quinn's farm had changed.

"Nolan."

Ray's calm and kind voice drew him from his troubled thoughts.

"Yes?" He began unrolling his sleeve.

"What you tell me, your condition, it all falls under doctor-patient confidentiality. You've been through an ordeal, and if you need to talk…"

That sinking feeling in his stomach took a nosedive. Canny Quinny had nothing to do with inviting her father out here to check him out; Quinn genuinely cared about his health. Probably to her, his lack of participation could only be chalked up to an injury. After all, who would agree to take a job, travel over three thousand miles and then not do anything unless he couldn't because he was hurt? But he'd never use his burn as an excuse when it rarely even pained him now.

He'd made promises to Quinn when she offered this job. Nolan hadn't done much carpentry, but he worked well with his hands and knew his way around a hammer. He could rebuild a sagging porch. Help knock down a crumbling building. He could help with a lot of projects around the farmhouse that didn't involve stepping inside the workshop.

Armed with that plan, he shoved past those prickles of guilt that had poked him since he arrived and found the remarkable Quinn Hardwick.

"Nolan?"

He shook his head. "Sorry, I was thinking. Thanks for coming out here. I'll join Quinn out in the Berry House and see what she needs help with. I don't know what the place looked like before, but she's made the living quarters nice and comfortable."

Ray glanced down at his watch. "I may pop over there for a few minutes, but I only snuck out here between patients." The doctor closed his medical bag and the two of them retrieved their coats from the mudroom and strolled the short distance to the Berry House. Once inside, they followed the pounding sound of a hammer against wood until they found Quinn breaking down what used to be a pallet.

Without her bulky red coat, Nolan could admire her strength as she tore apart two pieces of wood. She'd piled her hair high on her head, with only a few of the silky dark strands still wet from their impulsive snowball fight. Even with her safety goggles and thick flannel shirt, he'd never seen anyone so adorable.

After propping the hammer against the wall, Quinn gave her father a hug. "It's so good to see you. As you can probably surmise, I haven't done much with the old berry screening room, but it's perfect for organizing all the boxes. But the bunkhouse is looking pretty good."

"Why not get everything sorted in the workshop?" her father asked.

"I will once we get the new ventilation system and the sprinklers installed, but I still have to paint, and this way, I only have to move things once."

Ray kissed his daughter's cheek. "I'll take a rain check on seeing the bunkhouse. I'm afraid of what my waiting room will look like if I hang out here too much longer." He stuck his hands in his coat pocket to retrieve his gloves. "Oh, I almost forgot. These are for you." He pulled out a small wrapped package and extended the gift to Nolan.

"Me?" he asked, taking the ribbon-tied bundle. After Ray's nod, he tugged on the string to reveal a pair of hand-knitted gloves.

"Ah, I see you got one of Gram's signature gifts," Quinn said.

"Why would she make me anything?" But Nolan knew why. Like Quinn, her grandmother wanted him to feel welcome here. When she realized he didn't have a warm pair of gloves, she made sure Nolan wouldn't go without. He swallowed against a lump forming in his throat. Guilt reared up stronger than ever.

"She must like you. Gram doesn't knit for just anyone."

"Nice to meet you, Nolan." With a wave, Ray Hardwick left, whistling a cheery tune.

"I probably way overstepped my bounds in inviting

Dad out here. Okay, no probably about it, but I figured you hadn't even started searching for a doctor yet, and Dad is the best."

"No, I appreciate you keeping an eye out for me."

She sighed with relief, and then she handed him a crowbar.

"What's this for?"

"You said not a twinge of pain this morning, right?"

His opinion of her returned to Canny Quinny. Not that he minded in the least. He planned to help out from now on anyway. "Yes."

She motioned around the storeroom. "Somewhere in this mess should be the ventilation and sprinkler system. I can save money installing it myself. I found three great tutorials online, and watched them all last night. Probably could have got it done in an hour and a half if the internet worked better out here."

"What about safety?" he asked.

"It's okay. I talked about it with the inspector in town and she walked me through a few of the things I still had questions about. She's going to make sure everything is safe and sound. Plus, I won't fire up a single thing until she gives her seal of approval."

She handed him a pair of safety goggles. "Let's go."

Someone had helpfully stenciled the contents onto most of the larger boxes, so they shoved the furnace and the kiln into the corner to open once the workshop passed inspection. Other boxes came directly from the mail order businesses, either shipped to her or to the local hardware store in Bethany Springs. Quinn had already popped into town to retrieve them, and he carried them in from her truck. The older boxes, worn with frayed corners, came from Gram's attic.

"Was your grandmother okay with giving you all these?" he asked, eyeing the rows of boxes.

Quinn ran a finger down a cardboard side. "All the pictures and memorabilia from the old Hardwick Ornament Company should be in these. She loves the idea of me collecting everything to display in a mini-museum. If you find anything cool accidentally mixed in with the other stuff, we can stack it here."

"Will do." With a plan in mind, they set to work.

"Found part of the sprinkler system," she called a few minutes later after breaking open a box.

He discovered shears and the large tweezers used for shaping and scoring glass. The next box contained a blowtorch, and his pulse began to race. The sooner they unpacked, the sooner he'd be working with open flame. He dropped the blowtorch, his fingers nerveless, and grabbed a piece of wood.

"You're finding all the cool stuff. What's that for?"

He glanced down at the object in his hands. "It's, uh…it's a block. Sometimes we call it a spoon. It's for shaping the glass while it's still hot so it'll be round."

"Neat. Can't wait to see you with it in action. I bet you're ready to work on some of your own commissions."

His commissions. He'd almost forgotten they'd worked out a kind of time-share. "My clients aren't expecting anything until after January."

"Oh, that's good to know." She quickly moved to the next box, anxious to open another new "treasure."

Nolan took a few more deep breaths and shoved the panicky feelings so far down he'd never have to think about his reaction again. Still. The idea of the red-hot furnace. The roil and bubble of the molten glass. The thought of the open flame in the reheater caused sweat to break out on the back of his neck. The memories had a hold on him. He held his breath a moment, forcing his pulse to slow, and his mind to clear.

Although he'd been in the workshop before, tonight happened to be his first time around glass blowing supplies after the fire. Of course he'd reacted, but that deep-seated dread could now clear out. A one-time situation to be forgotten.

With new resolve, he attacked the next box revealing a shiny new blowpipe and his heart pounded. *Not* a one-time-only response. Another memory confronted him. When Quinn first brought him to the workshop to show the place off, his lungs constricted like a man holding his breath under water at four minutes and counting.

He glared at the blowpipe in his hand, lumbered to the wall and balanced the pipe against it. At his feet lay some of the older boxes that came out of Gram's attic. Opening those might be the answer. Laying off the glass blowing supplies and sorting through that stuff wouldn't cause an anxiety attack.

Whoa, slow down. He wasn't experiencing an anxiety

attack. No, he felt understandable apprehension. What if he couldn't get his negative association with fire and glass blowing under control? Not only would the HOC no longer play in his future, he'd be out of a career.

The blaze that took down his apartment had nothing to do with his shop. The fire investigator had provided that very conclusion to his insurance company days ago. In reality, he should be no different today than the day before the fire. *Slow down and focus.* With that plan in mind, he popped open one of the attic boxes.

The scent of mothballs and the earthen woody aroma of old papers touched his nose as he opened the first cardboard box. Row after row of large legal folders waited inside. Someone had scrawled the date in the corner in a fading cursive script. He found a lease for a building in Bethany Springs. One folder held several years of catalogues featuring Hardwick ornaments. Tucked behind the files he discovered an ornament in a metal tin. After carefully removing a protective layer of bubble wrap, Nolan smiled when he spotted a glass alligator ornament. He lifted the glass to the light for a better look. Hand blown, with the barest hint of lines from a mold.

Who put a gator on a Christmas tree? Nolan replaced the wrap, tucked the ornament inside and set the box aside. Besides the sprinklers, Quinn hoped to find items for inspiration, but also fun memorabilia to display in the part of the Berry House she planned to turn into the mini-museum of the old Hardwick Ornament Company.

His eyes strayed to the box again. Somewhere inside might be a clue about why Quinn's great-great-grandfather transferred ownership to the Vessers and why he never told anyone.

Nolan moved on to the next box, carrying the same musty scent as the other. This box revealed the kind of memorabilia Quinn had wished for. Nestled inside a mess of packing peanuts, he found another glass ornament, still in the old-fashioned packaging of what he'd guess dated to around the '50s. A smile tugged at his lips when he identified the ornament as a sea turtle. Like the alligator, the craftwork remained undeniable, a gorgeous blending of the colors of the sea. Green, blue and turquoise made up the body of the creature.

He itched to remove the ornament so he could hold it up to the window and watch as light shimmered through the glass. Only the box didn't appear worn, suggesting some long-ago Hardwick had put this away for safekeeping. Another mystery.

A prickle stung the back of his neck and he glanced up to notice Quinn had focused her brown eyes on him. She studied him, her expression a mix of curiosity and hope.

"Does the ornament inspire you to venture into the workshop? Because it does me, and I've pored through these catalogues and stared at ornaments on my family tree my whole life. Are you getting…anything?"

Ahhh, so that explained why hope lurked in those brown depths. Nolan knew she questioned why the workshop hadn't tempted him to step inside yet. Honestly, he wondered why too. His fingers trembled a little as he placed the ornament box on the table and gave her an encouraging smile, even though inside he felt nothing but confusion and dread at the thought of creating again.

Below where he'd discovered the ornament box, he found an ornately-carved wooden frame. A bit of dust clung to the glass, which he rubbed away with the pad of his thumb to reveal a black and white picture. Two men sporting the popular flat caps of the 1920s, wearing collarless shirts with their sleeves rolled up and smiling for the camera. A rarity, since most of the subjects of their generation wore serious expressions.

Wait a minute. He recognized the background. Nolan squinted, realizing the two men stood in the workshop on the Hardwick Farm. One man carried the tools of a glass blower. His jaw angled in such a manner that it reminded him of his dad. Milos Vesser. Had to be. His great-great ancestor, the original Vesser. And while Nolan couldn't make out the splotch of ink behind them, he knew they must have just carved his name and date in the wood.

His chest grew heavy.

The same workshop.

The same business plan.

A Hardwick and a Vesser.

Quinn attempted everything she could to mirror

the past. To recreate the magic of the Hardwick Ornament Company. His eyes strayed to her brown head, bent over as she worked to read the packing slip on the box beside her. She'd already poured so much of her time and energy and heart into the project. Her dream.

Nolan's gut clenched. He shouldn't feel guilty here. He wasn't doing anything wrong. The Hardwick Ornament Company belonged to him. He turned away from the picture and grabbed the crowbar. For a large storeroom, the walls sure hemmed him in, blocking his moves and clouding his thoughts. The sooner he got these crates unpacked, the sooner he could get out of here.

Chapter Seven

Quinn had no idea what had gotten into Nolan, but she'd never seen the man work so hard. Had opening all the deliveries filled with the glass blowing supplies finally made the dream real for him? Her fingers began to tingle, and for a moment, all the fear and worry and doubt disappeared and she felt weightless. She'd bake some cookies to celebrate.

Sweat pooled behind her neck and on the small of her back. Her limbs ached a bit from the unusual exertion and her stomach would grumble any time now. She sheathed the blade on the box cutter, tossed it onto the sorting table, and took off the heavy work gloves. Nolan still worked like a man on a mission, and she wandered over to some of Gram's boxes Nolan had already sorted. She giggled when she spotted the sea turtle ornament.

Her laugh must have caught his attention because he paused and glanced her way. A tiny line furrowed between his eyes, as he caught a glance at the funny ornament she examined. How could a confused expression look so amazing on a man? Maybe only this particular man.

"I was curious about that myself," he said, finally taking a break. His footsteps echoed as he approached her, his feet heavy on the old-fashioned plank and beam flooring. "What's with the strange ornament?"

She tapped the corner of the box. "This is part of the wedding tree ornament series. Other than the first heart ornament, these solidified the Hardwick Ornament Company's reputation and brand. Family and friends give the new couple an ornament that they open once each month."

"But a turtle?"

"Each ornament has a special meaning. For instance, this one is all about longevity and traveling together."

"A turtle means all that?" he asked, unable to hide the skepticism in his voice.

"Well, turtles live longer than almost any animal on earth, so they serve as an inspiration for a lifelong love. Turtles are found all over the world, in the ocean and on land."

"I found an alligator too," he said.

"That one represents patience, which is nice, but like a lot of those ornaments, there can be a negative meaning too. An alligator will wait a very long time to attack, so the message there is to not hold on to slights or grudges in your relationship." She bit the corner of her lip. "If you want to see wild ornaments, my parents' Christmas wedding tree has an artichoke."

"I'm almost afraid to ask," he said, then his chest began to rumble when he could no longer hold back a laugh.

Quinn giggled beside him. "You know, it's not as bad as it sounds. The ornament is actually sort of... okay."

His chest only shook harder. "That's great marketing. Hardwick Ornament Company. You'll want our ornaments on your tree. They're sort of okay."

She had to blink a few times to not tear up as she laughed. Almost every moment of every day since Gram had named Quinn caretaker of the HOC, she'd spent working and dreaming and planning, all while weighed down by worry and apprehension. But not once had she really laughed. She'd never felt lighter as she stood beside Nolan giggling over the absurdity of the really bad slogan idea.

Her phone vibrated in her pocket, and she paused to lift it from her jeans. *Oh, no.* Her screen lit up with an appointment reminder. Quinn lost her smile and a heaviness settled in over her heart. She'd set up the notification a week ago so she wouldn't forget a meeting with the loan officer at the Bethany Springs Savings and Loan. She'd been turned down for a loan to reopen the HOC, not once, not twice but... Maybe the third time would be the charm. How could she fail with her secret weapon—Nolan Vesser?

"I think we've done enough for now," she

announced, surveying the room. Flattened cardboard stacked several feet high in the corner. Packing peanuts and bubble wrap scattered across the floor. Many boxes remained untouched.

"Really?" Nolan asked.

No, not really. She'd rather be unpacking and emptying boxes in the storeroom with Nolan than wobbling on heels in a skirt and possibly facing another refusal from the loan officer. Should she tell Nolan about her past applications failing? No, better not. Why invite trouble if everything worked out on the third go-around?

So she plastered on a smile and brushed her hands together. "I don't want to wear you out." Quinn grabbed her coat and sprinted to the farmhouse to grab a quick shower and slap on a bit of make-up before heading into town.

Why did the chairs in the bank have to be so uncomfortable? To discourage pleading your case after a rejection of a loan? Maybe to remind patrons that under no circumstances would they want to come back inside the office again, so keep up with the loan payments. The armrests were more ornamental than practical, her feet didn't touch the carpet if she reclined all the way back, and the seat lacked padding.

Mrs. Henderson sat behind the desk, her readers at the tip of her nose, as she perused the paperwork in front of her. The woman had already rejected her twice, and Quinn would have asked for another loan officer, but Mrs. Henderson was it for the Bethany Springs Savings and Loan. She'd been kind, of course, her eyes a bit sad as she made suggestions to improve Quinn's chances for next time. But once someone got in the habit of rejecting you…

The loan officer cleared her throat and tugged the readers down where they suspended on a chain around her neck. "Your paperwork is in order and your assets are stronger than before, Ms. Hardwick."

"Thank you." Why did Quinn feel like she'd returned to second grade, waiting in front of the principal's office because MacKenna Crane wouldn't get off the bottom of the slide? Her knees began to tremble, too, just like they had when she had to explain that yes, she knew Mac was at the bottom and yes, Quinn slid down anyway.

"You've really strengthened your case, and I'm prepared to extend a loan," Mrs. Henderson announced with a smile.

It took everything inside Quinn not to slink down the seat and onto the floor like a cartoon character. Suddenly it felt easier to breathe and it took her two attempts to squeak out words. "Thank you."

Mrs. Henderson's smile widened, but her eyes filled with caution. "Unfortunately, the amount I approved was not your full asking total." The woman slid her gaze over the paperwork. The bank would give her about two-thirds, but the news she'd even gotten a penny amazed Quinn. One less penny she'd have to ask from her parents. And Gram. Or her grandparents who lived in Texas. She could pay off at least one of the credit cards she'd used to buy the furnace and the kiln.

"Where do I sign?" she asked.

Mrs. Henderson laughed. "I'm glad you're so excited. I want you to read through the entirety of this document, even the fine print, and you'll have to agree to enrollment in the bank's new pilot program on credit counseling. I have a short video for you to watch and then we can finalize everything." She turned the screen on her computer and pressed Play.

"Welcome to the next chapter in your financial independence..."

Nolan thought about continuing to work on the boxes in the cleaning room, but with Quinn gone, the place lost its energy and sparkle. He noticed the cracks in the walls and the gouges in the flooring. Funny, he hadn't realized the downright dreariness of the place while they'd worked together.

He eyed the box containing the files. It wouldn't be a big deal to take them into the bunk end of the Berry House, right? They had to go through the paperwork eventually—why not in comfort? If he managed to find the missing pieces to the mystery of the HOC ownership, even better. But something didn't settle right inside him. It felt sneaky, and he already felt conflicted with the ownership question anyway.

Instead, Nolan grabbed his coat, switched off the light, and walked down the hallway toward the bunkhouse. He strode into the kitchen but didn't feel like coffee. He strolled over to the bookcase, but all the books were about plants. In the corner, the battered Christmas tree Quinn had set up appeared bare and a little sad. The Bethany Springs General Store carried ornaments. He could buy decorations for the tree and do a little ornament research at the same time.

After a quick shower, Nolan tugged on the flannel shirt his sister bought him. He should call her while he was in town. And buy more flannels. His small rotation of winter clothes drove him to the small laundry room almost every three days. He'd rather open his wallet and buy a few more shirts to avoid that.

Once in Bethany Springs, he parked in the small lot off Main Street and hiked over to the general store, grabbing a few shirts off the rack as quickly as he'd picked out the coat days before with Quinn. He smiled at the memory. Already this woman felt interwoven with his life. He sucked in a deep breath and waited for the inevitable freakout to hit him. He'd avoided getting too close to others. First, he'd been so overwhelmed with the death of his parents, taking care of a grieving sister, and keeping Dad's business afloat so he could keep a roof over both their heads.

By the time Kaylee entered college, his urge to push others away had become habit.

But it hadn't been his natural inclination with Quinn Hardwick. Why?

You never got the chance to be carefree... Now you can. Was his sister right?

Nolan paid for his shirts and left the store, his steps slow, his thoughts a little dazed. Argh, and he forgot to buy the ornaments. He locked his new flannels in the Jeep and turned around so he could return to the store. As he circled back, a flash of red caught the corner of his eye. As if his earlier thoughts of the woman had conjured her up, Quinn exited the... He glanced at the granite sign in the grass. The Bethany Springs Savings and Loan. Did she need money?

Her dark hair curled around her shoulders, and she wore dark boots that matched her black skirt. He'd only seen Quinn in jeans and work boots, her long hair knotted on the top of her head or in a ponytail. All dressed up and beaming with pride, she stunned him. Before he realized it, his feet led him to her side.

"Thought you would've gotten enough of me at the farm," she teased as he approached. Her brown eyes sparkled, more brilliant than he'd ever seen them, and his thoughts strayed to the Savings and Loan.

She asked, "Everything okay?"

He flexed his jaw, releasing some of the tension. He'd been scowling at the thought of Quinn needing money. He mentally ran through the recent expenses his long list of supplies must have caused. He'd repay her with interest. "I stocked up at the GS," he finally said, not liking his mental math.

"Hey, look at you. Using the initials like a Bethany Super Berry."

"A what?"

Her eyes crinkled in the corners. "That's our high school mascot."

"A Super Berry? How intimidating. I'm surprised the other teams didn't run for cover immediately." He gave a fake shudder.

"Mock all you want," she said with a fluttery wave of her hand. "Until we rub your nose in our many state championships."

"What are you doing in town?" *And coming out of the bank?* He kept his tone casual, only polite curiosity involved, definitely no prying here.

The corners of her lips lifted and the smile she flashed him made his heart beat faster. "I finally got approved for a loan for the Hardwick Ornament Company. And I have you to thank for it."

"Me?" he asked, pointing to his chest. How could that be?

"Don't be so modest. Your work is world-class."

"You've seen my work?"

A light flush tinged her cheeks. "Of course. Your last name may be Vesser, but I wouldn't offer you a job just on that. Gram and I drove over to Mount Holyoke College to look at one of your installations. Stunning." She patted her face. "I promised myself I wouldn't fangirl all over you. I lasted over a week, that's pretty good."

Fangirl? He'd thought he could read Quinn fairly well, but he'd had no idea. She had some poker face.

She shook her head in embarrassment. "Anyway,

you're my good-luck charm. Let me buy you lunch to celebrate. Although we'll be celebrating on a budget, because you know, most of that money is basically spent," she teased.

Nolan knew she expected him to smile. To laugh. She made light and joked when stressed. That was her quirk. Her tell.

"How about the Giddings House?" she asked.

As someone used to locking away emotion, he wouldn't pick at her need to joke her problems away. He could play along, and asked, "Why do I think you would have chosen the Giddings House even if we weren't celebrating?"

She raised her hands in surrender. "You got me. I would have picked this place if I had to lift my spirits instead of celebrate, and I've been wanting some pumpkin bread toast."

Why'd she make that sound like a guilty confession? "Not cranberry?" he asked, intrigued.

Quinn lifted a brow and gave a cautious look from side to side like she starred in a Bethany Springs version of a spy movie. "Don't you dare tell anyone this. Cranberry might be the thing around here, but pumpkin is my favorite."

This time his chuckle came naturally. When had he ever laughed so much?

She shook out her hands. "I have so much energy. I know it's cold, but do you mind if we walk?"

He nodded toward the sidewalk in agreement.

They fell in easy step together as they strolled toward the older section of Bethany Springs.

"It wonderful you've been able to keep the glass blowing family tradition going through so many generations. We weren't so lucky," she said.

His breath lodged in his chest, his chance to learn more. "Kaylee and I were in the shop with Dad as soon we could understand the words hot and really hot," he answered instead, rather than prying. Why? He had no idea, but he breathed easier.

"I didn't find much about your father online," she said, then bit her lip as if she'd revealed too much. "I promise I wasn't being creepy."

"No, I understand. You're about to invite someone into your business. It's smart to want to find out everything you can," he assured her. If he'd performed his own due diligence before rushing out here, he'd have known the Hardwicks weren't rich.

He and Kaylee never spoke much about their parents after the car accident. At first, they avoided mentioning their mom and dad because it hurt to think of them. Being so young, dodging thoughts and memories turned out to be the way he and Kaylee coped with their pain. Later their silence became a habit, and neither one of them wanted to revisit a time they'd preferred to forget.

Now he allowed himself to picture their parents in his mind. Like how his tall, barrel-chested dad always seemed strong and unbreakable, but his mom's quick smiles turned their mighty father to mush. Or when traffic lights changed from red to green, and he could hear his mom's voice telling him, "It's not a race" as she taught him to drive. Kaylee got her determination and love of school from their mother, and he'd inherited the need to create from their dad.

Nolan waited for the familiar ache brought on by thoughts of his parents, but instead he felt his lips twitch into a grin. They'd be so proud of Kaylee graduating from law school and making her mark on the world. Would they be pleased with him? Happy he walked in the previous footsteps of elder Vessers?

He shook his head to break the spell of time and memories and focused on Quinn's question. "Dad had a small glass shop. He specialized in repairing broken glass for estates and museums, but he loved recreating vases and goblets of the past. He'd challenge himself by using only the techniques and tools available in that time period. There's evidence of glass blowing dating back to the time of Pompeii."

"Wow. It must have been fun to experiment without the ease of electricity to fire up a furnace or fireproof gloves. How did you move into creating those big installations?"

"After he died, I kept up with his repair work, but I didn't have his kind of artistry with the recreations." Embarrassment and shame blasted though him, colder than the swirling snow on this New England afternoon.

Her jaw firmed and her expression grew skeptical. "Lack of artistry? I doubt that. Look how many people are willing to wait any amount of time it takes for your sculptures. Don't forget, I've seen your stuff online. It's unique, and, well…" Pink tinged her cheeks. "Amazing."

Conviction laced every one of her words. With her hand on her hip, he had no doubt Quinn Hardwick would argue with him about *him*. The only other person in his corner like that was his sister. Quinn's belief in him warmed him like coffee, but she didn't really understand. "Compared to my father…"

Quinn rolled her eyes. "Oh, please. Don't even start with that comparison bunk. I have two overachiever siblings and a mess of cousins. I had to learn pretty quickly the only person you can really compete against is yourself. Today's Quinn is smarter than yesterday's, so believe me, in a fight, I can always take her."

Nolan laughed at the awkward boxing stance she followed up with. He rubbed at his chin because maybe she had a point. Comparison was natural because he'd inherited his dad's workshop, but over time he'd made Vesser GlassArts his own. "I didn't have the love for the recreations like he did."

"Now that makes sense. It about broke his heart when my great-grandpa shuttered up the Hardwick Ornament Company."

"Oh?" he asked, his voice encouraging. He didn't want to appear too eager to find out how the Hardwicks lost their legacy. And why not a single one seemed to know. "How did that happen?"

"My great-great-grandfather and great-grandfath—you know what, let's just refer to them as the greats.

Anyway, the greats were the ones with the vision, the brilliant marketing, which barely existed then, and the drive behind HOC. The Vessers wielded the skill and creativity. My great-grandfather held on until it became clear Grandpa's heart lay in medicine. At some point in the '60s, Great-Grandpa closed up shop."

"That's about the time my family moved to California," he said, fitting one of the pieces together.

"At one point, they talked about selling the business; they even had a few offers. But according to my dad, nothing felt right. I guess they thought a Hardwick should own the Hardwick Ornament Company, and now one does." She flashed him a sweet smile that made his heart dip. She linked her arm through his as she launched into her next thought. "And with you here, it's like it was meant to be. You and I have made the greats' dream live again."

After lunch, Nolan escorted Quinn to her vehicle. She tossed her purse and a sack filled with pumpkin bread onto the bench seat of the truck, then turned to face him. He'd expected her to climb in behind the wheel, but the muscles of her throat worked like she was struggling with needing to say something. The wind ruffled a strand of her light brown hair, and she tucked it behind her ear, her hands jerky. Quinn stood before him, a bundle of awkward.

The delicious meal they'd eaten settled in his stomach like a boulder because he knew she would say something grateful, and every part of him rebelled at that happening. Nolan already felt terrible about how things played out with his ownership of the HOC. She'd given him credit for changing her fortune, but Quinn set the new Hardwick Ornament Company on the path to success through her hard work from the beginning. He'd only lucked into a deed to the place.

Her fingers touched his forearm, and his body stiffened.

"Nolan, thank you."

"You don't have to thank me," he said, angling away from her, trying to put some distance between the two of them.

But she only gripped him tighter, her face so open and earnest. "You took a chance on me. Leaving everything you knew in California, your sister, and then crossing ten other states to get here. I, uh…"

Her eyes grew shiny with unshed tears and everything inside him ached. *Don't thank me again. Don't make me better than I am.*

Quinn gazed up at the sky, as if the right words could be found in the clouds, as she struggled not to let the tears slip. "I dreaded asking my family for money. Gram's already given me some, and so have my parents. The idea of it…" Her gaze met his again. "Well, with you here and the loan, I won't have to ask for more."

Her expression brightened like the heavy mist dimming her view had blown away. Her brown eyes sparkled and her tremulous smile radiated. Nolan couldn't stop himself from being swept up in her joy, even though he knew he shouldn't. He held the key to taking her dream away.

Her hand fell to her side, but she still grinned up at him. "I can tell I've embarrassed you. I'd apologize, but making others feel uneasy is kind of a Hardwick family trait," she told him with a playful wink. Her hair flew around her like a cloud as she rotated around and hopped into her truck. "Don't show any weaknesses to my cousins–they'll pounce."

After a quick wave, she drove off in the direction of the farm.

With Quinn gone, he noticed the bite of the winter air. The brisk wind cut into his cheeks and along the back of his neck. He rolled up his collar to block the chill. After stuffing his hands in his pockets, his fingers wrapped around the gloves Quinn's grandmother had knitted for him. Grateful, he slipped his hands inside. Joy chased away the gloom like sunlight as he noticed one of the fingers hung lopsided and way too long. But the gloves did the trick, kept him warm, and that's the only thing that mattered.

He didn't deserve to wear the handmade gift. Gram had knitted the gloves and given them to him in good faith. And he hadn't arrived in Bethany Springs in that same vein. Before he'd come to this town, the Hardwicks were a faceless group of people standing in the way between him and his property. *His* new beginning.

He zipped between the cars in the parking lot until he stood outside his vehicle.

Nothing had prepared him for Quinn Hardwick. She grabbed risk with both hands and blew away caution like the seeds of a dandelion. She worked from the moment the sun rose to well past it setting. Quinn had invited him into her world, shared her plans and her hopes, and he'd caught her contagious enthusiasm. She cared about everyone around her, and that included him.

He climbed into the Jeep and shut the door against the whistling cold air outside, but he didn't slide the key into the ignition. Instead Nolan sat, his fingers drumming along the steering wheel. So, pack up and leave? Drive back to California and spend Christmas alone? His sister's miserable lumpy couch loomed as an option, but he'd been sleeping on a twin bed, so clearly comfort no longer stood out as a huge priority for him. He could be out of the Berry House in ten minutes. Even with the few things he'd bought here in Bethany Springs, all his possessions still fit in the duffel bag.

The insurance money should be in after the new year. Kaylee would enjoy helping him find another apartment and setting up a studio with brand-new equipment. This time, he'd avoid the convenience of renting a place with an apartment above his business. He'd been burned. Literally.

He could say goodbye to cold, and mucking horse stalls, and dusty storerooms. Forget about running around with Quinn in the snow, and feeding Lulubelle a carrot after she escaped from her stall, and finding pieces of his family history.

Palm trees.

No more worrying about a life that wasn't his.

Christmas on the beach.

Home.

Only…he couldn't leave without seeing her at least once. Wish her well. Dread tore at his heart. Quinn had banked all her plans on him. If he left, she might lose the loan as well as being stuck without a designer.

His knuckles whitened around the steering wheel as his grip tightened. Bracing himself, he waited for the hemmed-in sensation of unwanted responsibility to wrap around him like an old, heavy blanket. Nothing happened. He centered his thoughts on how much Quinn relied on him, and still nothing but… acceptance.

The glass blowing community wasn't a large one; locating the right professional would take some time. Nolan could stay on in the Berry House until he found an artisan worthy of her.

With that plan in mind, he shoved the key into the ignition, and the engine roared to life. As he drove down Main Street, street workers hung banners wishing him a Merry Christmas from the streetlights. Every time he visited downtown, the decorations multiplied. Honestly, they'd passed the over-the-top mark on his last visit.

A sedan with a Christmas tree tied to the roof passed

him, the backseat filled with two happy, bouncing-in-their-seat, excited children. A light snow began to fall as he passed a sign on the outskirts of town.

Thank you for visiting Bethany Springs. Come back soon!

The city reminded him of a picture postcard, of both a time past and hope for the future. Just like Quinn. He'd expected to be greeted by wealthy heirs, but instead found a mud-splattered, intriguing woman chasing after a horse.

With a chuckle, Nolan reached for the knob on his radio and a lively Christmas song surrounded him. Quinn would like this music. She probably knew every word, and most likely could retell some story that went along with the tune about making snow angels, which reminded him of their game before her father showed up. Did snow ice cream really exist?

Here he had snow. And Christmas trees. Hardwicks who checked out his injured arm and knitted him gloves.

And he had Quinn.

Why not stay here for Christmas?

Why? Because the HOC title might as well be flashing with green and red strobe lights in his duffel bag right now. A blinking alert reminding him that he'd never fully allow himself to relax and enjoy Christmas in Bethany Springs. Not with the truth of his ownership jammed between them like a teacher breaking couples up at a prom. Even though Quinn had no idea what held him back, he knew, and the piece of paper acted like a wedge. He had to leave.

But did the deed have to be a barrier?

If two generations of Vessers hadn't moved forward to take full ownership, why should he? He might never discover how his family came to possess the HOC, but Quinn stood as the heart of the company, and the business should remain hers. Maybe someday, he'd draw up the paperwork so the Hardwick Ornament Company would be rightly hers, but right now he didn't have to do a thing. Problem solved. Snow instead of sand on Christmas Day sounded like a pretty great trade-off.

As he neared the farm, the heavy weight of the deed still pressed on his chest. His sister was waiting for an answer. He didn't want to drive onto Hardwick property with the ownership still between them. Nolan needed to drop that bulk off right now so he could breathe easy. "Call Kaylee," he instructed his smart radio.

"Hello," she answered on the third ring.

"Sis, it's Nolan."

"I'm so glad you called. I wanted to chat before I left for vacation," she said.

He heard the happiness in her voice. His sister loved him. His gaze strayed to the new knitted gloves on his hands. Until recently, Kaylee had been the only person to care about him. The urge to tell her about Quinn jolted him, but he reined in that instinct. Everything felt too new. Too unfamiliar.

Don't fall for her.

"Glad I caught you," he said, instead of mentioning Quinn.

"Sure you don't want to come to Colorado?"

Nolan remembered how he'd scoffed at the sleeping arrangements when she'd invited him to join in on the trip before he left for Bethany Springs. Nine people crammed into a two-bedroom house. Little did he know he'd still be spending his holiday on a twin bed. "I'm good where I am."

Satisfaction glowed inside him. Who'd have thought he'd be happy sleeping on a cramped bed, sharing the holiday with people he'd barely met? In fact, those were the very reasons he was turning down his sister's invitation.

"I can barely hear you, but I think that's a no, right?"

"Right. The reception out here is terrible. I should've called while I was still in town." That had been the plan, only he'd been so distracted by Quinn and learning about the loan and the choice he'd need to make. "It's about the deed."

"Ready for me to file? I can sneak that paperwork in before I leave for Colorado."

"I want you to file that paperwork in some drawer for now."

After a pause, she said, "Sure, sure, no problem. I'll take care of everything. Merry Christmas, Nolan."

The air rushed from his lungs in a huge blast of relief. For a moment, he'd thought his sister might argue with him, try to convince him to take full ownership of the HOC now, but she accepted his decision with quiet understanding.

"Merry Christmas, sis."

The Jeep ate the miles between Quinn's farm and Bethany Springs. With the decision made, his happy, almost weightless feeling reaffirmed he'd made the right choice. The light holiday tune playing on his radio echoed his mood. Now he could actually enjoy his time with Quinn and her family without guilt chipping away at his joy of Christmas.

What he'd do after the new year he had no idea, but for now, and for once, he'd live in the moment.

Chapter Eight

Quinn had lost her patience. Wait, no, her cool had officially vanished three days ago and she didn't plan on putting up any Lost and Found posters searching for it. She'd shelled out a ton of money for each and every supply Nolan said he'd need for crafting ornaments, and the man hadn't even picked up a measly blowpipe. Meanwhile, she'd been unpacking boxes as they came in, emptying the clutter from the workshop, and drawing—and discarding—one ornament idea after another while taking care of the horses every day.

As far as she could tell, Nolan Vesser, glass blower extraordinaire, had made a very elaborate job of doing…nothing. *That* ended today. She'd thought they'd reached some kind of understanding five days ago when they bumped into each other in Bethany Springs. Clearly, she'd made life too easy out here for him.

After finishing off her morning tea, she grabbed

a coat and headed outside. She found him crunching through the snow on his morning walk, his face relaxed as he deeply breathed in the crisp, cold air.

He'd really taken to winter, traipsing through the snow, and while she'd never spotted smoke coming from the chimney of the Berry House, she knew he'd picked up a second space heater. Probably, growing up in California, he'd not had much experience with fireplaces and preferred something that plugged into the wall.

Quinn almost felt guilty breaking up his morning solitude after such a trying time in his life. After all, the man probably only wanted to grab a little fun. Yesterday she'd found what could have been an attempt at a snow angel. Then her gaze fell to the newly earned calluses on her fingers. No, he'd basically been taking a nice, do-nothing vacation on her dime. Time to pay up!

"Hey, Nolan," she called.

He turned and flashed her a friendly smile. Guilt pricked at her conscience, and her lips began to turn up in an answering grin. *Toughen up.*

"Good morning," he said, and she forgot to brace herself for the buffet of feelings his deep baritone conjured inside her. Warmth and sunshine and dreams. She steeled herself against his dark eyes flecked with a golden brown.

Toughen up.

Really.

Do it this time.

"How's the designing going?" Okay, she kind of just blurted out that question. She'd meant to exchange a few pleasantries, maybe a breezy conversation, but somewhere she'd read a decisive leader asked direct questions.

His smile faded and he turned his gaze toward the line of trees. "Finding inspiration."

Irritation flared, and something a lot like anger began to bubble and overflow like boiling water on the stove. She was no artist, clearly, but simply waiting for inspiration to find him didn't seem like the first step to designing the new line of Hardwick Ornaments. Maybe something like—and she was just spit-balling this in her mind—maybe actually designing something, *anything,* would get the ball rolling. Design and discard and fine-tune and tweak might be the more productive approach. You couldn't fix what you never began.

If the man wanted to find inspiration, maybe he should try tackling the tasks she performed on a daily basis. Her mind never wandered so much as when—

That's it. She might have stumbled on the solution to fix both his problem and hers.

"You know what I've found really sparks my creativity?" Quinn asked as she propped her hand on her hip.

Nolan's expression grew skeptical. Good, because she was about to throw down some wisdom on him.

"Housework."

His brow furrowed. "Housework?"

She nodded. "Yeah, nothing like sweeping and mopping to get me ready to do something else." *Like design.* "Maybe mucking out the stalls will do the same for you. C'mon, there are plenty of rakes in the barn."

"Yeah. Good idea."

Good idea? She'd expected him to balk. He took off for the barn in a fast clip she hadn't seen him use since he'd arrived. Who looked forward to cleaning out a dirty horse stall? Maybe the man grew tired of waiting for inspiration, too.

Her belly fluttered in hope, but she beat that back. Hope she would reserve for actual designing. With a sigh, she followed him to the barn. She found him talking quietly to both the girls, and they listened, enraptured. Who would've guessed she'd also found a horse whisperer?

Although Nolan had never worked in a barn, he didn't need much instruction, and she had to admit he handled the unwieldy wheelbarrow much better than she did. It wasn't designing, but at least one less smelly task she had to do.

"What's next?" he asked after smoothing out the last of the fresh bedding for the horses.

Maybe design? "Any inspiration flash for you?"

He shook his head.

Hmmm, so dirty physical labor hadn't done the trick. Maybe the opposite would get Nolan picking up a pen to sketch out an ornament idea. Quinn angled her head toward the horses. "These ladies need a good brushing."

"Really?"

"Something about the repetitive motion really jolts my creativity. Might help you, too." *To design.*

"I've never taken care of a horse before."

She handed him Lulubelle's favorite type of groomer. "Perfect time to learn, then. This is called a curry comb; it takes out any caked-in mud or things caught in her coat." She gave the horse a slow rub down her neck with the comb. "You like that, girl. Feels good to get clean."

Nolan began to copy her motions on the other side of Lulubelle. "Am I doing this right?"

"Oh, she'll tell you if you're doing it wrong," she assured him.

"That's what I'm afraid of."

She laughed at his dry delivery, despite hoping this job would spur him on to get *out* of the barn. "I've never met a horse who hated the curry comb, especially on their muscles. Feels like a massage," she assured him. "We'll brush away any dirt and hair the comb picks up with the hard brush, and follow that up with a soft one."

"That's a lot of brushing."

"Well, these gals will take such excellent care of us on the sleigh rides, so we take good care of them all the other times."

"They deserve the best," he said, giving Lulubelle a good scratch to her withers.

Seeing that the ladies were in good hands with Nolan, Quinn left to check the food supply in the storeroom. Maybe leaving him alone with his thoughts as he brushed would get the creative juices flowing.

When she returned, he'd moved on to Maribelle, talking to her softly, his voice gentle and soothing. Quinn couldn't help but smile. Apparently, talking to the horses was catching.

In a half hour, both horses were brushed, and that ended the barn chores. "Good work," she told him. The girls looked happy and settled and clean.

"Thanks," he said, replacing the combs and brushes on the shelf where they belonged. He fell into step beside her as she aimed toward the double barn doors. "What now?"

Now might be the right time to turn up the pressure. She pretended to roll through her mental agenda. "Next item on the to-do list is in the workshop."

His steps slowed. "Oh, well—"

Something about the workshop bothered him. But what could it be? She'd thought it would be kind of cool to be working in the same place where the Hardwick Ornament Company first began. Maybe being surrounded by the memories of a family he never knew made him miss his sister, and regret leaving California to come here.

Toughen up. Decisive leadership.

Quinn plowed forward. "C'mon. Believe me, this is the second dirtiest place on the farm."

Maybe he'd hate cleaning up the workshop so much he'd fire up the furnace himself. With that image in mind, she almost danced up the steps that led to the workshop. After leaning on the frame, the door swung open on a now well-oiled hinge and she flipped on the overhead light.

"You've been busy in here," he said, his tone appreciative as he studied the swept floor.

"It's amazing what clearing a little clutter will do." She angled her head toward a crowbar waiting for him against the wall. "First thing you can do is remove the boards from the windows."

"What's the second thing?" he asked, his lips twisting in… what? Worry? No, distaste. Hmm, that wasn't it either.

Ignoring the twinge that told her something wasn't quite right with his reluctance, she crossed the room to a corner where she'd stowed her cleaning bucket. "It's either that or wash windows."

Nolan lifted the crowbar. "Boards it is."

Quinn laughed, until she realized she'd been stuck with window washing. Oh well, anything to get him moving, and he had finally stepped foot inside the workshop.

She fished out a pair of safety goggles from her cleaning bucket for him, and once they were over his eyes, Nolan tested the ladder. Satisfied the thing wouldn't collapse under his weight, he began to climb. It only took them a few moments to get a good system going. As he pried off each piece of plywood, she chased after any errant nails. He even helped clean the windows once the boards were off.

With the windows sparkling, she gazed through

the glass, taking in the snow, the farmhouse and the barn. She allowed her imagination to envision how this place would look in a few years. Families and students would mill around the yard, twinkle lights would welcome them to the workshop for a demonstration of the ancient art of glass blowing, and the horses would graze until it was time for the evening sleigh ride.

"You really love it here."

His words caught her off guard. With her mask down, Quinn knew every hope and dream must be etched on her face. "When I'm not muddy and chasing after horses," she told him with a laugh, trying to turn the moment light and playful. Good grief, she'd be in a lot of trouble if tearing down a few boards ratcheted up her emotions to an extreme high.

His golden eyes searched hers for a moment. That closed off vibe she'd felt earlier momentarily lifted. Quinn drank in the warmth in his gaze. Then bam! Closed again.

Good. Closed off was good. A decisive leader insulated her feelings and disconnected from sentiment.

Yeah, but having Nolan around had been pretty nice. Better than nice. She'd grown kind of lonely on the farm by herself. She tamped down the giddy restlessness of connection. *Don't get too used to that.* Once she proved the new ornament company would be viable, she could begin paying him a salary. He'd move into town. Get an apartment. Maybe work on his own designs, too. He wouldn't stay in the Berry House forever, and she'd be alone again.

"What's next?" he asked.

Quinn tugged the to do-list from her back pocket. "Mop down the walls to remove about fifty years of grime, then cover them with that fire-retardant paint, or drill the holes for the trusses so we can hang the water pipes for the overhead sprinkler system."

"I'll work on that sprinkler system," he offered.

"Good, I hoped you'd say that," she said, grabbing the drill and plans from the toolbox.

"Because of my manly strength?"

Hey, was that a joke? Was Mr. Dreamy being funny? On purpose?

"No, because you're taller," she said.

He laughed and followed her to the worktable where she unrolled the layout she'd sketched out with the designer. Quinn tried to keep her expression neutral, but inside she felt like melting. Nolan was taking an interest in the workshop.

"Since we don't need anything really fancy in here, a line of PVC pipes and the sprinkler heads will work. If the system detects smoke, out the water shoots. The plumber will finalize it by tying the whole thing into the water supply. No matter how many videos I watched on the internet, I couldn't find a way out of that expense."

"I'm glad you're putting safety first. It's important to me."

"I'd never dream of putting you in danger." She stared up into his eyes. Why did she have to find *this man* so alluring? A man she'd have to work beside, day after day. She cleared her throat and faced the table.

The lines around his mouth softened, and his hand fell away from her arm. Nolan returned his attention to her blueprints for the sprinklers, studying where to drill the holes for the brackets.

His words told a story. He didn't say safety was important. He said safety was important *to him*. Was she being a jerk, pushing him too quickly to roll up his sleeves and get to work? The man had lost everything he owned in a fire. He'd been injured and then drove cross-country to Bethany Springs. Had he even had time to process everything that had happened to him?

Her mouth dried. The idea of causing him distress… But what could she do? Even with the influx of new cash, bills loomed and her money ran thin. No way to forget she'd only secured the loan because *his* name was attached to HOC now. Quinn had to keep charging forward.

Her uncle and dad used to argue about which approach was the best way to teach a kid to swim. Uncle Travis believed in acclimating a child to the water at the child's pace. If it took an entire summer for a kid to dunk their head under water, then that's how long it took. Her dad thought tossing a kid into the pond was the way to go. Quinn remembered walking down the dock, her father explaining he'd watch her carefully, ready to jump in if needed.

Quinn felt a little too much like Dad right now. She could spare another day or two for Nolan to find his way, but after that, something had to give. She brushed off her hands on the sides of her jeans and straightened. "I don't know about you, but I'm beginning to get hungry."

"I could eat."

"Good. We've done a lot today—we deserve to celebrate. If you want to finish up in here, I'll go make us some sandwiches. Peanut butter and jelly good for you?"

Nolan's eyes crinkled in the corners and he began to laugh. "Quinn, if you celebrate with PB&J, we need to update your party technique."

"I'll cut them at an angle so they're fancy."

He laughed again then glanced at the ladder. "I think I can get these holes drilled in about twenty minutes."

"Okay, I'll meet you in the kitchen when you're done."

After donning her coat, she raced across the yard to the farmhouse. With a quick wash of her hands, she set about making them a light lunch, breaking out the good buttermilk bread. She might even have time to bake half a dozen cookies from the leftover dough she'd whipped up the night before.

Quinn heard his footsteps in the hallway five minutes after she slid the cookie tray into the oven.

"Smells good in here," he said, sniffing the air.

A few snowflakes clung to the hair at his temples, and Quinn stuffed her hands in her pockets to keep from smoothing away a melting flake. "Chocolate chip cookies. Just to prove I know how to celebrate."

He laughed as he approached the kitchen sink so he could wash his hands, and then he joined her at the booth seat. "You really did cut these into triangles."

"But I didn't cut the crusts off. Can't get too wild."

"You said no one's lived out here in years, so how did Lulubelle and Maribelle end up here?" he asked after a few bites.

"Oh, they're part of the dream, chapter two. They just came into the story a little early," she said with a wave of her hand.

He lifted a brow. "chapter two?"

She glanced out the window, surveying the land beyond the glass. "Reopening the Hardwick Ornament Company was the beginning. The old-fashioned sleigh rides, with carols and stories and a campfire, would be chapter two. Glass blowing demonstrations and maybe even classes come later."

"Chapter three?" he asked, but it wasn't really a question.

"Exactly. When I can't sleep at night, I run through their route, plan activities, debate hay or cushion." She didn't mention she usually paced a bow into the hardwood floors of the hallway, worrying what to do next.

"So you already have it mapped out?" he asked.

"Right down to where we'll stop to build the fire." The timer on the oven dinged. "Cookies are ready."

He flattened his palms on the table as she stood

and reached for the potholders. "Great. Then let's go tonight."

"Wait, what?" she asked as she slid the baking sheet onto the stovetop.

"I'll be your trial run."

Her mind raced through all the things she'd have to do. Ready the horses. Gather the wood and s'mores supplies. Did she even have marshmallows? And chocolate. No, she always had chocolate. How about—

"It's just a ride through the woods, Quinn. You don't need to construct a to-do list and a plan of attack on the fly," he reassured her. "No reason to cancel the fun."

The tension eased from her neck. Nolan was right. Besides, she didn't cancel fun. She *brought* the party. To prove it she grabbed a spatula and slid the cookies off the baking sheet to a plate.

Quinn spotted the challenge in his eyes. Was this payback for the heavy lifting she'd had him do or every box she'd made him open? Of course. Did he think she'd back down? On to his game now, she began gathering their empty plates.

"If we finish up in the workshop around five, that should give us plenty of time to clean up and eat dinner. We can meet outside the barn at seven," she said. The man would be caroling by the time she finished with him tonight.

"Sounds like a plan," he said, grabbing their glasses and placing them near the sink.

"Those should be cool enough to eat now."

He grabbed a cookie, closing his eyes after the first bite. "Mmm. These are great."

"Have as many as you want." Warmth filled her chest. Despite the heavy lifting, she'd enjoyed their day together so far. It felt nice to share lunch with someone and talk over plans. When she'd quit her travel agent job in Bethany Springs, she'd also left behind meals with co-workers and after-work get-togethers.

After finishing off the first cookie, he snagged another. She'd have to add a second bag of chocolate chips to her grocery list. Quinn dropped the stopper into the sink and began filling up the basin with warm water and dish detergent.

"Need help? I can dry."

She turned, almost bumping into him. He towered above her, making the kitchen feel tiny and intimate and the prospect of washing dishes together too much like a couple. "No, I'm good," she said. A strand of hair fell forward.

"Here, let me," he said, tucking the errant lock of hair behind her ear.

"Thanks," she mumbled. *Focus on what you're doing, not how cozy splitting tasks would be.*

Quinn rubbed the plate with the washcloth, wiping away a smear of peanut butter. She wouldn't be able to construct a to-do list and form a plan of attack on the fly with him hanging around. Her stomach sank like a dish in the rinse water. That eliminated spontaneity. She *did* cancel fun. Okay, no to-do list and only a tiny plan.

After snagging the last cookie from the plate, Nolan slid out of the booth and followed her to the sink. He slipped the empty cookie plate into the sudsy water. "See you then."

Now why did that sound like a promise?

Chapter Nine

The double barn doors opened, and Nolan watched as Quinn led the horses by their reins into the paddock. His breath stalled in his chest. Would he ever get over what all she'd accomplished in such a short time? Nolan hopped off the fence. "I'll get the door," he offered.

"Thanks," Quinn said, her cheeks rosy and her voice a bit breathless. She wore a black knitted stocking cap, lopsided to the left. Must have been a gift from Gram.

He should have asked if she needed any help with the horses, but she'd already hitched them to a large, beautiful sled, painted in what could only be described as Santa Claus red and trimmed in black.

"Do we need that big of a sled?" he asked.

Quinn shook her head. "No. Originally I tried one horse pulling a two-person sled, but Lulubelle and Maribelle were so used to working as a team, they'd balk at going it alone. Now the girls can be together. I found this four-person sled used. It only needed a new layer of paint and I updated the upholstery."

He admired the tufted velvet cushions. "Let me guess, you learned how to upholster from a video online."

"Yes, and I'll add that it looked a lot easier on the internet, but this fabric is very forgiving." She reached up and tweaked the fringe. "Adding the fringe to the canopy was a whole lot faster. Hot glue is way more my style."

"These rope lights have your name written all over them," Nolan told her before he thought about the implications of his words. He *was* getting to know this woman's quirks, habits and whims.

"I thought they could be fun. If you want to grab that basket by the gate, I packed some supplies."

Nolan placed the basket in the back seat, then swung up beside her on the driver's bench. She tucked a heavy red and green fleece blanket over their legs.

"Ready to sing?" she asked, grabbing the reins from where she'd secured them on the brake.

"You've got to be kidding," he said. But he was sitting beside Quinn Hardwick; the woman wouldn't kid about something like caroling.

"It's a horse-drawn sleigh ride," she pointed out, her face and tone deadpan.

So much for thinking he knew Quinn. He couldn't tell if she was teasing him or not. Actually, she'd probably always surprise him. Warmth filled his chest at the idea of a December of wonder.

The corner of her lip turned up in a smile. "But I'll let you off the hook. For now." Her tone turned conspiratorial. "After all, you may be a horrible singer."

He pretended to tug at a piece of fuzz on the cuff of his jacket. "And now you'll never know."

The teasing glint vanished from her eyes. "Hmmm, seems like I've overplayed my hand. Well done, Mr. Vesser, you've left me with a lifetime of curiosity."

His shoulders began to shake with laughter. Not counting in the shower, when had he last sung? The one semester of choir in his freshman year of high school? He preferred to listen to music, not make it.

Quinn's hands flew to her mouth. "Oh, wait." She hopped off the sled, raced into the barn and then returned carrying two large leather straps with at least twenty brass bells that jingled with each step. Her words were low and gentle as she carefully slipped the jingling leather around the Belles' necks. "Don't you look pretty," she told both horses.

He chuckled as she returned to the cushioned seat beside him. This woman never did anything halfway.

"I know you're laughing at the bells, but you have to admit, it's not a sleigh ride without them." Playful defense filled her voice as she tugged the fleece back over her legs.

He lifted his palms in surrender. "You got me there."

"Believe me, I could've made it even more festive. There's Christmas quarter blankets, red and white halters, reindeer horse caps."

"I'm impressed by your restraint."

"They're in my online cart," she admitted with a grin and then released the brake. With a quick whistle to the horses, they were off, the sled gently gliding over the snow.

"Aren't your hands cold?" he asked.

"A little, but the reins feel better in my bare hands."

They rode in silence for a moment, breathing in the crisp woodsy scent of winter and enjoying the chill of the air on their cheeks while the bells provided joyful background music.

She dragged in a deep breath, then exhaled with a cheerful sigh. "Sleigh rides always make me a little antsy for Christmas. Of course, when you live in Bethany Springs, there's one event after another that builds the anticipation."

"Like what?" he asked.

"Oh, well there's the Longest Night of Light in the town square. Then the dance and auction at the community center a few days before Christmas."

Without the weight of the deed and ownership of HOC on his mind, he could fully enjoy his time with Quinn. His breath lodged in his throat. Why'd he single out Quinn? *Maybe because you're looking forward to Christmas for the first time in a long time, and the reasons have nothing to do with dances and a town square.*

"What do you normally do in Pasadena?" she asked, breaking him away from his momentary panic.

"After our parents died, Kaylee and I sort of made

our own traditions. We'd drive down to Newport Beach and walk along the pier. We'd make a picnic lunch and even though it was chilly, we'd take off our shoes and wade in the water and get sand between our toes."

"That sounds nice."

He'd loved it, and while he missed his sister, the traditions they'd built together felt like filler. Temporary Christmas habits to pass the time until his sister had her own family. "Once Kaylee went to college, she'd rent someplace with a bunch of her friends. This year they're in Colorado," he said, enjoying the sound of the sled gliding through the snow and the view of the trees.

"Ahh."

He glanced her way. "I can tell by that sound you just made that you think spending the holiday by myself is lonely."

"You got that from one sound?"

"And more. I can read your game face." Yeah, he was beginning to know her. Really know her. And the idea of that didn't scare him. "Spending Christmas alone isn't really that bad. The shop is closed, and it's about putting my feet up and ordering a pizza. Football for the rest of the day and night."

"Well, your pizza-and-sportsball day self is in for a shocker. I forgot about the Hot Chocolate Happy Hour. That's always fun. Then of course the Hardwick family party. You can't miss that."

"I don't want to intrude."

"Ha! When I said you can't miss that, I should have said Gram won't let you miss that. Besides, you came all this way out here and no one's leaving you to spend Christmas by yourself at the Berry House with that sad excuse for a tree. The way Gram tells the story, Vessers and Hardwicks did everything together. We're simply carrying on the tradition."

Nolan braced for his usual reaction to celebration and family stuff – to slam on the brakes and backpedal. He didn't want to hurt Quinn's feelings. In the end, inviting him into her world underscored everything he'd learned about her. Except keeping a part of himself separate had developed into a fundamental element at the core of his nature, a part of himself he knew well.

Only, his compulsion to recoil… never happened.

He sat beside her, stunned. Quinn didn't seem to notice, but he only caught bits and pieces of her words.

"When we were little, we used to have this big party with my grandparents and every one of my cousins…"

Where was the panic? The dread? Nolan rarely grew close to people. It was one of the reasons he enjoyed his solitary job. Learning how to make a person smile or interpreting a co-worker's tone never once played into his career. Until now, he'd written that off to being simply the way he preferred it.

"…but since there are no longer any small children, the whole family gets together a week before Christmas for a Hardwick version of a gift exchange, and…"

Yet here he sat beside Quinn and he wouldn't trade it for a million moments alone watching football.

"Whoa," Quinn said, and tugged on the reins. The horses slowed and Nolan tried to shake the realization that hit him as unexpectedly as sleet in L.A. She smiled up at him. "We're here."

His reaction to his *non*-reaction surprised him. Nolan smiled back, and something lightened inside him. He hopped off the sled and extended his arm to help her down.

"Thank you," she said, as she placed her hand in his. He broke the contact as soon as both her feet were planted on the ground, but minutes later he still felt the impact of her touch. The softness of the back of her hand. The urge to not let go.

"I'll, uh, unhitch the horses," she said and turned away from Nolan. Quinn felt her cheeks with the back of her hand, hoping they weren't flushed. *Nolan helped you out of the sled like a gentleman. Only being polite. No big deal.*

Then why had her breath hitched? Why had her heart *thump-thump-thumped* up a notch? And her cheeks, oh, they always gave her away. Here, now, they burned.

"He's only a guy, right?" she asked Lulubelle. But the horse only stared at her with soft brown eyes. No, that horse was a goner for Nolan, too. Wow, had she just admitted something to herself? She wanted to be near the man...and her reasons had nothing to do with the Hardwick Ornament Company.

"You're no help," she grumbled to the horse. Quinn tied both horses to a lead so they could graze and roam a bit. She returned to the sled to grab the bucket of water she'd brought.

Nolan had already unloaded the wood next to the fire pit. He stood staring down at the darkened bits of charcoal and wood that remained from fires in the past. "My grandpa used to take us out here and light a fire and tell us stories." She set the bucket on the ground and took off the plastic lid.

"Are we supposed to drink that?" he asked.

She shook her head with a smile. "It's for the fire. Always have to keep a bucket of water nearby in case the flames get out of control."

Nolan shifted his weight and shuddered. She hated that he must be cold. California with its sun and sandy beaches must feel a lifetime away.

"He'd tell you ghost stories?" he asked, his gaze still locked on the pit.

"No way. Now, my cousins, that's a different story." She crouched to begin arranging the logs, kindling, and tinder in the way she'd learned in Scouts. "Mostly legends and fables. He would have been a perfect history teacher. He liked stuff that reached into the past."

Once the fire caught and the flames rose and wood crackled, she stood with a smile. Only Nolan no longer stood near her. Quinn wheeled around to find Nolan with his back almost plastered against a tree. "You'll never get warm all the way over there."

"Nah, I'm good."

Hmmm, strange. She loved nothing better than the heat of the fire against her cheeks and the scent of wood smoke in the air. She stepped to the back of the sled where they'd stowed the supplies. "Mind grabbing the s'mores stuff?"

His nod was tight, his body language off. Where had the carefree, easy-going Nolan Vesser gone? The one who'd traded snowballs with her and joked with her about caroling? The closed off vibe returned. He advanced on the sled and grabbed the box that contained the chocolate, graham crackers, and marshmallows. Lines creased his forehead, like he didn't exactly know what to do next.

It's the fire, Miss Unobservant. Grr, how could she be so insensitive? Probably the last time he'd been around the smell of burning wood, his home had been in flames. Why hadn't he mentioned it before? *Well, would you?* Maybe spotting the fire pit dredged the emotions up. Quinn wanted to offer him some kind of comfort, but she suspected that would be the last thing he'd want.

Long ago, her grandpa had fashioned benches out of long logs. With plenty of room on the bench she patted the spot beside her. Nolan's gaze fell on the bucket of water for a moment. Was he going to turn her down? Then he awkwardly stretched out beside her.

She handed him one of the tiny twigs she'd raked away from the fire pit. A large clearing circled around the stone ring, so nothing could catch fire accidentally, but that didn't prevent the wind from blowing small branches and leaves into the area. They'd always taken the precaution of keeping a rake nearby, as well as water.

"What's this for?" he asked, twirling the stick between his thumb and fingers.

"My gram calls them worry wood. You put your worries on them, and then toss them into the flames. You watch as the twigs catch fire, turn orange and then finally burn away. Your cares will go with them."

"Does it work?" he asked.

"Worth a shot to try." She closed her eyes, but oh, how much worry could one little stick carry? So she focused on only one—making the workshop a place Nolan could create all the beautiful ornaments she knew he was capable of. Her eyes fluttered open and she tossed the stick into the flames. Nolan's stick followed, and they watched in silence as the flames caught and consumed the tiny pieces of wood, blazed for a moment, and then faded into nothing.

Quinn breathed in deep, already feeling lighter.

She studied his profile as he stared into the flames for a moment. His arms didn't seem as stiff, and after a moment he lifted his palms to the flame, soaking up the warmth. A slow smile spread across his face, and that deep breath she'd just taken lodged in her chest. "Did it work?" she asked.

"Yeah, I think so," he said, his voice filled with wonder. "Thank you."

He faced her, and his smile warmed her more than the blazing fire in front of them. "You're welcome." She focused her attention to the s'mores supplies before she lost track of everything and decided to stare into his golden-brown eyes. He leaned to the side, and something slipped out from beneath his shirt. She pivoted on the wooden bench to see a ring suspended from a chain around his neck. The gold caught the firelight and glinted as he moved.

"I've never noticed that before," she said, indicating the golden ring. "Why do you keep it hidden?" Quinn popped her fingers against her lips. "Never mind, you don't have to respond to that."

Way to go, getting too personal. She stabbed two marshmallows on a stick and handed the branch to him, and then stabbed two more for her.

"It was my dad's wedding ring," Nolan told her. "My sister kept both of their rings in her jewelry box, but after the fire, she gave me his."

"Oh, that's so thoughtful. Your sister must be pretty special." Nolan must enjoy a tight bond with Kaylee. That fact made Quinn happy. Before, he'd struck her as kind of a loner. Until he came to work with her, he'd created alone. Since arriving, he'd never mentioned his hometown or seemed to long for Pasadena the way she would for Bethany Springs.

"She's pretty great. She got all the best of our parents."

Quinn liked how Nolan never shied away from

complimenting another. He had all the qualities of a generous man. A trait he shared with her grandpa.

A winter bird called in the distance and the wind rustled in the bare branches of the trees as they rotated their marshmallows above the flames. Despite his earlier hesitancy at the fire pit, Nolan appeared to be enjoying himself. He'd chosen the longest stick and she worried how the marshmallow would balance. Her foot tapped against the packed ground. She loved s'mores. Hated how long it took to make them.

"I've heard there are two kinds of people in this world," she finally said with a sigh. "Those who get frustrated, unable to deal with the wait, and shove their marshmallow right into the flames. The others are happy to sit patiently, knowing that ooey goodness is way better than a burnt piece of fluff."

"So which are you?" he asked.

"I'm charred all the way," she told him ruefully.

He lifted his carefully browned marshmallow. "It's like you read my mind."

She giggled, and his smile widened.

"You mentioned your grandpa told stories here. Tell me your favorite," he invited.

She squirmed on the bench, suddenly nervous about sharing such an intimate story of love: the tale that inspired the first Hardwick Heart. "Oh, it's okay."

"You're going to have to tell them when you get this going for real. You might as well practice on me," he said, finally pulling his stick from near the fire. As she'd predicted, his marshmallow appeared perfect.

"You sure you wouldn't rather sing some carols?"

"And scare the horses?"

She laughed, as he'd probably intended her to do, and after steeling her nerves, she dug into the story. "This is the legend of The Hardwick Heart. Our great-great grandfathers based the very first Hardwick ornament on this legend of love. Once upon a time, because that's how stories like this begin, a brave and gallant knight named—"

"Nolan?" he offered.

"Close, but no. His name was Roland." She cleared her throat and began again. "Once upon a time, a brave and gallant knight named Roland rode into a village on a quest of great import. Only our brave knight forgot his quest when he happened upon Natalia in the village square. The two fell in love at first sight. Okay, *he* fell in love at first sight; she fell in love after he chased away a thief from her stall in the market."

"As all good knights should."

"Absolutely. Roland asked Natalia's father for her hand in marriage, but before they could exchange their vows, Natalia discovered something terrible about her intended."

"Let me guess. He was really an alien? He trapped unicorns? At midnight he became a hideous beast?"

"What? No. Nolan, exactly what kind of bedtime stories were you told as a child?"

"I guess you were told the boring kind," he said.

"Actually, it's worse than that. He'd been keeping a deep, dark secret from her."

His smile vanished.

Good. She'd surprised him. Guess she'd finally dropped a detail into her story that would keep him interested. "Roland had really come to her realm seeking a lost treasure, and he'd been secretly questioning her for clues the whole time. Heartbroken, Natalia demanded an explanation. Of course, our not-so-brave-as we-first-thought knight apologized."

He relaxed. "See, it turned out okay."

She shook her head. "No, the damage was already done. His words meant nothing if his actions didn't match. She broke off their engagement, and the other villagers banished him."

After few moments of silence, he asked, "Why are you pausing?"

"I waited for you to interrupt. That seemed like the kind of moment you'd choose."

"I like a good fairy-tale banishing as much as the next guy, but I'm anxious to hear how this ends."

"Okay, here we go. He may have kept a secret, but Roland's heart was true, and to convince her of his love, he devised a plan."

"Good for him."

She lifted a finger. "But it wasn't easy. He faced a lot of threats. All of them grave. First, of course, being thrown into the dungeon."

"Always a winner."

"Enchanted into…"

"A sword."

"Nope."

"A mighty lion," he said.

"Not even close."

"Surely not a frog."

"Already done. Our villagers wanted something truly unique. The last threat was enchantment into a babbling brook."

"A what? Did you say a brook? What kind of village turns a person into water?"

"I actually thought it kind of poetic. This way a part of him would flow out into the world as a warning to all," she said in mock defense.

"Maybe he thought she'd never find out. Once he arrived, Roland realized Natalia to be the real treasure. Why hurt her with the knowledge of his original intention when he never planned to follow through?"

"Hmm, interesting premise. I typically lean on the side that keeping secrets from the one you love is wrong. Despite the threat of imminent transformation over his head, Roland would sneak into her village every night to leave proof of his unending devotion. Wherever Natalia ventured, she found a heart. Notched into the trunk of a tree. Traced in the sand along the riverbank. But her favorite was the carved heart she found nestled among the branches of her Christmas tree. On Christmas morning, he vowed his love to her once more, and again asked for her hand. After everything he'd done, she decided to forgive him, and said yes. From that day on, Roland and Natalia placed a heart on every Christmas tree."

"He didn't fully earn her love until his actions

matched his words," he said, almost lost in thought. "He gave her his heart every day."

"Exactly. I don't think either of my grandparents could tell any kind of story without it imparting some kind of life lesson." She added more marshmallows to their sticks.

His focus snapped back on her. "I like it. I can see why they based their first ornament on that legend."

Her gaze locked with his. "Yeah, it's kind of special."

The wood in the fire popped and hissed, and he glanced over to the water safety bucket. Quinn propped her stick against a rock and reached for the thermos she'd tucked in with the s'mores supplies. "You thirsty? I packed some hot chocolate."

At his nod, she twisted the lid off the thermos. Steam rose from the heated beverage, and she poured the hot chocolate into two collapsible mugs she'd brought along.

As she raised the mug to just under her nose and breathed in the delicious scent, her marshmallow branch dipped under the weight and caught on fire. Quinn drew the stick toward her and blew on the flames.

"Quinn," he called, his voice harsh and alarmed.

"What?" she asked, after she'd blown out her burning marshmallow.

The lines on his forehead softened. "It's fine. You're good."

She melted a little inside over his concern. He

wouldn't appreciate her drawing any more attention to that, so she changed the subject to something lighter. "I love hot chocolate, but now I'm thinking maybe some wine would be good too."

"Is there a wine that goes with s'mores?" he asked, handing the graham crackers to her since there was no point in her continuing to roast her burnt marshmallow.

"If it's out there, I'll find it." She slid a piece of chocolate onto the cracker and took a bite.

"I know you will," he said, still continuing to roast his marshmallow. Once again, she knew his s'more would be perfect.

Her breath came out in a heavy sigh. "Glad you have faith in me. And I don't mean about the wine."

He scratched at his chin. "Honestly, Quinn, how could I not? You're the most determined person I've ever met. Look at what you've done in only a few months. I've never seen you slow down the whole time I've been here."

Maybe it was the crackling of the fire or the stars shining so brilliantly above them, but the need to unburden herself flowed. She stared into the flames, the pop of the wood soothing.

"If I slow down, I'll have to feel it," she finally confessed.

"Feel what?"

She avoided the need to meet his eyes. "All of it. My grandpa entrusted me with our family's legacy. Gram believes in me in a way I don't even believe in myself. I've borrowed money from every Hardwick I know. And every morning, for just a moment, I think maybe I should pull the covers over my head and give up. What if I'm a flop? What if I disappoint the people I love?"

"You're not going to disappoint them."

She wanted to wrap herself up in the reassurance of his words and the conviction in his voice. Quinn only wished she had that kind of faith. "You're right, because it would be worse than disappointment. I'd be the family dream killer, and I—"

The warmth of Nolan's hand covered hers. Surprise cut off her words, and a fluttering took over her stomach.

"No one as persistent as you would fail." His thumb stroked the back of her hand, and tingles raced along her skin.

Quinn glanced from his hand on hers and met his eyes. The firelight flickered against his cheeks, and tenderness dwelled in his gaze. Nolan believed in her. Lightness chased away the heavy worry that had battered her confidence. She squeezed his hand, thankful for this moment, for the opportunity of the Hardwick Ornament Company she'd been gifted, but mostly she felt thankful for him.

Something heavy inside her lifted, and she breathed in a deep breath, savoring the smell of winter and wood smoke in the air. It uplifted her to share the burden with him. "I haven't told anyone how worried I've been." The words tumbled out of her like a confession.

His eyes narrowed in confusion. "How come?"

"Because they're my family, and they'd give the same kind of support if I said I wanted to be the first astronaut on Mars or that I wanted to snap photos of plastic bags trapped in barbed wire for a coffee table book," she said with a shrug. "That sounds like a complaint, but it's not. They're amazing, but kind of biased. Plus, I know what it's like to carry around this burden, and I don't want that for any of them. Anyway, thank you."

"You're welcome." Nolan's gaze dropped to her lips, and her heart began to pound. Quinn leaned into his chest and his head lowered.

The soft whicker of a horse and the thumping of an impatient hoof broke them apart before his lips touched hers.

"There's a horse right behind me, isn't there?" Nolan asked.

Quinn poked her head around his shoulder to spy Lulubelle, dragging her reins and the tether spike in back of her. "She pulled the stake right out of the ground. Must be too soft."

He stood and gave Lulubelle a gentle scratch behind her ears.

Nolan had been going to kiss her, right? She hadn't imagined that. She glanced around the area. With the sleigh ride, fire, stories of love… she'd created quite the romantic scene here. An embarrassed panic made her jumpy. Would Nolan think she'd deliberately set this up?

Had she?

"We should go." She surged to her feet and quickly stuffed the leftover marshmallows, chocolate and other provisions into the picnic hamper. Her steps were stiff as she darted to the sled and stowed the basket.

"Quinn."

Nolan's deep voice sent a shiver down her spine. *Don't react. You'll only embarrass yourself.* She squared her shoulders, whipped around and faced him. She couldn't read his expression this far away from the light of the fire. Good. That meant he couldn't read hers. "I'll put out the fire. Can you hitch the horses to the sled?"

"Yes, but–"

"Thanks," she directed the comment at the night, returning to the pit. Fifteen minutes later, they were back in the sled and on their way to the farm. Silence stretched between them, but not the comfortable kind she'd grown used to with Nolan.

Get to the barn.

Say good night.

Tomorrow, pretend they hadn't almost kissed. Good plan.

She scrambled out of the sled the second the horses slowed to a stop. "I got it from here, Nolan. Thanks."

"Oh, but… Do you want some help?" he asked, his voice friendly, but his body stiff.

She shook her head, not bothering to look up, and concentrated on Maribelle's sleigh bell as she slipped it over her head. "Just open the barn. Good night."

Quinn sensed him staring at her, as the creak of the doors opening filled the chilled air between them.

"'Night," he called.

Her shoulders sagged, his footsteps echoing as he walked away toward the Berry House. Parts one and two of her plan were complete.

She secured Maribelle inside her stall, making sure she had plenty of clean hay and fresh water. "Sweet dreams, girl." Then she brought Lulubelle inside. "Don't look at me like that. I get it. You think things would've been awkward with me and Nolan if we'd kissed, because what if we'd gotten more involved with each other, only to break up later? What would that have done to our working relationship and the HOC?" Here she was, talking out loud to the horses again.

Quinn glanced over her shoulder, her gaze finding the Berry House through the window. A light flashed on inside. Then another. *You're being weird.* Lulubelle gave an impatient grunt, anxious to get into her stall for a drink. "Sorry girl," she said leading her inside.

After latching the gate, she watched as the horses settled down for the night. "Maybe you're right. Mixing in anything, uh, romantic with him could get awkward." She gave the horse a final pat down the side of her long neck. "Thanks for looking out for me."

Chapter Ten

Quinn might not ever find a harder worker than Nolan Vesser. When it came to taking care of the horses, he became the perfect cowhand... er, horsehand? He joined her on every trip into town to "carry the heavy stuff." He also tested and retested the new ventilation and fire suppressant system in the workshop. No box remained taped and packed for longer than ten minutes after arrival. The man resembled FedEx but in reverse. He did everything—except the job she'd actually hired him for. The design sketchpad waited on the table unopened, the furnace stayed cold to the touch, and the switch on the kiln remained in the off position.

With a pang, Quinn dismissed Nolan's confused expression as she waved goodbye and drove away from the farmhouse. She didn't invite him along. Oh, she'd told herself she'd drive around on the outskirts of Bethany Springs for hours. She loved to admire the sun shining through the bare limbs of the trees.

Let her thoughts wander as she drove past the gently rolling, snow-covered hills. Recharge and decompress alone in the cab of her truck. And maybe not think about Nolan.

She only lasted four minutes.

Frustrated, Quinn finally sought the help of the one person who usually had the answers—Gram. Her grandmother had the door open and ushered Quinn into the kitchen as the sound of the doorbell still reverberated through the house.

"The kettle is already on the stove," Gram said, her wreath earrings shaking back and forth with each move of her head.

"Are those new?" Quinn asked, angling her head toward Gram's earrings.

Green garland twisted into a circle with the tiniest red bows, and they almost matched the wreaths on the vest she wore over a bright red turtleneck. Gram's fingers flew to the dangling jewelry. "I made these in one of the craft classes at the community center. Happy to make you a pair," she offered with a wink, knowing full well no one in the family shared her eccentric taste in ear wear.

"Well, you did an amazing job."

"Thank you, dear."

Quinn unwound the long black scarf Gram had knitted for her two winters ago, one of the first projects her grandmother had tackled after retiring. "It smells good in here."

"It should. I'm making gingerbread cookies for Reindeer Ruckus."

"Hope you made an extra batch," Quinn said, after slipping out of her red coat. She hung it on the back of one of Gram's wooden kitchen chairs, freeing herself to give her grandmother a hug. "Thanks for the invite."

"Honey, you know you're always welcome," Gram said, smoothing a wayward strand of hair from Quinn's face. "You can tell me why you're missing your smile later."

Gram never told anyone to smile or tried to fix their problems for them, one of the great things about her. She allowed a person a moment to be gloomy and gave a sympathetic ear when anyone in the family needed someone to listen. Not that she'd allow anyone to travel too far down the self-pity highway, but something about Gram's house smoothed away the rough edges of any trouble.

"You want to help me roll out the next batch?"

"Absolutely." Quinn steered toward the farmhouse sink to wash her hands. The shiny white porcelain stood as a direct contrast to the modern, stainless steel sink Nolan insisted they'd need in the workshop. Her patience with the man faded faster than a summer tan in October. She would do anything to get her mind away from the brand new and very expensive equipment sitting idle in her workshop, and her hopes for mockup ornaments by Christmas. She dried her hands with a sigh.

"You ready to tell me what's wrong?" Gram asked, as she floured the kitchen countertop.

"That obvious, huh?" Quinn dusted her palms with flour.

Gram handed her the rolling pin. "You were never one for subtlety."

The dough for the gingerbread landed on the countertop with a plop, the spicy aroma of the ground ginger tickling her nose. Quinn attacked the blob with the pin. She really put her back into the task, evening out and flattening the dough from different angles. "I don't understand what's going on. The man's done nothing yet," she finally said as she compressed the dough more. "Okay, that's not altogether true. Nolan's been great with the horses, and anytime I need something from town, he's always so helpful."

"Yeah, I'm surprised to see you alone," Gram said, her tone full of meaning.

She lifted the pin from the dough and twisted to eye her grandmother. "I know you're trying to say something. Something valuable and important that I'm supposed to glean for myself because you brought up the point, but honestly, I'm so frazzled I can't figure it out. Can you just tell me?"

"Where's the fun in that? If I have to be both old and wise, the least you could do is let me enjoy it." Gram's lips twisted as she raised her hand to cut off Quinn's reply. "Okay, okay. I'll even use the phrase all your cousins say: The man is into you."

The pin hit the counter with a clang. "I wish."

Okay, that rang out as a *huge* admission she hadn't meant to make in front of her grandmother.

"I'll let that one slide," Gram said, catching Quinn's confession. "But not before pointing out that you're into him, too. And what's with this wish part? Why wouldn't he be into you?"

Quinn refocused her attention to the dough now rolled flat and thin, but she reached for the pin again anyway. "Because I'm a mess, and he's this great artist biding his time here in Bethany Springs until…"

"Until what?"

"Until his own inspiration hits him or whatever," she said with a shrug, then flattened the dough further. "I think he's so used to working alone. It's unusual for him to have someone who can help him hanging around."

"You don't have to be a journalist like your cousin Chloe to figure out that man's expression when he sees you."

"What's the expression?" Quinn asked, stopping the pin mid-roll. Her heart began to pound and her grip around the handles loosened. Then she shook her head and thumped the pin back onto the dough. "No, never mind. I don't want to know. Wait, I do. No, he's only here to do a job."

Gram made a scoffing sound. "I've seen the Berry House. Believe me, the man could find a better gig than the one you're offering."

And there went her heart again. She couldn't forget that moment of awareness on their sleigh ride. There under a blanket of stars and the crackle of the fire… he had been going to kiss her. But since then, nothing. Had she imagined the whole thing? Had it made living on the farm awkward for him? She worked the dough with a vengeance. "If he's looking at me in any special way, it's probably because he's trying to figure out how he wound up in Bethany Springs in the first place. Maybe his confusion is the reason he's done next to nothing to design an ornament."

Gram's hand stilled the rolling pin. "That explains the heavy sigh. And why you rolled this dough so thin it's see-through."

Tension eased from Quinn's shoulders as she put the pin aside and began pounding and thumping the dough back into a ball. "When I talked to him on the phone, he seemed so eager to get here. Wanted to know all about the Hardwick Ornament Company, what still remained of the old place. Maybe it's me."

"How could anything be my precious granddaughter's fault?" Gram teased.

Quinn stared hard at the dough, avoiding meeting her grandmother's eyes. "I kind of fell in love with the idea of rebuilding the HOC, you know, with a Vesser and a Hardwick creating together again. But he seemed stunned when he finally arrived and I showed him around. I get that maybe on the outside the place needs a lot of work. Okay, and the inside too, but I've got that squared away now. Mostly."

"And he's still not designing?" Gram asked, her expression thoughtful.

“At first I thought it was his arm—that maybe the burn hurt more than he wanted to let on. I even asked Dad to come out in case Nolan wanted to discuss his injury with a professional. But Nolan assured me he wasn’t in any pain. Let’s just say it’s easier to convince Lulubelle to trot into the barn than to get him to talk ornament design.”

“Hmmm.” Gram seemed somewhere else, like her engineer’s mind was busy processing differential equations.

“You know, I actually searched his name all over again on the internet to make sure the man in the Berry House was the real Nolan Vesser. Like maybe the guy who showed up on the farm hoped to pass himself off as an artist for free room and board,” she said, her tone rueful.

Gram’s brows shot up in alarm.

“Rest easy, it’s definitely him. Although it wouldn’t take much for an imposter to take over. Nolan doesn’t have his picture on his website. In fact, he’s kind of stingy with his face being online but I finally found a photo of him on a write-up for some gala. And another from the night of the fire.”

He’d been cradling a dog against his chest, ash dusting his forehead and one shirtsleeve singed. Quinn had stared at that picture on a newspaper’s website for a full ten minutes. Bright orange flames snaked from the broken windows of the building he’d just escaped. The blur of red emergency lights flickered in the background as two young boys approached him, but she only studied Nolan.

The courage it had taken to return to that burning building. The determined set of his jaw. The unwavering glint in his eyes. The emotion of the moment had been raw and powerful. Even now, her breath seized in her chest. Upon discovering that photo, she'd felt like an intruder, as if she had no business witnessing such a private moment, but she'd also felt a connection to the man who'd risk his life for a scared and defenseless animal.

"I didn't realize there was a problem. He's always so helpful when I run into you two in town."

Gram's words broke the spell over Quinn. "It's all so very confusing," she managed to say, and yes, if she examined that statement more closely, she admitted to being confused about more than Nolan's lack of ornament design.

"He's helpful with the animals, and with other tasks around the farm, you said."

Quinn nodded and grabbed the rolling pin, ready to attack the dough again.

"A fourth inch, Quinn dear, no less," Gram cautioned.

"I'll let the dough win this battle, Gram," she teased. "I don't know if it was the dust or what, but the first time I took him to the workshop he couldn't wait to leave. I thought he'd be more anxious to get the place up and running. After all, he must have orders of his own he needs to take care of."

"Was he in his workshop when it caught fire?" Gram asked as she opened a drawer under the cabinet and pulled out a second metal gingerbread man cookie cutter.

Quinn smiled at the cutter her grandmother had been using for as long as she could remember. "No, in his apartment, but it's above the studio. He got hurt when he went back inside the building to find a neighbor's dog."

"He suffered a burn in a fire that took away both his home and his business in one night. Well, it's no wonder he's hesitant to work around molten glass and fire again," Gram said.

"But he told me..." Quinn replayed their earlier conversation in her mind. A cool shaft of realization zipped down her spine, and Quinn straightened as she faced her grandmother. "He told me not to worry, and that the burn no longer hurt, not that *he* felt okay. I feel like kind of a jerk for not understanding it before. All the clues were there, especially at the fire pit. How did I miss it?"

"Because he wanted you to," Gram replied.

"You figured it all out easily enough," she countered.

"Because I'm not emotionally invested in him and the future of the HOC the way you are. In addition to the benefits of wrinkles around my eyes and gray in my hair, getting older makes it easier to understand how people work. What makes them tick. The man hopes you see him as capable and strong. Not afraid of anything."

She tapped her fingers on the floured countertop.

"I'd never think of him as weak because fire makes him nervous. I'd think he's normal."

Gram's eyes turned thoughtful. "But he doesn't know that. Believe me, figuring out another person's problem gets easier with time. It's understanding your own that's tough."

Quinn set the pin aside and reached for the cookie cutter. "You got that right. So how do I fix this?"

"You don't." Gram laughed at what must be Quinn's outraged and confused expression. "What I mean is, all you can do is help people help themselves. Just how you couldn't see the problem earlier, Nolan might not see it either."

"How do I do that?" Quinn cut the cookie dough into gingerbread men.

"You have to give him a reason to want to go into the workshop," Gram said as she lifted the excess dough away from the shapes.

"I know I'm supposed to be understanding more here and learn something about myself and working with others, but I'm not getting that part. You're probably not suggesting I trick him into the workshop and then lock him inside shouting, 'You can come out when you're ready to work!' as I leave him in there."

Gram chuckled as she handed Quinn a spatula, and then grabbed a greased cookie sheet. "No, you make the person think the alternative is worse. Honestly, is this how it's going to be with all you grandkids? So much easier to lead your parents to love."

"Gram, this isn't about love."

Her beloved Gram made a coughing sound.

Quinn rolled her shoulders like a swimmer ready to approach the block. "Why can't I just say, 'Look, the reason you're not firing up that furnace is because you're scared. That's perfectly understandable. I get it, but you have to work to overcome the problem, and I'll be here for you as you try.'"

But Gram already shook her head. "Because these are emotions and feelings, and when have either of those ever responded to logic?"

"Good point." Sort of like why she never had a conversation with Nolan about their almost-kiss, although the reason flashed crystal clear. No one wanted to have that kind of discussion. Not only potentially embarrassing, but also potentially soul crushing. Who wanted to face the prospect of dashed hopes? She'd take blissful ignorance any day of the week, thank you.

Gram popped the pan of cookies into the oven and set the timer. "You plan on sticking around to decorate these?"

Quinn shook her head. "I have a worse scenario to strategize."

"Should I be worried?"

"Absolutely." Quinn had a few videos to watch on the internet, an instruction manual to read and a furnace to fire up.

"That's my girl," Gram said, kissing her on the cheek.

Nolan had seen little of Quinn in the last few days except for a few flashes of her red coat as she darted in and out of the workshop. Watching her rushed activity piqued his curiosity. What was she doing? Of course his interest was normal, natural, and had absolutely nothing to do with the woman herself. He'd stopped himself from following her into the workshop at least three times.

You're trying to slow her down.

He'd already sent out a few emails to other glass blowers, but with the holidays, the only responses he'd received suggested they'd touch base in the new year. Still, he'd almost slowed his steps and leaned on the door and turned the handle in the special way she opened the workshop. Good thing he'd given up the idea of keeping the place. He'd been in dozens of hot shops; why did this one make him pause?

The weight of the history waiting in that building? Quinn's optimistic expectations of him? No, he'd experienced plenty of pressure to create in his past. First, after his parents' unexpected deaths, and then when interest in his original glasswork grew.

A streak of red caught his eye. Quinn. She headed toward the barn this morning rather than the workshop. Finally. Stuffing his hands in his pockets, he trailed her footsteps to the horse stalls. Lulubelle's ears perked as he closed the double doors behind him. He found Quinn measuring oats for the horses. Her dark brown hair fell down her back in a windblown wave. His throat tightened when he realized he'd missed their daily conversations the last two days, and for the first time since he was a little boy staring at the chimney and gazing up at the lights on the tree, Nolan wished he could stretch out Christmas.

"Need any help?" he asked.

Her body stiffened. She rolled her shoulders before spinning on her heel to face him. Quinn grinned up at him, but something was off. Her smile didn't reach her eyes. Instead he found… Determination. "Good morning," she said.

"Need help?" he asked again.

She shook her head. "I'm almost done here. I've been thinking about the Hardwick party. It kicks off in a few days. We'll need gifts for Reindeer Ruckus."

"You want to go into town, then?"

Her gaze dropped for a moment, then her brown eyes met his. The determination intensified, now tinged with resolve. "I thought we could make the presents ourselves. We have a whole workshop full of equipment, so why not?"

"Oh, uh…" Nolan angled away from Quinn as sweat broke out on his brow. He spotted Lulubelle, and even she seemed to be glaring at him.

"Nolan, why not?" Quinn's tone was gentle, and concern brimmed in her eyes.

He had a million reasons why not. But none of them made sense. How could he explain what he didn't fully understand? A disquiet that blocked out everything but the eerie whoosh of flames sucking the oxygen from a room and the jarring shatter of glass breaking?

"I know you told me earlier you were fine, but-"

"You don't need to worry about me," he told her.

Her eyes narrowed as she studied him, then she took a deep breath. "So listen. I've been viewing a ton of videos online and I'm pretty sure I have this whole glass blowing thing figured out."

Wait, what? Nolan's brow lifted. "Oh, you do?"

Quinn nodded. "Absolutely. I've learned how to change the oil on the truck, how to weave holly into the horse's mane... I'm telling you, the guy on the video made glass blowing look really easy."

Nolan watched, stunned, as Quinn gave him a sweet smile and then whirled around to rush out of the barn...toward the workshop? His gut seized. His nose filled with the heavy scent of ash and smoke. His chest tightened and for a moment he couldn't drag air into his lungs. He rubbed at his arm. *Not yet.* He'd blow glass again, just not yet. He remembered the worry wood, watching that stick burn his cares away, and the tightness between his shoulder blades relaxed.

Then he imagined Quinn getting hurt. Burning herself with molten glass or cutting herself as she tapped her creation off the pipe. She'd be careful–if he knew one thing about the woman, she took care of business. Still, his father had stressed safety in the workshop since he was old enough to hold a blowpipe. Honestly, he couldn't imagine a worse scenario than Quinn working in a hot shop armed with only what she'd learned online. With a sigh, he gave chase. She seemed to hesitate outside the workshop for a split second.

Once inside, he shucked his coat and placed it on a peg beside her red coat. The temperature was warmer in here than he'd expected. He tamped down that useless worry. It's warm in here; it's not on fire. After one last glance toward the exit, he braced himself. *It's only another hot shop. This. Is. No. Big. Deal.*

Nolan pivoted, bracing himself against the place, but Quinn stood in front of him. The corners of her lips turned up in the barest of smiles, and he stood close enough to enjoy the honeysuckle fragrance of her hair. She'd already secured her long tresses in a ponytail, the first step in safety, and he breathed a bit easier.

Quinn had really transformed the workshop since he'd last stepped inside. She'd wiped away any trace of dust, and the light scent of pine cleaner hung in the air. She'd scrubbed the walls clean, repainting them a color that reminded him of the warm, soft sand of the beaches back home. Coincidence, or had she done that for him? To make him feel comfortable in this space?

The furnace, reheater and kiln he'd specified had been installed, as were the new ventilation system and sprinklers. In addition to the equipment, Quinn had framed a few of the older catalogues and pictures he'd found and displayed them along one of the walls. A black and white photo caught his eye, and he recognized the blown up replica of the grainy one from the 1930s, when their families had worked to build the Hardwick Ornament Company together. A shaft of guilt uncoiled inside him. This special place came alive under her supervision. The two of them working together was the only thing missing. He couldn't make that happen for her.

No, he could. He could do this. Let muscle memory take over. He'd held a blowpipe in his hands a thousand times. A rush of excitement used to flow through him when he felt the blast of heat from the furnace. His lungs would burn as he held his breath, ready to create. *You can still feel all those things.*

His gaze strayed toward the spot where his relative had left his mark. She'd painted the entire workshop except for one small area the shape of a rectangle where Milos Vesser had marked his name on the wall. With the building filled with furniture and equipment, his footsteps no longer echoed as he walked across the flagstone flooring. He studied the signature.

"Hand me that hammer, would you?" she asked.

Her words broke his concentration. He searched around him until he found a neat row of tools on a workbench. He lifted the hammer and offered it to her. Nolan watched as she tapped a nail in place, then picked up a wooden frame she'd left leaning against the wall. She affixed it to the nail, neatly framing the signature and date like a picture.

"Nice touch," he told her as he glanced around the room. Anything to avoid meeting her searching brown eyes. "I can't believe you got all this done so quickly."

"I was inspired. By you."

Those last two words jabbed at his heart, and he couldn't prevent his gaze from slamming into hers. An array of emotions flickered across her face. Hope and confusion and doggedness.

"I think you were afraid to see me dust," he countered, ready to break the intensity of feeling surrounding them both.

Her mouth relaxed, and she even giggled. "You may be right."

Hearing her laugh filled some corner deep inside him with light. He'd never really felt connected with another person before, not like he did with Quinn. He could live off the bond between them. The link he felt with her warmed a cold wintry afternoon. He still planned to leave, right? It wasn't right to keep this… this… whatever it was between them. He was playing with her emotions. And his own. Understanding that made him find his voice. Finally.

He examined the room, grabbing for some kind of excuse. Then he spotted the open box of glass rods. She must have already added the raw material to the heat. "It's going to take two days at least for the glass in the furnace to get molten."

Instead of appearing crestfallen, Quinn's face lit up. She even reached for a pair of safety goggles and pushed them down over her face. "Just checked the pyrometer and we're set. Good thing I turned the furnace on two days ago."

His mouth fell open. Quinn grabbed another

pair of safety glasses and extended them toward him. Everything about her from the firm set of her jaw to the determined glint in her eyes told him—*you're not getting out of this*.

And suddenly, he didn't want to. A shot of adrenaline overshadowed his unease, and for the first time in forever, he ached to create something. To build something with Quinn. And as quick as a match turned to flame, he shoved back his remaining qualms and fears of what could happen.

Quinn's expression softened to one of satisfaction, and the truth hit him. Her challenging him with tackling the hot shop all on her own must have been her plan this entire time. She hadn't only hoped he'd follow her inside the workshop, she'd counted on him doing exactly that. Her pausing at the door made sense now.

His admiration for the woman standing in front of him grew. But he certainly wasn't going to show her that. With all her other burdens, Quinn shouldn't have to deal with his growing, and probably unwanted, feelings. She'd backed away from that kiss. He settled the goggles over his face and then folded his arms across his chest. "Okay, show me what you learned from the internet."

Quinn's soft grin faltered a hint, but then her innate instinct for accepting a challenge surfaced. With a sassy salute, she angled toward the wall where several brand new blowpipes waited. "The blowpipe is a hollow steel tube that can withstand the heat of the furnace," she told him, and he couldn't help but smile. She grabbed the closest and instead of bringing it to him, she blew into the pipe the way every glassworker did, checking to ensure nothing would block good airflow.

He nodded, not bothering to hide that he was impressed she knew the first steps to the process. Actually, he never should have doubted her. Quinn struck him as a woman who rarely took half measures. If she planned to tempt him to follow her inside the workshop, she would learn all she could before she tried to challenge him.

"What's next?" he asked.

"I dip the pipe into the reheater first."

"Right. Warming the end prevents bubbles from forming in the glass later. Ready?"

"Absolutely."

He donned some heat resistant gloves and opened the hatch on the reheater. Quinn fed the pipe inside, twirling it as she must have learned from the video. "The metal is beginning to turn color."

The excitement in her voice spurred his own, and he almost wished he'd grabbed a blowpipe too. Almost. She deserved the opportunity to savor the experience. To feel the thrill of creating beauty out of something that was once only sand. "That's good. We want it nice and hot. Eventually that end will get charred and dark, but this middle part should stay silvery. See this shiny part? That's where your hands live."

He peered inside the heater, examining the end of the pipe. "Pull the pipe out before it turns red."

Once satisfied with the color, she removed the end of the pipe from the heat.

"Now the real fun can start," he said, surprised as his own excitement jumpstarted to life. He pointed toward the furnace and she walked in that direction, her steps careful and her eyes focused on the end of the pipe. Good. His dad would have approved.

He pried back the hatch, and a blast of red-hot heat warmed their cheeks. A slight tremble invaded his fingers. Nolan forced himself to steady and clenched his fists tight for a moment, then shook them loose. The fire remained contained. The workshop had been inspected. They were both safe.

He took a deep breath. "This opening here is called the crucible. Keep your blowpipe level, and begin to coat the end with the glass." The words tumbled from him. The way one generation shared with another, he now shared with this amazing woman beside him.

She stuck her pipe inside the crucible that glowed orange and yellow. "Oh wow, I feel the weight of the glass. It's heavier than I expected."

Nolan remembered the time his dad brought him into the hot shop to craft his first glass. His words of encouragement. His calm reassurance. He waited for the familiar pang of loss that usually followed thoughts of his father, but felt…nothing negative. Only the lightness of a good memory.

"I can't believe how much fun this is. I'm not really even doing anything," Quinn said.

He felt a heat inside his chest not due to the over

two thousand degrees bubbling in the furnace. "Yeah, it can be a blast." What's more, his muscles hadn't seized and his gut hadn't clenched. Like the worry wood, his fears were little more than smoke.

"Nolan," she said, catching his attention. "Should I start twirling the pipe now?"

He focused on the crucible and the woman beside him, her fingers white around the grip of the blowpipe. "Yes, but rotate the tube slowly. That's it, you're doing great. You want a good, even cover of glass," he instructed. "I'm going to back away as you pull the pipe from the furnace."

"Keep it hip level, right?" she asked.

"Exactly. I'll have to be careful or those videos might put me out of business." He stepped out of range of her pipe and she slowly pulled the molten glass from the furnace.

The fiery red and orange blob glowed at the end of her blowpipe. "Art class in school was never this fun. Of course, that was mostly watered-down tempera paint, glue, and tissue paper."

The ball started to wilt and she watched in frustration as it drooped down toward the ground.

"Oh, no. What did I do wrong? I wanted it to be a goblet."

"You gotta keep spinning your pipe. Gravity is not a glass blower's friend," he said.

"I ruined it."

He shook his head and tried not to laugh at how crestfallen she looked. "Not at all. That's the beauty of glass blowing. You can melt your mistakes away. C'mon."

She followed him to the second furnace. "Here we reheat the glass to do the detail work, and not that any glass blower would admit it, but to hide our mistakes too."

Nolan opened the second furnace for her and she inserted her quickly cooling goo that resembled a lump of coal more than it did a wineglass. "Good thing glass gives you a second chance."

"And thirds and fourths too," he told her, his tone rueful.

They watched together as the glass began to heat and glow until it resembled the same blob as before. "I think it's ready," she said, her voice excited again.

He eyed the room until he found the stand she could use for the next step. After adjusting it for her height, he nodded in her direction. Quinn pulled the pipe out of the reheater, rotating as she walked. She positioned the pipe and lowered her mouth to the end and slowly began to blow. The glass bubble grew and expanded.

"Wow," she said, but then her beautiful glass bubble deflated and leaned to one side. "Grrr. I got so excited I forgot to spin."

"Exactly, and this is why the reheater is your friend."

"We're going to be best friends by the time this whole project is over. I'll probably wear out the hinge before this thing is made."

Chapter Eleven

Nolan's warm chuckle made Quinn feel a little bit better about her first attempt at glass blowing. Okay, he made her feel a lot better. "Quinn, don't be disappointed. I must use this thing to reheat a project hundreds of times. Honestly, it's no big deal."

She loved his reassurance, but something about that blob of melted glass intrigued her and made her think maybe not all was lost. "You know what, instead of making an elegant chalice, I'll now be presenting to the Hardwick clan a functional paperweight."

His laugh filled the workspace around them and she couldn't help but join him. She'd never seen Nolan this carefree. Two laughs in the space of a few minutes. Allowing himself to work again, she sensed he felt most comfortable in a hot shop. There could be no other explanation for his easier manner and quick smiles.

Not that she could blame him. Something very comforting hung in the air. Maybe it was the warmth from the furnace. Or perhaps how the sweet, almost earthen scent of the molten glass seemed to bring her closer to the elements. Probably the thrill that what she made could be hit or miss, but her mistakes could be melted away.

"Well, if you're going in that direction, now we can really have some fun." He handed her a tool that basically appeared to be a large pair of tweezers.

"You can use the tweezers now and pinch and twirl the glass while it's still hot."

So the equipment looked like tweezers because they were exactly that. She sunk the metal tines into the glass, squeezed the ends together and tugged. "It's like taffy."

"Yeah, it's a lot like that at this temp." Next he gave her a pair of oversized scissors. "You can cut the glass with the sheers and fold the ends around. Go nuts. You can't make a mistake."

"'Cause we'll melt any mess up away."

"Exactly. Want to add some color?" he asked.

"Does Lulubelle love carrots?"

"Give the paperweight a little heat so it will be sticky, then come over to the worktable," he said over his shoulder as he left her side to search one of the supply trays. A few minutes later, she met him at the old wooden table that had managed to survive in this building for several generations.

He set out several steel bowls in front of her. "You can add some color to your paperweight by dipping the end into this crushed glass. This is your creation, you can do whatever you want."

His warm voice was pure encouragement, and she bit the corner of her lip as she dipped the end in each of the bowls he'd set out. "What do I do next?"

"You happy with that?"

She glanced down at her blob now stuck with tiny pieces of glass. It didn't appear to be much, but she loved the thing. Although she did feel a kindred moment with her Hardwick ancestors whose talents lay more in vision than in creativity. So yes, happy and having fun with Nolan. She gave him an enthusiastic nod.

"Now you take your project back to the furnace."

She liked how he called her artwork a project, like a real creation, rather than a hodgepodge mess. He opened the hatch and she slid the blowpipe back inside. The crushed glass melted from the heat and was encased under a clear layer of glass. "Cool, but am I doing this right? Why does this thing seem like a light bulb?"

He nodded. "Bring your pipe back to the table and we'll give it a little shape. We'll mold and smooth your paperweight with the block." The block resembled a wooden spoon soaked in water rather than a child's toy. "Don't press too hard. Keep spinning and rolling."

"That should go on a T-shirt – When It's Hot, Keep Spinning and Rolling," she said, concentrating on his instructions.

After a few moments, her blob of glass could probably pass as a paperweight. "I think you're ready for the jacks now."

The jacks also looked like giant tweezers. "See this spot just below the end of the pipe, I'm going to score the glass with jacks while you keep spinning and rolling. You want to trade places so you can do it yourself?"

While she could watch Nolan work the glass as an artist, she loved how he included her in every step. She enjoyed being more than an observer. With a nod, he took over rotating the blowpipe and she positioned the sides of the jacks on the quickly cooling glass where he'd indicated.

"A light touch is all you need, and then slowly begin to pinch." The glass thinned and closed off. "We call this the neckline."

Excitement made her fingers tingle. A paperweight instead of an ornament, but this colorful clump of glass would be the first thing they created. Together.

"I know what comes next. I tap the pipe and the paperweight should fall right into my heat-safe gloves," she said, grabbing the gloves and shoving her hands beneath her project.

She tapped the pipe with the jack as she'd seen in the online video. Sure enough, the glass broke off in the exact place where she'd scored it earlier. Nolan left the pipe on the stand and handed her the block again. "Press the back at the neckline so the paperweight will have a flat surface to rest on when it's on a desk."

"Hey, that also hides the neckline. Clever."

"You happy with it?" he asked, a twinkle in his golden brown eyes.

She forced herself to glance down at the colorful paperweight resting in her gloved hand. She loved it, but she spotted a few bubbles in the glass, and the sides weren't perfectly rounded. Hmmm, maybe it would be best if one of her parents won this at the Reindeer Ruckus party. Then they'd have to love it too. Her cousins… they'd be a harder sell.

"Yeah, I'm thrilled." Including the bubbles and wonky sides.

"Okay, last step, the kiln." He swung open the door and she carefully placed her paperweight inside. "The glass can cool more slowly in here, and lessens the chance it will break."

"How long does it stay inside the kiln?"

"At least twenty-four hours," he replied, checking the settings on the kiln's keypad. He stood beside her, towering over her, really. They hadn't been this close since the night of their almost-kiss. He stared at the controls on the machinery, but she knew he'd lost himself in thought. Or maybe in another place altogether. Perhaps a burning workshop in California. The muscles of his jaw twitched, and his fingers drummed against his legs. The man seemed encased in tension, and she fought the urge to reach for his fingers to give him a comforting squeeze. Wherever he was, Nolan needed this beat for himself.

His chest rose as he sucked in a deep breath, then Nolan seemed to give himself a shake. He blinked down at her, a quiet peace in his eyes. Her stomach grew fluttery as his mouth opened and closed like he wanted to say something to her, but didn't know what. Or how. The moment should have been awkward, but a calm surrounded them. Neither of them needed words.

"You still haven't made your gift yet," she reminded him.

He grinned at her, his smile almost boyish and a hundred-percent-infectious. "You want me to show you the first thing I ever made?"

She nodded with enthusiasm and they strolled toward the stand where he'd left the blowpipe. He crossed the shop to open the door to the furnace and inserted the end of the pipe. "I can never get enough of the clean scent of molten glass. I love pitching in the rods of glass and watching as impurities melt away."

"I know what you mean. When I ordered those glass rods, I had no idea how fascinated I'd be seeing them liquefy."

He tossed her a sheepish glance over his shoulder. "So how long have you been planning to drag me in here?"

She studied the muscles of his back as he rotated the pipe inside the furnace, coating the end of the tube with glass. She sensed no resentment or irritation in his tone, and he held himself relaxed in a way she'd never really seen him. "Only a few days. And we both do need a gift for the party."

"I'll give you that," he told her, his lips twisting.

"How come you went into glasswork? I mean, obviously you're talented," she added quickly, "but neither my dad or his brothers felt any need to stick with the family business."

He studied the fire in the furnace. "Glass is nothing more than sand and heat. I guess I'm drawn to the elemental nature of it all. How I can magically transform glass into something functional like a dish or beautiful sculptures with nothing but my own breath."

He tugged the pipe from the crucible and walked over to the stand.

"What are you making?" she asked.

"A vase. My dad loved this design, dating clear to ancient Rome."

Nolan worked with the large tweezers and glass effortlessly, his voice smooth and warm as he explained his actions to her, his slight West Coast accent wrapping around her like a blanket on an easy Saturday morning. She observed in awe as he rolled the metal tube, just like she'd done earlier, but when he did it, he created something amazing. He tapered and elongated the neck so the sides would support flower stems. He reheated the bubble and then flattened the bottom.

"I can't believe your dad taught you to make a vase first thing. Especially now that I know what goes into the entire process. The videos online made that whole thing look a lot easier," she said, waving toward the furnace.

"I had a lot more experience around dad's shop before I ever picked up a blowpipe," he said, walking toward the reheater. "All I have to do now is break away the vase, and smooth over the rim so the glass won't be sharp. What do you think?"

"Cute, but how does it compare to a paperweight?" she teased. Watching him create the vase in front of her was one of the coolest things she'd ever seen. Now she couldn't wait to begin working on ornaments with the man.

Baby steps. Quinn beat back her impatience.

"You're right."

She gasped when he stuck his beautiful vase inside the furnace. Stunned, she watched his amazing creation melt into a blob that matched hers. "I can't believe you did that." Then her shoulders began to shake with laughter. Quinn giggled until he finished his paperweight and slid it into the kiln beside hers.

"I had so much fun, Nolan. Thanks," she said as he latched the kiln closed.

His brown eyes darkened, his expression distant and far off. "Yeah, so did I," he said, surprise lacing his words.

Then his attention snapped into focus. On her. Her breath lodged in her throat and her pulse ran wild because he gazed at her with curious amazement.

"Thank you," he finally said, his words slow and careful.

Quinn gave herself the space to enjoy the excitement of their first project together. A moment for her thoughts to wander. And to wonder. To speculate about the future. The Hardwick Ornament

Company's, but also hers. She found herself leaning toward him. Only inches separated them.

His gaze narrowed and she hoped he might lean in toward her too. Closer. But instead his spine straightened and he backed away. "I'll clean up in here. We've been in here for a while. I know you'll want to see to the horses."

Dismissed. A helpful dismissal. A practical one even. But a dismissal all the same. Disappointment shafted through her. His rejection confused her.

She scrambled to the hook where she'd left her coat and scarf. She lifted her hand in a wave, but his attention centered on replacing the tools and returning the safety equipment to the cabinet.

She rammed her arms into her coat, anxious to escape. What if she'd followed her instinct by smoothing a lock of his sandy blond hair away from his temple? Touching the back of his hand? Her cheeks heated and she rushed away, thankful she hadn't embarrassed herself further.

The cold air worked its way over the backs of her ears and the tip of her nose as she concentrated on not stomping her way to the barn.

She. Was. Being. Ridiculous.

But what about that night by the fire? And how many times had she asked herself about that? This last time officially put her in the *one time too many* column. No, they were business partners. Keeping it professional between them wasn't the smart move, it was the *only* move. *Don't focus on lost opportunities.* She should be excited for Nolan. Not only had he joined her in the workshop, he'd blown glass and now worked in there alone.

Things would only go up from here. Tomorrow was the Longest Night of Light celebration in town. It would also be his first real exposure to both her parents. And Gram. She almost felt sorry for him.

Chapter Twelve

Snowflake arches graced each entrance into the Town Square of Bethany Springs. Quinn always looked forward to how the Square fully shined this time of year, completely decked out in garland, hand-painted red and white candy canes, and wooden snowmen. She usually loved the bright banners that hung from the light poles and stretched across the street at Main and First. Red wire-framed reindeer dotted the lawn along with giant fiberglass Christmas bulbs, but she couldn't enjoy a moment of it because Nolan hadn't arrived yet.

"Have we scared off your boyfriend?"

Quinn pushed back the exasperated sound but didn't hold back on glaring at her cousin Alara. "He's not my boyfriend."

The corners of Alara's brown eyes crinkled as she tried not to laugh at Quinn's unintended vehement denial. She'd pinned her dark hair up in a messy bun, and a few curly tendrils fell down her temple, but that cute look couldn't fool Quinn.

"No one would know that. I hear you two are never two feet away from each other," Alara said, ignoring Quinn's stare.

"You know, it will always be a mystery to me. Uncle Travis and Aunt Katherine are so great. How did they manage to produce three of the most annoying children?"

Alara draped her arm around Quinn's shoulders and gave her a hug. "You know you love us. I should probably take you to lunch since you're dragging some of the family focus off me, but you'll probably want to go to the Giddings House and order toast."

"Toast never lets you down. But hey, speaking of love, you and Derrick are driving everyone ragged wondering when he's going to propose. You know, there's even a bet."

Alara bit the corner of her lip. "Uh, about that–"

Quinn gripped her cousin's arm. "You're not secretly broken up and just keeping up appearances fake-almost-fiancé-style until after the holiday, are you? No? I got it: he's won the lottery and you're secretly pretending to be his girlfriend to throw off the many women clamoring after his money. If we're all on some dating show and this is a home visit, I'm going to be really irritated. I would have watched one of those videos online about smoky eye and contouring."

Her cousin only rolled her eyes. "Your imagination. No, actually Derrick and I are–"

"Don't you two look lovely," Gram sang out, and Alara fell silent. Their grandmother kissed each of her granddaughters on the cheek. Tonight she sported green tree earrings with silver and gold ribbon. Although Gram's coat hid her holiday vest, Quinn knew it would be a matching tree design. "Where's Nolan?" Gram asked, and then glanced at Alara. "For that matter, where's Derrick?"

"He's chasing after Lulubelle." Quinn scowled up at the clock decked with a giant red bow in the center of the Square. "I thought he might be here by now."

Gram patted her hand. "Don't worry, that man won't pass up a chance to spend the evening with you."

Alara's eyes widened, and her lips compressed into a tight line. "Who is Lulubelle?"

"Relax, she's a horse. She's growing more and more stubborn, and for some reason Nolan is the only one who can get her to mind. Plus, we aren't dating, but thanks for wanting to defend me."

"Not dating? Sure," Alara said, her tone scoffing.

After flashing another glare in her cousin's direction, Quinn glanced at Gram. Her grandmother only shrugged. "Don't look at me. You're together all the time."

Quinn huffed a little too loudly. "That's because we're working together. It's a professional relationship. He's the designer. I handle the details of the business."

"Do I have to remind you again that I've seen the way you two act together? Hesitant glances and secret smiles."

Her mouth gaped. Butterflies began to flutter in her stomach. She'd thought she managed to keep her growing feelings for Nolan from becoming even more obvious. Oh no, had Nolan noticed? Was that why he'd opted to drive out here alone rather than tagging along with her? She could have waited for him to get Lulubelle in her stall. Quinn's mouth dried, and she found herself scanning the Square for the most direct path to her truck.

She caught sight of Nolan's familiar blond hair. Her chest tightened, and her gaze strayed to his despite her embarrassment. He perused the crowd, but stopped when his eyes caught hers. A rugged smile tugged at his mouth as he aimed straight in her direction.

"Yeah, that's all very professional," Gram said.

Quinn concentrated on breathing normally in front of her family. And not allowing her mind to speculate if Gram and Alara might be onto something. Nope, that was hope talking. Hadn't she just yesterday told hope to back down? She didn't need that Pandora-ish problem.

"I'll be over there minding my own business," Alara said, laughter in her voice, but Quinn also detected a bit of an offer. Alara wouldn't question her about Nolan, if Quinn didn't interrogate her about Derrick. She gave her cousin a small nod, one only Alara would understand.

"I should probably go find Derrick," Alara said, but her cousin didn't move.

If Quinn knew her family, they'd probably tasked

Alara to hang around and check out how Nolan acted around Quinn. With a sigh, her gaze strayed in Nolan's direction as he weaved through the throng toward her. She tamped down the way her heart kicked up at the sight of him. Every part of her forgot the pep talk she'd given herself as she left the workshop yesterday afternoon. *Keep it professional.* But yesterday, she hadn't yet spotted the way he smiled at her as he found her in the crowd.

"This is a good spot to meet for the lighting ceremony. Reconvene back here?" Gram asked.

"Sounds good," her cousin said, and then Alara disappeared among their neighbors. Maybe Quinn had guessed wrong about Alara's motives for sticking around earlier. Or maybe she'd rather be with her boyfriend.

Quinn watched as her cousin strolled away. She sensed a story about those two, something Alara and Derrick wanted kept secret. Normally, she and Landon and Emmaline followed a "no rules apply" policy when it came to their cousins, but she'd back off. For now.

"We've done this Longest Night of Light thing for decades. You'd think we'd come up with a centralized meetup spot and stick with it," Gram said, a frown in her voice.

"That's what you say every year," Quinn replied, trying to keep her tone light as Nolan neared.

"True," Gram said. "Oh, look, Nolan's nearly made it through the crowd."

"Really?" Quinn asked, trying to keep her tone

nonchalant like she hadn't tracked his progress through the throng of people. So close she could almost smell the scent of his soap and see the flecks of gold in his brown eyes.

"I almost didn't find you," he said as he approached. "Had no idea there would be this kind of crowd."

Quinn's friends and neighbors filled the Square. The beloved faces of people she went to high school with, the woman who'd tried to teach her piano, and the officer who'd conducted Quinn's first driving test. And her second. Tonight didn't feel jam-packed to her because she knew these people, almost like an extended family. "Next year it won't seem this way to you."

"Good point. I'll enjoy my anonymity while I have it tonight."

Oh, he didn't have privacy here, but she'd let him hold onto that illusion. Small towns latched onto new faces the way– Wait. Nolan had just confirmed he'd be here next year. Kind of. Excitement bubbled inside her.

"You look much warmer tonight," Gram told him.

He lifted his gloved hand. "Someone left me some knitted gloves."

"And you're still wearing them, even though the pinky fingers are twice as long as they should be. Good man."

"So what's so special about this date?" he asked.

Quinn loved how easy Nolan acted with her grandmother.

Gram pointed to the darkened sky above their

heads. "It's the longest night of the year. Beginning tomorrow, the days will start getting longer, but tonight the dark reigns. So we're all about filling the dark with light. It's been our tradition since the '30s." She glanced toward Quinn. "And before you say anything, no, I hadn't been born yet."

Quinn raised her hands. "I'd never suggest that."

Gram's tree earrings began to swing. "For over eighty years, everyone from Bethany Springs has gathered in the Town Square. We sing, make our wreaths, and then light the tree and gazebo."

Nolan searched the Square. "I hadn't noticed this until you mentioned it, but there are no Christmas lights on. Which is strange, considering how this town is like a second North Pole."

Gram nodded. "Our tradition used to be different. Bethany Springs decked the halls the day after Thanksgiving. That all changed after the crash. Similar to every town back during the depression, money became tight. So the town leadership decided to make the tree lighting a special, but very limited time."

"So we keep the lights on from the longest night of the year to December twenty-sixth, and it's never changed," Quinn added.

"If you hurry, you'll have enough time to make a wreath before the lighting ceremony." Gram kissed her cheek. "I'm going to find Alara. Engagement countdown is coming to a close. Mark my words, tonight's the night."

"You really think Derrick will ask in front of the whole town?"

"It's too romantic not to. The longest night of the year, and wanting to fill the darkness of night with their love. Hey, that's a pretty good line. I might even suggest it to him," she said with a wink. Quinn waved and then Gram faded into the crowd.

"I'm almost afraid to consider this, but would she really suggest a line to Derrick?" Nolan asked.

"Yes. No." Quinn shrugged her shoulder. "Honestly, I don't know. She's just ready to see the six of us settled, even better if it's in Bethany Springs."

"So what's this about building a wreath?" he asked.

She pointed to a large tent striped in red and white. "Under that tent is a high school rite of passage. The juniors staff every one of these tables. Table one, you choose a wreath. Table two, a bow. Table three, decorations, and so on. They divide the proceeds between Special Olympics and the cost of prom. In January, when school starts up again, everyone returns the decorations and stuff to be reused the next year. This way everyone in town gets a new wreath each year, and the kids get an idea about how to run a business while at the same time doing something good for the community."

"Sounds fun," he said, adjusting his long legs to her pace as they headed toward the tent.

"It is. *Now.* Sometimes it could be such a drag when the only thing you wanted to do was hang out with your friends. It's like the principal knew exactly who we shouldn't be paired with so we'd work instead of talk. It could also get so hot in the gym sorting tons of those things. Ready to make a wreath?"

"Where would I put it?" he asked.

"The Berry House hasn't had a wreath on it for years. I believe it's due. Besides, when it comes to wreath building, I'm pretty sure I can take you."

His expression turned skeptical. "You know I'm an artist. People actually pay me to design artwork for them."

"But I have years of experience. Loser has to pay for lunch at Giddings House."

"You set this up," he said, shaking his head. "Whether you win or lose, you're eating some weird kind of toast."

"Grandpa always said to never make a bet you couldn't afford to lose," she told him with a laugh.

"You're on."

"Oh, I should probably warn you. The people you didn't meet while in town the other day, you're going to meet now."

Nolan drew in a deep breath, closed his eyes and sighed. When his lashes fluttered open, she spotted the twinkle in the golden depths. "I've braced myself. I'm ready."

She looped her arm through his and led him through the entrance of the tent. "C'mon. It won't be that bad."

Actually, it turned out to be worse. The scent of pine and resiny smell of plastic filled the tent. They couldn't walk a few yards without someone popping over to say "hi" or to ask about the HOC. But instead of retreating, Nolan took the not-so-subtle attention in stride. Finally, they made it to the wreath line.

"Wow, you even made small talk with people you don't know," she said.

"I'm getting used to it." He pretended to pat his shoulder, but resignation laced his every word.

She hadn't counted on being trapped in line, like mannequins behind store glass.

There were the comments… "So glad you two are reopening the Hardwick."

And the questions…"When will we see the first ornament?"

But the worst… "Introduce us to your new guy, Quinn."

Eventually they stood at the front of the line, and Nolan whipped out his wallet to pay for both their wreaths before she had a chance to dig for some money in her purse. "Thank you," she said, grabbing each of them a wreath. She'd planned to treat him tonight, but by the speed he produced his wallet, Nolan might not let her pay for anything. Luckily she knew the location of the hot chocolate booth. She'd be better prepared to pay for that one.

"You'll have to show me how to do this," he said once they were situated at one of the long rows of tables. Due to the space heaters scattered throughout the tent, they could take their gloves off inside to work.

She lifted a brow. "You're the artist. In fact, weren't you the one challenging me not five minutes ago?"

"I'm kidding you," he said.

They left their wreaths at the table to grab some decorations displayed on several tables in a corner. She carefully eyed all the different bows and bells, and played around with a few themes in her mind. To get her in the mood for her new business, she chose a selection of small colorful balls. Nolan had promised to teach her how to blow glass ball ornaments next. Quinn glanced toward him. He'd grabbed what appeared to be one thing from every bin and theme. He wore a grin like a boy who'd just discovered he could spiral a football.

Cheery Christmas music played and the scents of roasted chestnuts and hot chocolate filled the air as they worked. She kept stealing glances as Nolan constructed his masterpiece. "What do you think?" he asked, finally holding his wreath up for her to see.

His creation struck her as if he'd tried to jam twenty-five years of missed wreath making into his first attempt. She sucked on the bottom of her lip. "Well, uhm…"

"That is a mess," Gram said, sneaking up behind him. "But I think you know that." She patted his shoulder, and Quinn was struck again how well he joked around with Gram. "The kids are about to sing."

Near the gazebo several rows of children were lining up, wearing an assortment of Santa hats, reindeer antlers and elf caps. She waved to her sister Emmaline, who'd been chosen as the announcer for tonight. Her sister did a double take when she noticed

Quinn walking with a man, so Quinn quickened their pace. The last thing she needed was for her sister to draw attention to Quinn's usual single state in front of Nolan. Their parents waited in the area Gram had suggested they meet, along with her Aunt Katherine and Uncle Travis.

Might as well get the introductions out of the way. "Mom, this is Nolan Vesser."

Nolan shook her parents' hands, and her mom greeted him with a big smile. Everyone said Quinn favored her mom. She didn't see it, but hoped she'd inherited her mother's always-friendly smile.

"Please call me Barb. It's so nice to meet you, and at such a great time of year. With a Vesser back, it feels like the season has finally come full circle."

Her dad lifted a brow. "How much work has Quinn piled on you? You know you have the perfect excuse to skip being in your studio. I can always write you a doctor's note. I'm told they hold some weight around here."

Quinn's mouth dropped. "Landon and I asked you at least fifteen times a semester for a doctor's note, but you always said no."

"You were children; that was to build character. If it makes you feel any better, I'll happily write you a note now."

"I'm self-employed," she replied drily. "What good will it do me?"

"Exactly," he said with a wink, then he focused his

trained eye on Nolan. "So what's the verdict on the note?"

The man beside her laughed. "I'm good right now, but she does have me mucking stalls, chasing after horses…"

Her dad flashed him a sympathetic glance. "She gets that from her mother."

Not bothering to deny it, her mom simply rolled her eyes. It warmed her to see how well Nolan fit in with her parents. He didn't seem uneasy, and, fingers crossed, there hadn't been a single awkward moment.

"Oh, look there, Mrs. Dane has taken the stage." Quinn pointed her out in an attempt to prevent her dad from saying anything truly embarrassing. Sometimes a woman had to add action to her finger crossing. She leaned toward Nolan so he could hear her as Landon and her cousin Chloe joined their small group. "Mrs. Dane has been leading the second grade choir for as long as I can remember."

Emmaline stepped to the microphone. Her sister sported a lopsided knit hat that could only have come from Gram. Her long light brown hair curled down her back. "Welcome to Bethany Springs' Longest Night of Light celebration."

"How did Emmaline get chosen to be on stage?" she asked her mom.

"They put names in a hat. I knew as soon as she entered, she'd win. You remember how lucky she is." True, her sister had the wildest luck. She'd won every raffle she entered. Once she answered a wrong number on her cell and ended up getting a job offer.

Her sister waved toward the risers, drawing the attention of the crowd to the children. "To start off our evening, please give a warm welcome to the second grade classes of Bethany Springs Elementary School."

The kids were restless, so excited to be on stage. Some even hopped up and down. After a quick hum through a pitch pipe, Mrs. Dane led the children through a sweet and festive rendition of *Deck the Halls* followed by the junior high bell choir playing, of course, *Jingle Bells*.

"And now Mayor Allen Kingston will welcome light into the night," Emmaline announced.

A man sporting a red and green Christmas tie and suspenders approached the microphone. "Welcome to the Bethany Springs tree lighting ceremony. We're thrilled to have you here with us tonight. Please join us this Saturday for our annual auction and Christmas dance at the Rec Center. Tickets are on sale at the wreath stand and all food trucks. Now, without further ado, count down with me," he invited.

"Three." She and Nolan exchanged a glance, and joined in with the rest of crowd to chant. "Two. One."

Mayor Kingston pressed the button with a flourish and the lights along the gazebo brightened to oohs and ahhs from the children. The star on top of the Christmas tree lit up, followed by the strings that wrapped through the branches.

"Merry Christmas," the mayor called, and the crowd returned the greeting.

The high school band began playing carols and people began to mingle. Her mother turned toward Nolan. "I'm so glad you could join us tonight. It's kind of fun seeing our town and traditions through the eyes of someone else."

"What did you think?" she asked Nolan.

"Pretty cool."

Gram waved her hands. "Now don't put him on the spot, you two. What's he going to say in front of us?"

"I guess it would be hard to beat whale watching and the beach," Quinn added.

"Different, but both are special," he told her, still taking in the sights around him.

Quinn paused to simply enjoy this moment. Seeing the excited faces of children greeting their parents after their performance. The tired teens cleaning up the tent. The clear happiness on her Gram's face as she watched her family gather around. A sadness tugged at her mouth too and Quinn sighed. This would be their first Christmas without Grandpa.

Nolan lightly squeezed her hand, drawing her attention. "I guess what makes a moment something to remember is who you spend it with."

The warmth in his words cast tingles to her heart.

Just then two ladies swooped in. One had short gray hair with green tips, the other had short gray hair with red tips. "Don't mind us, we're going to steal your grandmother. There's some hot chocolate with our name on it."

"See you all Thursday night," Quinn said with a wave. Good. Gram's friends were exactly what she needed.

"Don't forget to get a designated driver," her dad called.

Nolan flashed her a confused look.

Her father clarified. "The Bethany Springs Bed and Breakfast has a hot chocolate bar this time of year, and don't ask me why, but Gram likes hers with a dash of whisky and plenty of marshmallows." He draped his arm over his wife's shoulders and faced Nolan. "We'll be seeing you at Reindeer Ruckus?"

"Wouldn't miss it," Nolan said. "Thanks for inviting me."

"We made our gifts this year." Quinn lifted a hand to tamp down her parents' excited reaction. "Not ornaments."

"Then what?" her mom asked.

"It will have to be a surprise."

"I have early rounds tomorrow. Nolan, good to see you again." Dad bent and gave Quinn a quick hug and Mom kissed her temple.

Quinn and Nolan stood alone, surrounded by shimmering lights and a thinning crowd. Her hand fluttered to her mouth. "Oh, I just realized Gram lost her bet."

"Derrick didn't propose."

"You were right. Gram almost had me convinced,

but you said he wouldn't. You've never even met him, so how'd you know?" she asked.

"A man should take some pride when asking a woman to be his wife. This is a night of little kids and town tradition. That shouldn't be upstaged by a proposal. If Alara is anything like you, she'd feel the same way about Bethany Springs that you do. I doubt either one of you would spend time with a man who didn't understand that about you."

She peered up at him, impressed and yet a little exposed at how well he could read her. "I, uh, guess I'll see you tomorrow morning."

"I'll walk you back to your truck."

After a quick wave to those friends of hers still milling around, she and Nolan weaved through the crowd. "Great job tonight," she called to her sister as they passed the gazebo.

Who's that? her sister mouthed with a lift of her eyebrow.

Please don't. Please don't. Save this silent interrogation for another time.

Cute, her sister added the exact same moment Nolan focused his gaze in the direction where Quinn also looked.

His head snapped back, and he stared straight ahead.

Ugh. He must have witnessed her sister calling him cute. Her body froze. It was Nolan catching her calling him "dreamy" all over again. *Move.* Her muscles unstuck and she forced herself to keep her stride natural and fluid rather than jerky. Or from taking off in a full-on sprint.

She'd parked in one of the large lots behind a row of shops that lined Main Street. They reached for the handle at the same moment, the warmth of his hand closing around hers. She lifted her gaze to him. The night air ruffled his blond hair. Quinn fought the urge to cup his cheek and smooth her thumb over the light stubble along his chin.

Nolan, surrounded by a backdrop of stars, made her heart pound and her knees a little wobbly. How had it happened? How had she felt drawn to him so soon, like she couldn't imagine a day without him so quickly? She'd started to fall the moment he offered to dry the dishes. Then he followed it up by fitting in with her family, his easy manner with Gram, how her horses followed his lead. He'd sealed the deal by facing his fears and trailing her into the workshop to check her safety.

"Quinn, thanks for inviting me tonight," he said.

"I was happy to."

"But you didn't have to share your family with me. Make me feel part of something. Thank you." His voice grew deeper and laced with something she couldn't quite make out. "I'm glad I'm here."

"I'm glad you're here too. Better put your gloves on so your hands won't get cold."

"I guess I never put them back on after the wreath tent, but that reminder's rich coming from someone who always forgets hers," he said with a chuckle. After giving her hand a gentle squeeze, Nolan helped her up into the cab of the truck.

With a final wave, she turned the engine. As she exited the parking lot, she couldn't help peeking at the rearview mirror. Nolan still stood there, watching her drive away.

Chapter Thirteen

Nolan didn't do big families. Or Christmas parties. Correction – he hadn't. Being self-employed, he had the luck of always missing the Christmas office party season. Once his sister had moved off to college, she'd usually spend her break with friends, like this year. He'd grown used to his solitary, no-party and definitely no-tree lifestyle.

Not this year.

He glanced at the woman next to him in the Jeep. Her arrow-straight attention focused on the dial on his radio, as she searched for a station that played something fun and festive. Quinn balanced two brightly wrapped gifts on her lap. The soft strands of a carol floated from his speakers and she straightened. She flashed him a reassuring smile, but his grip around the steering wheel tightened each mile closer to the Hardwick family gathering. He had absolutely zero idea how to act over the next three hours. Hopefully it would be shorter. A lot shorter.

Of course he'd kind of dreaded the Longest Night of Light with her family, and it turned out he'd had a wonderful time. And his wreath rocked. So if this party was even half as fun, he'd be okay.

"My aunt and uncle's house is right down that street," Quinn told him.

For some reason, she wanted to give him directions rather than letting the GPS tell him where to go. The chance of him mishearing and then missing a turn or a street only added to the excitement of the festivities. He flipped his turn signal and pulled onto a residential street dotted with homes decorated with lights, wooden reindeer, and waving inflatable snowmen. Wreaths decked the front doors and glowing luminaries lined the sidewalks. Yeah, nothing in his past holidays had prepared him for this.

"See that haze of light ahead?" Quinn asked.

A bright twinkling glimmer radiated near the end of the street. "Is that…?"

"Yeah, about half a million Christmas lights. Welcome to a Hardwick family Christmas."

Nolan parked across the street and shut off the engine, but sat staring out his window. It might be pitch black outside, but he could probably read a business contract by the glow coming off the house. Clear down to the fine print.

"Wild, right?"

He nodded, taking in the display. Twinkling lights outlined every window, gutter and frame. More lights twined around tree trunks, along the limbs, and draped across every bush. The yard seemed to be some kind of tribute to what would happen if a candy store and the North Pole got married and had a million babies. Along with coordinated music. "I don't think you could even prepare me for this."

Quinn made a scoffing sound and rolled her eyes. "I know, right? Emmaline, Landon and I were so jealous growing up. Dad refuses to play along."

He caught the wistfulness in her tone. "But not jealous now?" he teased.

She shrugged. "I'm a Hardwick. Christmas decs are in my blood, so maybe just a teeny bit. One time my dad painted this sign that said 'Bah Humbug'. It was huge; no one would have been able to miss it. My mom drove up to the house right as he dug a hole for it in the front yard. I think it's the one and only time I've ever seen my mom yell at him."

Nolan couldn't prevent his laugh, and after a moment Quinn joined him. "You're not supposed to laugh. You're supposed to join me in sadness." Her comment only made him laugh harder. He had no doubt that once the HOC was fully up and running, the farmhouse and every outbuilding would be covered in lights.

She bit the corner of her lip. "Believe it or not, it's going to be worse inside."

His fingers twitched, and he had to force himself not to reach for the Jeep keys he'd stowed in his pocket.

Quinn shook her head. "Oh, no. You already made the gift. It's even wrapped."

"I can easily fix that," he said eyeing the packages.

She twisted in her seat to protect the present on her lap. "No way. You're committed."

Committed. Strange how the sound of that didn't feel oppressive. He'd always imagined it would.

She chatted happily beside him as they crossed the street and walked up the sidewalk, sharing a story about a particular yard ornament, and he found himself breathing easier. They'd barely stepped inside the house when one Hardwick took his coat, another confiscated the presents and still another shoved a cold glass at him. Quinn ushered him to a tastefully trimmed Christmas tree, where they stood with a cup of eggnog in each hand, and he tried to remember each person's name.

Holly was draped over the mantel, above a roaring fire. Red and green throw pillows decorated the couch. Quinn's aunt must have raided every store in Bethany Springs because flickering candles adorned each available surface in the room and filled the living area with the festive scents of pine, berry and ginger.

"I thought you said it would be worse inside," he whispered to Quinn. "This is just a tree and some garland. Sure, about a million candles, and the tree brushes the ceiling, but I was prepared for an animatronic Santa or LED light display in here. This is basically…friendly. And warm. Downright merry."

"That almost sounds accusatory." Quinn's warm laugh floated above the din of the room, a sound he grew to like more and more each day. "I meant every member of my family would be gathered. When we're all together, we can be more overwhelming than a dozen inflatable reindeer. Or so I've been told."

A woman with dark curly hair and yet another cup of eggnog zeroed in on them, intent dwelling in her hazel eyes. Quinn hissed in air between her teeth. "Brace yourself. First round."

"That's not reassuring," he told her.

"It's not meant to be," she said with a giggle.

"You must be Nolan," the woman said as she descended upon them. "I missed meeting you at the Night of Light, but I had to work the soundboard. Let me take those glasses and give you a refresher."

He glanced down at the cups in his grip. "I haven't had any yet."

The woman waved her arms. "No matter. Someone else made those. *This* is the eggnog you'll want." She carefully tugged one eggnog mug from his grip and then exchanged her glass for the remaining one in his hand.

"Nolan, this is my aunt, Katherine Hardwick. She's Alara and Silas and Chloe's mom."

Ahhh, the mom of the woman everyone expected to get engaged.

Quinn scanned the crowd. "I don't see Alara and Derrick yet. You think he's proposing now so they can make a big entrance? I think that's Landon's bet."

Katherine wrinkled her nose. "Quinn, I find all this betting on the proposal distasteful." Her stern expression faded. "But my money's on him popping the question at the Christmas Auction and Ball." Her gaze focused to his right. "Oh no. Gram's trying to foist her eggnog on Uncle Joe. So nice to meet you, Nolan."

He examined the cup he held. "What's with the eggnog?"

Quinn closed her eyes for a moment and sighed. "It's a competition. One that goes back decades, and believe me, it can get ugly."

"Over eggnog?"

"Of course. Eggnog is serious stuff."

He examined the creamy concoction in his glass. "I'm not sure I've ever had any before."

Quinn flashed him a look that he expected she'd also wear if he'd stood and announced to the room he spoke fluent Dog. "That's so weird."

He couldn't keep a smile from spreading across his face. "We're standing in a house so bright from the lights, an astronaut in space could use it as a navigation tool."

She covered her mouth with her fingers. "It's not that bad." She leaned in, and he caught the slight honeysuckle scent of her perfume. "Hmm, maybe you have a point. Anyway, about five years ago Grandpa put an end to the judging—"

"Wait a minute, you had actual judging?" he asked, unable to hide his incredulousness.

She nodded. "And a trophy. Aunt Katherine won last, so she's displayed the trophy in her china cabinet for the last several years, which really irks my mom."

Quinn angled her head toward a wooden display case, covered with lights and holly and filled with white china embellished by delicate blue flowers. On the bottom shelf, he spotted the "trophy," but the thing looked more like a yard sale reject with a rickety base that leaned to the side and was spray painted gold. A goblet served as topper, also painted, and swathed in press-on gems and rhinestones.

"Your family once worked to earn that hunk of plastic and glitter, and *I'm* the weird one."

Her shoulders began to shake. "I hadn't realized how many things a person can accept as normal because it's their family. Aunt Katherine might like to rub her win in everyone's face, but Gram is the worst."

"That sweet lady?"

"Man, she really has you fooled. Let's just say, Gram tried to sway the judges by adding a dash of rum."

"That is only a rumor," Gram said, handing him a new glass of eggnog, and taking away Aunt Katherine's award-winning brew. She sported bright jingle bell earrings that tinkled with every move she made.

Quinn reached over and gave Gram's earring a tiny tap. "These are cute."

"The only downside is I can't sneak up on anyone," she said with a wink.

Nolan chuckled, but he doubted the Hardwick matriarch missed much.

"Adding a touch of rum would only make the eggnog that much more authentic. How do you think the drink got its name? From the pirate word of grog. No worries, take a sip, my 'nog is spirit-free."

Nolan brought the glass to his mouth, sniffing the scent of molasses and nutmeg. The cool drink was thick and sweet. "Yum," he said to Gram.

She patted his cheek. "Good boy."

The lilting notes of *Jingle Bells* began to sound through the house. "Did the doorbell play a song?" he asked, as more than one Hardwick focused their attention on the door.

"Yeah, Uncle Travis rigs that up only at Christmas," Quinn said.

"I bet you wanted that in your house too. Any feelings of jealousy?" he asked.

She rolled a loose strand of her hair tight around her finger. "Tons," she confessed.

The front door opened, and in walked a couple. "Oh, there's Derrick and Alara," Quinn said.

Derrick wore that short cut of the military, jogging his memory that one of Quinn's many relatives had mentioned he served in the Air Force. Alara's brown eyes sparkled, but nothing sparkled on her ring finger. Great, now even *he* was speculating on the poor pair and checking for signs of engagement.

Quinn propped her hands on her hips. "See that? Alara lived here. She doesn't need to ring the bell. *I* don't even ring the bell when I drop by Uncle Travis and Aunt Katherine's place. She's only doing that because she knows we never got a Christmas-themed doorbell."

Maybe he should investigate how to replace the farmhouse chime as a gift for Quinn before he left town. Maybe a programmable one so she could change the tune to match every festival of Bethany Springs.

Darkness clouded his thoughts. The idea of leaving Quinn and Bethany Springs weighed heavier in his chest than leaving Pasadena had. No. This party wasn't the time or the place to think about leaving. *But when was?*

A hush fell over every Hardwick as they glanced down at Alara's bare left ring finger. If this room could be a balloon, someone had just popped it with a particularly sharp pin. One by one shoulders slumped and faces drooped. Except the older woman in front of him. She beamed.

"I knew he'd wait until we were gathered together to get on bended knee," Gram said.

Nolan lifted his palm to high five with Quinn's grandmother.

Quinn glanced at him, her eyes wide and her lips trembling with suppressed laughter. "C'mon."

"Where are we going?" he asked.

"We're escaping from my family trying to draw you into Hardwick intrigues for a few minutes."

He followed her to a closed door. She twisted the handle, and past the threshold waited a large kitchen, filled with elementary school-type ceramics and framed handprints. "I don't think I've ever seen a kitchen with a door before."

"Aunt Katherine says open concept houses are for

people without kids. Or dogs. Or unexpected guests. She had this added during a kitchen remodel." She led him to a small dining table in the corner of the kitchen, with an assortment of finger foods, vegetable trays, and platters of fresh fruit spread across the surface.

The door swung open and in burst Alara and Derrick, both laughing like they shared a particularly funny secret. "Oh," Alara said when she caught the two of them. Her spine straightened. Derrick's eyes were tender as he gazed down at her. Nolan suspected it wouldn't be long before the pilot ended the speculation and made the engagement real. They even held hands. Yeah, a real master at deductive reasoning. If he could roll his eyes at himself, he would.

The smile faded from Derrick's face and they dropped hands. But not before they shared another glance. The back of Nolan's neck tingled. He narrowed his eyes and studied the pair. Something seemed... off. Alara crossed the distance to the table to give her cousin a hug in greeting.

Alara waved her arm at her boyfriend. "Derrick, come meet Nolan. He's the genius who's going to save the Hardwick Ornament Company."

His breath hitched in his chest at the introduction. This family did expect him to save the business. Quinn had never really spelled it out as plainly as Alara just had, but there it was. Guilt nagged at him. He shook hands with the off-duty Air Force pilot, but the way Alara built Nolan up felt off too. Like she was trying to direct focus away from them, but neither of them appeared embarrassed at being caught sneaking into the kitchen or exasperated about all the attention directed their way.

Realization struck him like a lightning bolt. The couple knew everyone speculated on when their engagement would take place. Probably even recognized some Hardwicks were making bets. Hmm, that could be a sweet racket, to make bets using another clued-in family member, and then go have a nice dinner at the expense of the nosy relatives.

Nolan's gaze swung to Quinn. Her brown eyes slightly squinted, like she was sizing up her cousin and her boyfriend for clues.

He had to hand it to Derrick and Alara. They were dragging the whole engagement thing out to torture the rest of the family. He should clue in Quinn on his suspicions. The two of them were a team. *A team you plan to break apart as soon as you find another designer and glass blower.*

He hadn't even attempted that search. His earlier good humor drained away. A carrot stick broke between his fingers. Quinn glanced in his direction, flashed him an expression that seemed to ask—*you okay?*—then returned her attention to her cousin. Both of them shrugged as if to say *who knows.*

Having a large family must be so strange. It came with a bunch of complicated, unwritten rules he didn't understand. He mentally wished good luck to Derrick. Why would anyone put themselves though that?

Then his gaze fell on Quinn as she followed the details of a story Derrick and Alara were telling. Quinn's plump lower lip curved in a smile as the story progressed. He loved how quick to laugh she was. How she always included him in every aspect of the HOC and shared her dreams and hopes with him, along with her wild family life.

When he'd agreed to come to Bethany Springs, he'd never imagined ending up in a kitchen at a family Christmas party. Quinn blew him away from the very beginning when he'd found her chasing after a horse, her dark hair tousled by the wind. Tonight she'd twisted her hair into a knot on the top of her head. He'd stood on her porch stunned for an instant when he'd arrived to pick her up and take her to the party. She wore a dress the color of emeralds, rich and elegant. She reminded him of multifaceted glass, continually revealing some new and intriguing detail for him to discover.

No matter what Quinn wore, jeans with a piece of hay in her hair in the barn, pink-cheeked from the cold in her red coat walking beside him on Main Street, or graceful in a vintage dress like tonight, he always found her remarkable. Sometimes he couldn't wait to finish his morning coffee to go seek her out to learn what she planned to do that day. He'd come to resent the sun for setting so early, making him have to head back to the lonely exclusion of the Berry House.

The woman invaded his thoughts. His mouth dried and a chill went down his back. Invaded his thoughts?

What was happening to him? *Look anywhere but her.* Such silly advice. As if him watching her would make his feelings for her grow stronger.

Across from him, Derrick stared at Alara as she shared some tidbit about a time she'd visited Las Vegas. He seemed thunderstruck. Like a man who couldn't wait to spend the rest of his life with the woman he loved. And Nolan had his answer as to why someone put themselves though speculative engagements, betting family members, and the goofiness of the Hardwicks.

Alara finished her story, and he tried to steer the conversation away from anything personal or with heavy emotion. "So, explain to me how this gift exchange will unfold. Something tells me this isn't going to be like any party I've ever attended."

"It's cutthroat, man. These Hardwicks don't mess around," Derrick said, his tone serious, his eyes crinkling in the corners as he tried to hold back a smile.

Alara giggled. "No, we don't. So you don't know about Ruckus?"

He shook his head.

Quinn pretended to appear confused. "But he's the rudest reindeer of all. He's famous worldwide."

"If he's so famous, how come I've never heard of this reindeer?" he asked, teasing her right back.

"Because Santa doesn't put up with being impolite," Quinn explained with her hands on her hips, taking the manner of a teacher in front of an unruly classroom full of first graders.

"Santa thought the reindeer was impolite or that the people talking about a poor woodland creature were ill-mannered?"

Alara snorted.

"Both. Probably." Quinn shook her head as if to get the details of her story straight. "But in this case Santa made Ruckus stay in the stable and miss out on the fun."

"And that's how our parents kept us in line for years," Alara added, shaking her head at the playful sneakiness of their family.

He gave a mock shudder. "I'm afraid to ask how this game is played. Maybe I should check out now."

"Not a chance," Derrick said, "not when there's finally a first-timer."

Quinn eventually took some pity on him. "So, after everyone arrives and the presents are under the tree, then the caller reads out questions, like Most Likely to Leave Their Christmas Lights Up Until Summer."

"Or Who Eats the Most Fruitcake," Alara added. "Then everyone points at the person who most fits that description."

Nolan began to nod. "Hmm, now I get it. It's rude to point."

Quinn snapped her fingers. "That's Reindeer Ruckus. The person with the most 'accusations' gets to choose a gift from under the tree. But there's always one special prize, the last one given – The Ruckus."

"Think of it as the Hardwick family version of Most Valuable Player," Derrick said, as he draped his arm around Alara's shoulders.

"Do I want this prize?" Nolan asked, eyeing the three of them, gauging for truthfulness and deceit.

Gram poked her head into the kitchen, the bells of her earrings tinkling as she moved her head. "Time to play Reindeer Ruckus. Everyone skedaddle."

The four of them ambled toward the door to follow Gram's instructions, Derrick making a flourish of motioning Alara out before him. But Nolan still didn't have his answer. He prevented Quinn from leaving the kitchen with a light tap on her arm. "Do I want to win MVP?"

"Guess you'll have to play to find out," she replied with a wink.

He chuckled at how this woman always seemed to keep him on his toes. He followed Quinn back into the living area. A few more Hardwicks had arrived while he'd holed up in the kitchen. The area was packed and the tree overflowed with gifts.

Quinn's mother, Barb, clapped three quick claps and the room quieted.

"Have I mentioned that my mom teaches second grade?"

"Remember, family," Barb said, "this is your one and only time a Hardwick ever gets to be rude, so make it good, and don't hold back. New rules this year: if you pull out your phone to consult another Hardwick, I get to send a text to anyone in your contacts list—

from your phone. I one hundred percent guarantee what I type will be embarrassing. Also, at the halfway point, we switch it up and point with our elbows."

"Wow, it's like my mom is drunk with power," Quinn whispered to him.

Barb raised her arms like someone waving the flag to signal the start of a drag race. "Let Reindeer Ruckus commence."

A small cheer rose up around him. This family was *into* the game. He hadn't realized how much Quinn looked like her mom, both with their round faces and dark brown eyes.

Quinn's mom plopped her reading glasses on the end of her nose and started to read the first of a clump of lined index cards. "First question. Who's the bossiest when building snowmen?"

The question met with several good-natured laughs and a few points toward Gram, but Nolan practically guffawed as the majority aimed their finger in Quinn's direction. Yeah, he could believe it.

"Well, that's really unfair," she said with a heavy sigh, but a smile graced her face. "Actually, no one in this family can follow instructions. You have to get a little loud."

"I don't think you're doing yourself any good there, honey," Barb called.

Quinn crossed to the Christmas tree, her family members cheering her on. "For that, I'll pick the biggest package under the tree."

With a dramatic flair, she did indeed grab the

largest gift. He watched as she unwrapped her chosen package to reveal a red-leafed poinsettia. Her smile widened and Nolan knew she loved the present. Was she overplaying her hand? Acting like she loved the plant so some other family member might be tempted? "Can people steal?" he asked.

"No, we tried that a couple of years ago, but it made the game go on too long," Alara's sister Chloe told him. She worked in Boston as a reporter. They'd first met at The Giddings House. Yeah, he was starting to know who was who.

Why are you working at this when you'll be leaving soon?

"When you finally get to be rude to your cousin, no game is long enough," a man called, a new arrival Nolan hadn't met yet.

"And that loudmouth is Quinn's brother Landon," Chloe told him.

Nolan immediately went on alert. Protective older brother or the laid-back, accepting kind of brother? Nolan's money was on protective. Dressed more formally in dress slacks and oxford shirt, no way was this guy laid-back. Although he had rolled up his sleeves.

And why did he care what kind of brother Landon was to Quinn? Nolan wasn't dating her. He'd be out of Bethany Springs as soon as… *You have no timeframe because you've avoided making one.*

Barb cleared her throat and addressed the family. "Zip it, lock it, put it in your pocket."

Nolan laughed because this was the first time he'd been told that as an adult. Quinn brushed his shoulder with hers. "Imagine living your whole life with a second grade teacher and hearing her say these rhyming instructions over and over."

"Next question. When it comes to eggnog, who'd forget you were family and go for the win?" Barb asked the family.

This time every single one of the accusations were unanimous and all in Gram's direction. Even his.

"What? But everyone loves my 'nog," she told them with a bright smile, her large jingle bell earrings tinkling as she walked to the tree. She chose Quinn's gift. Beside him, Quinn stiffened as she watched her grandmother rip off the paper. The brightly colored paperweight fell into the older woman's hand.

Gram cocked her head to one side as she studied the blown glass. She lifted it toward the chandelier and the many colors suspended inside the smoothed clear glass caught the light and sparkled. "Oh, this is so pretty. I want to hear the story."

"I made it with my newly acquired glass-blowing skills," Quinn said, her voice a little hesitant.

Nolan knew how thrilled Quinn had been with her handmade gift as they created it together, but debuting it here, among her family with their one-time-a-year permission to be rude had her rethinking her decision. But her parents leaned in to give her creation a better examination.

"That's lovely, honey," Barb said, but Quinn

didn't appear reassured. After all, her mother taught elementary school and was used to giving praise for effort alone. He opened his mouth to say how wonderful the paperweight was when Quinn's younger sister Emmaline spoke up.

"Hey, that's great, sis."

"Cool," Alara said.

Gram glanced between Quinn and Nolan, her eyes narrowed a bit, and Quinn gave her the tiniest nod. "Glad to hear you've got the workshop up and running," Gram said, the bells at her ears emphasizing her words with a jingle.

Why did he have the oddest feeling he'd just missed something between Quinn and her grandmother?

"Okay, people, listen and silent have the same letters for a reason," Barb called over the Hardwicks as they drifted into dozens of different conversations. "Next question – the person who only scans for cash in their Christmas cards."

"Without a doubt, my cousin Landon," Chloe said. Apparently the rest of the family agreed because he won with the most accusations.

"I'll remember this indignity when you conveniently forget your wallet and it's time to cash out your tabs next time we're out in Boston," he quipped.

Emmaline, Quinn's youngest sister, won with The Person Who Could Name Every Single Reindeer Pulling Santa's Sleigh.

Chloe won with Who Would Have To Drive Back To The House To Check That The Christmas Lights

Were Unplugged. And then go back a second time to double check the first checking.

"The person who never sends a thank you note," Barb announced.

Alara won that round, but Derrick cleared his throat. "Let me pick your gift."

Katherine Hardwick gasped and tugged her phone from her pocket so she could film a potential proposal.

"I should take that phone, Kat, but you get a pass this time," Barb said. The two women clasped hands, clearly friends and not only sisters-in-law.

"You think he's hidden a ring box under the tree?" Quinn asked Nolan as she scanned the presents.

"I don't see him proposing like that," he whispered back to her as he shook his head.

Derrick proved him right as he chose the present Nolan had brought to the party, and presented it to Alara with a bit of bravado. Katherine gasped, and Nolan realized Quinn's aunt had no idea the package was his gift.

Alara opened the present with a smile, slowly peeling back the clear tape on the wrapping paper, careful not to rip the colorful decorative wrap. The crowd nearly lost its collective cool as she unhurriedly smoothed back layer after layer of tissue paper, but there were audible groans as she showed the crowd the paperweight he'd made. Nolan didn't take their displeasure personally.

Derrick spoke above the restless murmurs of her family. "I saw how much you liked the one your grandmother opened. It's about the same size and shape as the present Quinn donated, so I'd *betted* the one in the same paper was Nolan's and probably the same thing."

Alara cupped her boyfriend's chin and kissed his cheek. "Such a smart guy. What great deductive reasoning." The discarded wrapping paper drifted to the floor and Derrick crouched down on bended knee.

Anticipation hung heavy in the air. Round two.

He crumpled the paper into a tight ball and stood. "Don't want to litter." Then Derrick and Alara shared a secret smile.

Yeah, those two were hamming it up and drawing out the family's expectant agony.

Quinn leaned toward Nolan, and he caught a touch of her inviting honeysuckle scent again. "I'm beginning to think those two are messing with us."

"I think you're onto something."

The rest of the presents were distributed with good-natured allegations and defenses, and soon all the wrapped gifts were gone. Only he waited empty-handed. No one had accused him of anything. Of course, no one here really knew him.

Barb raised an arm, and slowly everyone else in the room raised theirs as they fell silent. "Hocus-pocus, time to focus. And now for our final gift of the night – the Ruckus prize. Okay, fam, who here is most likely to regret attending a Hardwick Christmas Party?"

Every fingertip pointed at him.

Nolan had to laugh at his own naiveté. The

Hardwicks might be loud and boisterous and large, but they wouldn't have forgotten him. He'd been welcomed and included the moment he stepped foot in Bethany Springs. And right on schedule, round two of guilt blasted him. Or was that the third?

Quinn's grandmother presented him with his gift, one that hadn't been under the tree, which explained why he'd first thought he'd been forgotten. He carefully set the heavy box on a coffee table decorated with a dozen candles. Everyone in the room watched as he tore away at the brightly-wrapped packaging to reveal a wooden box, aged by time along with dozens of nicks and scratches.

"I can't wait to see what's inside." Quinn's voice was hushed and excited, and his own anticipation grew.

But Nolan already knew they'd find nothing inside. The box wasn't a container; it turned out to be *the* gift. He unlatched the clasp holding the top and bottom together and carefully separated the two pieces to reveal the hollowed inside. "It's a mold we use in glass blowing. This is where the molten glass goes."

"Look at the lettering on the side of the box," Quinn's grandmother suggested.

Someone had long ago burned "MV" into the side. Exactly like the wall in the workshop back at Quinn's farm. His relative apparently had a quirk about marking what belonged to him.

"For Milos Vesser?" Quinn asked, and her Gram nodded.

"How does it feel to have held a piece of your own history in your hands?" Gram asked.

"Kind of incredible."

This had been his great-great-grandfather's. Created by Milos Vesser's own sweat and brilliance. And now he owned this piece of history. His throat tightened, and he fought off a rush of almost overwhelming nostalgia and exhilaration. Nolan had never considered himself a sentimental guy. After losing every picture and memento in the fire that destroyed his shop, he now gripped something that linked him to parts of the past he thought he'd never hold again.

"Can you tell what it is?" Quinn asked.

He traced the inside of the cast, worn by the heat of molten glass. "It looks like a... heart."

"The Hardwick heart," Gram confirmed.

The heart inspired by Natalia and Roland's love that Quinn had shared with him around the campfire a few days ago. If he'd kissed her then...

He forced his attention to the gift and not to what could have happened. This mold would be as important to Quinn's family as it was to him. Gram gifting him with a prize so important to their shared history touched him. *She gave it to you because she thinks you're going to hang around and build something special in Bethany Springs.* He didn't know what official guilt round he'd entered, but it hit him like a left hook.

The Hardwicks liked and included him, and accepting their easy friendships along with their gifts made him uneasy. He'd never really intended to hurt or deceive anyone, but he also couldn't ignore the wrongness of the situation. A situation he'd created, and now had to fix.

"They had steel back then; why would they make their molds out of wood?" Derrick asked. "I'd think red-hot glass would catch it on fire."

Nolan traced the scorched block, any jagged edges from carving by hand long burned away. "It damaged the wood for sure, but you could still cast quite a few ornaments out of something like this. Wood is cheap, and good to use when you're experimenting on a design. Once perfected, then you make the mold out of something like graphite."

"Think you could use this mold still?" Gram asked.

He eyed the two pieces with a skeptical eye. Some parts of the wood appeared warped from water, while others were brittle from being left in a dry attic. He shook his head. "No. A little charring in a mold is expected, but this one has had a lot of use, so most of the finer details are lost."

"But you could still use it for inspiration?" Gram asked, her voice hopeful. His answer was important to her.

He nodded, glad he wouldn't be disappointing her. "Absolutely." In fact, his fingers almost itched to break open the carving tools Quinn had ordered off the internet and begin working up his own mold. That would mean staying here. Remaining with Quinn rather than finding another designer to take his place.

The rightness of the idea stunned him.

"This could really mean something if you give it a chance," Quinn's grandmother said, her hazel eyes direct. Her meaning went beyond the glass mold in his hands.

Nolan wasn't ready to think what his time with Quinn and being part of her family could mean. Could do to him.

Gram straightened and gave him a comforting pat on the shoulder. "Excellent. Because I entered the first ornament from the new Hardwick Ornament Company into the charity auction to benefit the recreation center in Bethany Springs."

Now he understood. The older woman never intended her pat to his shoulder to comfort, but to fortify. Toughening him up for this new bombshell she'd just dropped. "Oh, but—"

"Gram, that's Christmas Eve," Quinn protested. "As in two days away."

She flashed him a grin filled with pride, but also a challenge. "Then I guess you'd better get to work."

Chapter Fourteen

Lulubelle greeted Nolan with a happy neigh as he and Quinn emerged from his Jeep. They'd both been silent on the return trip to the farm, lost in thought and trying not to panic. At least she tried not to panic. Nolan appeared nowhere near panic mode. If anything, the harsh lines of his face could pass for a solid block of wood. Like the mold now stowed on the backseat. He gave away nothing.

She followed him to the fence where Lulubelle waited for her nightly scratch behind the ears from him. "The vet said she'd bond with her caregiver. I sort of expected it to be me," she teased. Not that she blamed the horse. Nolan rocked Quinn's world too.

"Maybe it's because you called her Lulubelle," he said, opening the gate to the paddock. Lulubelle accompanied him to the barn. The man didn't even have to coax her with the sweet carrots she loved so much.

"Hold the phone. Lulubelle is a perfectly respectable horse name," she defended.

He made a scoffing sound. "It's a cow name. Everyone knows that."

Quinn couldn't contain her laugh. His pretend animal-name expertise struck her as kind of cute. "Oh, is it now? What would you name her instead?"

"Maybe something fierce and strong like Racer."

"More like Chaser," she scoffed.

"No, that'd be you."

Quinn groaned, because he might be right.

Maribelle turned to trail after them. Inside the stable, they both worked together to ready the horses for the long night. When had this easy camaraderie between them developed? Shocking, since she'd only known the man a couple of weeks. They acted almost seamlessly together, and soon both horses were tucked in their stalls with fresh hay and water. With their nightly chores done, they left the barn to be greeted by a delightful canopy of stars. The bright full moon invited them to slow their steps and stroll. Even though they had a lot of work to do, Quinn hated for this night to end.

How was she supposed to hide her excitement at being with Nolan? He sent her heartbeat racing. Of course, the chance to design and build and create with him also made her breath catch and the blood race in her veins. She'd finally found the confidence in herself to back up all her dreams.

The way that sleigh ride ended should've

extinguished any feelings toward him. And yet here they paused in the middle of the clearing to stare up at the sky. Could he be as reluctant for their time together to end? It was both of them, right? Quinn needed not to be alone in this situation. Just one glance… a single word…

"I can't believe how big and bright the moon is tonight," he said.

"Gram calls it the Yule Moon, nature's way of extending the time for people to be with one another before electricity and the invention of streetlights."

Somehow, they both broke their gaze away from the moon at the same time. The moonlight gifted her with enough light to spot promise in his golden eyes. And conflict. Did he want to take advantage of the Yule Moon's light too?

"How come you knew Derrick wouldn't want to propose in front of the family tonight?" she finally asked.

"I didn't. Not really. A proposal…that's the real deal. You're giving the woman you want to spend the rest of your life with a glimpse at your future together, so you've got to bring your A game. Not that sharing everything with family isn't the way to go, but I'd…"

Quinn tried not to stare as the muscles of his neck worked. Would he tell her his ideal proposal? Revealing his vision to her felt so personal. Raw, even.

He lifted his head and gazed at the full moon once more. "I'd take the woman I loved to our favorite place together. There, I'd reach for her hand and tell her I can't imagine the rest of my life without her in it."

Her heart began to race. "That sounds…" She searched for the right word. Amazing? Perfect?

"It's late, and tomorrow we'll have to decide on something to enter into the auction," he said, already rotating toward his Jeep.

Her hammering heart slowed at his abrupt change of subject. Her cheeks heated. Did he fear he'd given her some kind of false hope? Had her breathless response revealed her wishes? She schooled her features to appear nice and bland.

"I have dozens of ideas I've sketched in my notebook. I'll pore through those tonight and see what's workable," she said, aiming for a casual tone.

"Good idea. I took some photos of my dad's scrapbook. I'll pull up the pictures on my phone. Between the two of us, there might be something we can use." He snapped his fingers like he remembered something. "I'll grab that poinsettia for you."

They stepped across the clearing to his truck, where he fished out the plant from the back, the wooden mold sitting beside the flowerpot. Quinn caught the barest hint of his cologne, a verdant scent of rich earth and wood smoke.

"I don't think I've seen a poinsettia this big before," he said, transferring the plastic base into her hands.

The bright red leaves stretched high, completely blocking her face. Even if she'd been overcome with some silly notion to kiss him, the stupid flower blocked her lips. *Saved by the plant.*

Nolan laughed. "You able to see through the foliage?"

"I think I'll make it." He didn't shadow her up the steps to the porch of the farmhouse; instead he leaned against the banister, waiting to watch her step inside.

She set the poinsettia on the stoop, and then shook her clutch to make her house keys jingle. After fishing them from the bottom of her purse, she turned to tell Nolan good night. Framed in moonlight, his sandy blond hair tousled by the light winter breeze, he made her breath hitch in her chest. *Don't fall for him.*

Might be too late.

"Thanks for coming tonight," she finally said.

"Wouldn't have missed it," he replied. He readjusted the mold in his hands.

Her eyes narrowed on the block of wood. Gram expected a lot from them. Maybe too much. "You know, I can always call the auction coordinator and ask to have our name removed from the lineup."

Nolan glanced down at the mold he held. "Another cousin?"

She shook her head. "No, but I did go to high school with Abbie, so I can finagle a favor from her."

"Growing up in a small town must've been wild, but it does have its perks."

She laughed. "That's the problem. You could never be wild. Someone would've told."

His fingers drummed along the scarred edge of the mold, then gripped the side. "Don't call her. Not yet."

A flicker of hope and excitement lodged in her chest. "Okay. Good night, Nolan."

"'Night."

She closed the door behind her and leaned against the wall, knowing the man outside wouldn't turn away until he'd seen her safely inside her home.

Nolan stood staring at Quinn's closed door. What had he wanted? For her to invite him inside? Offer him the coffee he knew she didn't drink?

Well…yes.

He'd never seen anything more breathtaking than Quinn Hardwick bathed in moonlight. Nolan had never wanted anything like he had wanted to draw Quinn into his arms. To hold her close. To finally discover for himself the softness of her lips.

Gloom clawed in his gut.

Secrets blocked his path toward her. Secrets and a deed. Oh, he'd asked his sister to hold off on filing any paperwork, but was that enough? He could only imagine how Kaylee would react when he asked her to redraw the ownership paperwork. For sure, there'd be some dismay that he would throw away the opportunity to own a business again and the potential of some profit. Maybe she'd be satisfied that she'd guessed he'd grown interested in the rightful owner of the HOC despite her warning not to fall for Quinn.

He pivoted on his heel and stalked to the Berry House. The star on the top of the little Christmas tree Quinn had placed near the window caught the light of the moon and twinkled. The ornaments he'd bought in town improved the looks of the thing, but every day more of the fake needles fell to the hardwood floor. After he unlocked the bunkhouse, he plunked the mold onto the kitchen table and stared at it, tracing his fingers along the ridges and grooves Milos Vesser had carved into the wood decades before.

Nolan owned the Hardwick Ornament Company, but the business wasn't really his. And yet it was the reason why he never followed up on reaching for Quinn's hand. His mouth opened and closed and his stomach pitched as the realization hit him. His ownership of the HOC prevented him from drawing her beside him under the starlight, even when every part of him longed to hold her. The lurking guilt he hadn't worked through before had saved him from making that mistake.

He had no right to kiss her, touch her cheek, or explore the growing affection he felt for her. To probe the excited way his heart jumped in his chest when she smiled at him and her eyes lit up as he entered a room. And he certainly had no business discovering if her feelings for him grew, too.

Before he'd only asked his sister not to act on the paperwork, but he should've requested she draw up a contract returning the deed of the HOC fully to Quinn Hardwick. As if his ownership had never even existed. An urgent need seized him. Return the business to her. No waiting to file the paperwork later, no selling it back eventually. *Now.*

His shoulders sagged in relief. The Hardwick Ornament Company was only ever Quinn's. Something inside him always knew, which explained the ever-present guilt and dread he'd felt. After digging his phone from his pocket, Nolan dialed his sister's number. It was late, but she lived a couple time zones behind him.

Like every other attempt he'd made to call her near the farm, static and dead air plagued the connection. Her number only rang a few times then went straight to voicemail. Of course, she'd already flown to Colorado. Between his terrible connection out at the farm and hers in the mountains, he might never make contact with her until after Christmas.

He left a quick message for his sister of his intentions. Of course she wouldn't be able to do anything until she made it back to Pasadena, but his ownership was officially over. At least in his mind. His signature would follow as soon as the holiday passed. He smiled down at the mold, still touched by Gram's gift to him. He left the fire in the past. With the deed forgotten, he could finally lose himself in creating something special for Quinn. For the Hardwick Ornament Company.

He rapped his knuckles on the lid of the mold. He couldn't wait until tomorrow; he'd get to work creating the first ornament of the new company now.

He flipped on the coffeemaker Quinn had bought him to help him work long into the night, but he almost didn't need the jolt from the caffeine.

With mug in hand, he headed over to the workshop. Although he was a long way from doing actual glasswork—he still had a lot of designing to do—Nolan went through his ritual of checking the temperature on the furnace. His tools waited for him against the wall and moonlight streamed through the windows Quinn had so painstakingly cleaned. This may be his studio, but she'd stamped her influence everywhere. From the pictures and framed catalogue posters on the wall, to his memory of Quinn sharing her dreams for the company.

He smiled as he pried apart the mold and grabbed his sketchpad. Her gram was right: time to get to work. He rubbed his fingers along the inside of the mold. The sides weren't smooth, but had swirls and lines. If there'd been a pattern to the designs in the glass, he couldn't detect it from the worn mold. Nolan made a note to ask Quinn if she had access to one of the original ornaments, as he'd really like to examine his ancestor's finished product.

He turned the page on the design pad Quinn had bought for him weeks ago, and dove into sketching.

The scent of cranberry bread finally broke his concentration. Quinn stood beside him, offering a plate of the homemade treat. "Thought you could use a snack."

His stomach rumbled and he accepted the dish. "I got so caught up in drafting my ideas, I lost track of time. How'd you know I was out here?"

"I saw the light on. I couldn't sleep either, so I decided to bake."

"I'm glad you did. This smells delicious," he said, breaking off a corner of the bread and taking a bite.

"You've been out here for hours. I didn't know if I should disturb you or not."

He glanced up at the clock. Wow, he really had been lost in his creations. "For the record, you can always interrupt me."

"Good to know," she said, her voice light and happy. He'd helped to give her that smile, put some of that joy etched in the soft lines of her face. The idea of taking away even a few of her burdens of running this place filled him with satisfaction.

"This is good." His eyes closed as he savored the taste. "I thought you didn't like cranberry bread."

"But I know you like it," she said.

Warmth blasted the center of his chest. He couldn't tear his gaze away from Quinn as she bent her head to study his sketchpad. "Mind if I take a look?"

"Only if you want to see a bunch of rejects. I don't have it right yet," he told her with a shrug. But he would.

She pointed at one of his notes. "Does this say cranberry glass?"

He nodded. "Ever heard of it?"

"No, but I'm so intrigued."

"Artisans have played around with it for eons, but it didn't really come into fashion until the seventeenth century. They call it cranberry glass because the colors are so similar. It's one of the ideas I've been toying around with. Something about tying two traditions of your farm together."

She propped her chin on her hands. "Ornaments and cranberries. Tell me more."

Nolan had to force himself to look away from her deep brown eyes. "Since I know you're one for stories, legend has it that cranberry glass first originated when a noble tossed his last gold coin into molten glass."

She lifted her eyebrows, and lines crossed her forehead. "Wait. Why would he throw his last coin into molten glass?"

"I don't know, the story never mentions that." He opened his mouth to finish his tale, but Quinn lifted her finger.

"And is there a place where there's molten glass lying around? And if you have one gold coin, could you trade that in for a lot of smaller non-gold ones? I have a lot of questions about this legend of yours, Nolan."

His shoulders began to shake. "It's not my legend. It's been around for a while."

"The beginning is solid. I like it, but we need to fill in some details for sure."

"You can't just make up legends."

Quinn shrugged. "Sure you can. Someone had to make up the Big Bad Wolf once upon a time."

He rubbed his chin. "Can't argue with that logic. Now I won't feel bad when I tell you the legend doesn't make much sense anyway, because the gold has to be added to something called aqua regia first before going into the molten glass."

"Hmmm, aqua regia. That sounds cool."

"It means royal water," he added.

"Even better. People are especially intrigued if there's a royal element."

"But really aqua regia is basic chemistry, and the technique has been around since the Romans."

She tapped the tabletop as she thought. "Hmm, now I could do something with that tidbit. I've got gold and royal water and ancient times. This is all workable stuff, Nolan. Well done."

"We just need the actual gold to make it."

Her eyes widened. "Oh, like real *real* gold. I kind of hoped with that basic chemistry talk from a moment ago that maybe we could use something that *acted* like gold."

"Hate to break it to you, but people have been looking for something to act like gold for centuries without much luck."

"Good point. Okay, I guess we should table this plan until we have a pile of gold and some royalty," she said, her tone teasing and light.

"So next year then?" he joked.

"There's the spirit." Her gaze fell away and her

smile faded. She played with the edge of his sketchpad. "You have ideas in there for, uh…next year?"

His muscles tensed briefly, then he felt himself relax as heat spread from his chest, down his arms and to his fingertips. He reached for his sketchpad to show her his designs, but instead his fingers found hers. Twined together. The softness of her hands against his calloused palm intrigued him.

"Yes," he told her and suddenly a feeling of rightness flooded him. The fire. Finding the deed. If he hadn't lost it all… Tragedy had led Nolan to this moment. To her.

She flashed him a smile filled with relief and excitement. A light flush touched her cheeks, and she gave his hand a gentle squeeze. "I, uh… guess I better let you get back to work." She scooped up his empty plate and rushed out of the workshop, pausing for a second to offer him a smile that made his pulse kick up.

Nolan knew he must be giving her a ridiculous smile in return, but he no longer cared. While he'd only known her for such a short amount of time, now he couldn't ever imagine her not being part of his life. Something struck him. This marked the first time she'd left him alone first. He felt his grin droop into a frown. Not that he cared to take a deep dive into his feelings, but he hated this sensation. Had Quinn felt this same way each time he'd escaped when emotion came into play?

Nolan strolled to the table and opened to a clean

page in the sketchpad. He started with the outline of a heart, smooth and elegant, but with a hint of a medieval flair to it. A way to tie in the twenty-first century to the past.

Nolan almost laughed at his full-force excitement to create. At the thrill he thought he'd lost as he stood in a smoke-filled parking lot in California. After choosing a solid piece of cherry wood, he used a saw to cut the mold in half, and then a lathe to hollow out the center.

Time to break open the woodworking tools Quinn had bought for him. In the past, he'd dreaded the long hours the painstaking detail work required. Necessary steps he must take in order to get to the fun part – the glass blowing. Except now he reveled in every part of creating.

As he carved, he experienced the first stirring of connection to his old self. He could also envision the possibility of a new future with Quinn.

By the end of the night, he had a fully-crafted mold, and was ready to fire his first ornament. *Their* first ornament.

Chapter Fifteen

Quinn gasped when she found Nolan slumped over the worktable the next morning, using his jacket as a pillow. The chain for the wedding ring around his neck poked out of his shirt. The sharp scent of sawdust hung in the air, and he'd left carving tools scattered around.

So Nolan Vesser was messy as he worked. Good to know.

She'd only planned to pop into the workshop this morning to take a peek at Nolan's designs, but the man had barely stirred as she'd closed the door behind her. Should she wake him? A thin layer of stubble covered his cheeks and chin and he wore the same shirt as last night. Poor man, he must have pulled an all-nighter. Sleep. She should definitely let him sleep.

But wouldn't he be more comfortable in the Berry House? His back slouched at a weird angle, and sleeping on the hard stool with his steel-toed work boots on couldn't be comfortable. She lightly tapped his shoulder. "Nolan."

He awoke with a start, his golden eyes filled with confusion. He blinked a few times, stretched, then tackled her heart with a lazy smile she felt to the tips of her toes. "Good morning," he said, his voice still heavy with sleep but filled with satisfaction.

"Did you finish the design?" she asked.

He stood, towering over her, delightfully sleep-rumpled. "Better than that. The mold is done."

"What? Really?" She scanned the table anxious to discover everything he'd done. "Where is it?"

He pointed to a large tub where two wooden blocks waited inside, fully submerged in water. "The wood has to soak up the water for a few hours before I can blow the glass. That way it won't catch on fire."

"So you can start today? We'll make the auction with time to spare." She felt so excited she could dance. No, that could wait for the night of the auction. Maybe even with Nolan. "I can't believe you did all this overnight."

His eyes softened and his gaze met hers. "I was inspired."

Her chest swelled and hope bubbled up inside her. Maybe her feelings for him weren't completely one-sided. "How much longer do we have to wait?"

His brows drew together; his eyes grew confused, then cleared. "Oh, you mean before I can blow the glass. Another hour."

"I can't wait to start."

Nolan rubbed at his chin. "I… this first casting, I want to do alone."

"Oh." Her shoulders slumped. No way could she mask the disappointment on her face. Nope. At least she now knew the answer. Her feelings were definitely one-sided.

He stepped toward her. "Quinn, it's because I want to surprise you. I want to look at your face the first time you see a Hardwick Ornament for a new generation."

Emotion swelled inside her chest, and she had to be flashing him some kind of goofy smile. She'd never been able to hide her emotions. Concealment wasn't the Hardwick style. Well, maybe Landon's style.

While she'd love to work beside Nolan on the ornament, she understood his need to present it to her completed and not a mid-way mess. As if this man could ever create anything that wasn't stunning.

"Okay. I need to run into town anyway to find some supplies to decorate our booth for the auction."

The corners of his lips curved in a grin, and she fled the workshop before she did something really embarrassing like ask him to stay forever. After grabbing the keys to the truck and her purse from the farmhouse, she left for Bethany Springs. She'd told Nolan the truth, she did need some supplies, but she aimed the truck in the direction of Landon's law office instead of heading to the general store.

Watching Nolan work with glass as they'd made the paperweights and discovering him last night sketching and carving, Quinn knew, felt it in her bones, that her wild idea of restarting the Hardwick Ornament Company would succeed. She felt confident enough to make it official. Her fear of failure had kept her from registering the company earlier, but she was done being afraid when it came to her dreams and hopes.

At the first stoplight, she texted her brother to let him know she was on her way. Then she stopped at Jitters, Bethany Springs' new coffee shop—her brother's requirement for an early meeting.

He'd rented space in an area of town everyone referred to as ProRow; made sense, considering the businesses in this area were in a long line of renovated row houses. In two stories and a mix of brick and clapboard, the citizens of Bethany Springs could take care of all their law, real estate, and accounting needs in one convenient location.

Landon greeted her with a grumpy smile. Ah, so he was in a good mood. If she'd entered this world a dreamer, her older brother arrived a realist to the core. The man was a doer, pragmatic and stoic, but always passionate about justice and the law. He'd even volunteered to review all the contracts for the auction tomorrow night. She shoved the coffee cup into his hand.

"I'm ready," she announced, pride lacing her words.

"Ready for what?" he asked, as he took the cup of coffee. Black. No sugar, no milk, no foam or any of the millions of things people seemed to add to the bitter brew to make it palatable.

"To officially file the paperwo—oh, that's your idea of a joke. You've only been asking me when I'll be ready to file since I came up with the bizarre idea of restarting the old family business."

He winked, and with a sigh she followed him down the hall to his office, a bag of cranberry muffins she'd purchased at Jitters in hand. Quinn paused to leave one of the sweet treats on Janet's desk. Everyone with the last name of Hardwick appreciated the receptionist. Landon had gone through four before Gram had suggested the woman who'd finally taken over the management of her brother's office. A friend of their grandmother's, Janet wasn't quite ready to retire, and there were zero circumstances where Quinn's gruff brother intimidated the woman.

Landon collapsed in the large executive office chair behind his desk. His fingers traced across the track pad to wake his computer. "You know these forms are online. You didn't have to come in."

She stopped herself from rolling her eyes just in time. "There's something very anti-climactic about downloading forms and scanning them. I want to grab a number in some bureaucratic office, stand in line while watching the clock and have someone stamp my form in person."

"I think you're the only one, ever."

"Well, the internet at the farmhouse is the worst," she pointed out.

A reluctant smile tugged at her brother's lips. "Now that makes sense."

Quinn plopped down in one of the smaller chairs in front of his desk. He typed behind the large desk carved from a deep, rich cherry wood. She'd been shocked when he'd ordered the expensive piece of furniture, but Landon had insisted people wouldn't trust a lawyer who didn't appear like a success. She had to hand it to him; the room impressed. His framed degrees decorated the wall behind him, along with several tasteful, although thoroughly bland, original paintings of geometric designs. The décor radiated slick lines and sophistication. No personal snapshots or playful little doodads littered the top of his credenza. Only a few potted plants softened the office, due, Quinn was sure, to Janet's touch. Still the leaves held no hint of brown. Clearly they were too afraid to wilt.

Quinn figured the paperwork would take about an hour or so, and then she could pop over to The Junk Drawer for the ribbon she needed. If she didn't lose herself in the craft store and only marched down the ribbons aisle instead of browsing all the rows of fun stuff, she'd have enough money left over to treat Gram and Landon to something at the Giddings House before she left Bethany Springs. That should give Nolan plenty of time to finish up the ornament and she wouldn't ruin his surprise. She bounced in her seat like an excited six-year-old, and Landon flashed her a look.

She forced herself to settle down, and then with a mental shake, she whipped out her phone. Landon had top notch WiFi. Why hadn't she been taking advantage of it and catching up with her friends?

"Hmm," her brother said a few minutes later.

She straightened in her chair. She recognized that *hmm*. Had lived with it all her life. That was not a good *hmm*. "What's wrong?"

Landon's lips were pursed. "This can't be right. I'm going to run this inquiry again."

She scooted to the end of her seat and gripped the edge of his desk. "Landon, tell me what's wrong."

"There's something wonky with the ownership of the Hardwick Ornament Company."

Her shoulders relaxed. "Oh, well the will was clear. Is this whole mess because of a probate thing?"

He shook his head. "No; according to this, you're not the owner. No one in our family is, and it's been that way for decades."

She rose to her feet. "What? That makes no sense."

"We'll get to the bottom of this," her brother said. He gave her no false reassurance, in full professional lawyer mode right now.

Landon crossed to a filing cabinet, tugged open the bottom drawer and lifted out a large box. The cardboard appeared worn and a bit beaten up and resembled the boxes Gram had brought down from her attic. This one was marked "Legal Stuff" instead of "Catalogues and Pictures" like the boxes she and Nolan had unpacked.

"What's that?" she asked her brother.

"It's all the legal paperwork from before the

Hardwick Ornament Company closed. Most of it could all be shredded, leases and agreements with other companies long since gone. Janet screened everything and scanned the important documents. This box has the stuff she thought I should take another look at, but I put it aside since you weren't ready to tackle the paperwork yet. I'm sorry, I probably should have sorted through this sooner."

Quinn waved her hand. "Don't beat yourself up over this. I wasn't in any hurry myself to get the ball rolling." Being honest with herself, filing the paperwork would have made her dreams all the more real. If the company crashed, her failure would be in black and white and documented forever.

Landon pulled out a specific file. It landed on his desk with a slap, and he launched into sifting through the papers. The pages were yellowed, and clearly typed on a manual typewriter. After locating a specific document, her brother ran his index finger down the columns of text, his eyes squinting as he read. His face paled as he paused on a passage in the document. "Here it is."

His gaze met hers, his eyes bleak. Quinn braced herself for what she'd hear.

"This is the original agreement between Nathanial Hardwick and Milos Vesser. It states here that if continuous operation of the Hardwick Ornament Company is not maintained, the Vesser family will be deeded with the ownership."

Her hands wrung together. “But Grandpa left me the company.”

“He probably didn’t know of this provision. None of us did.”

Did Nolan know about the details behind her ownership—er, lack of ownership of the HOC? No, of course he hadn’t, because he would have mentioned that detail long ago.

“This isn’t usual contract language, more like a private agreement between two friends,” he said, tapping his finger against his desk.

“No Vesser has ever taken ownership in all these years, so it must not have been important to them, either.” She hated the desperation in her voice. Why did it sound like she was grasping at straws? Probably because she was.

Landon angled his head toward the computer. “That’s just it. A Vesser has.”

He pointed to the screen and she read the name where he’d indicated. Nolan Vesser.

Every molecule of air left her lungs in a whoosh.

“Wh—”

She swallowed and tried again. If he’d filed years ago, that was understandable. He took ownership of a company that was rightfully his. Sure, he shouldn’t have been keeping a secret from her, but… She had to know.

“When did he file?”

“A week ago. According to this, he owns the workshop and storefront on the farm, the business name and a few other odds and ends.” If her brain could not register Landon's words, the dark tone of his voice relayed all the information she needed to know.

The flames that she'd thought had taken everything away from him, had really taken everything away from her.

She gripped the armrests of the chair as Landon's printer churned out a copy of the paperwork.

Nolan had lied to her. He'd been lying to her all along. But why? It made no sense. If he owned the HOC, knew it when they'd first discussed him coming here to design, why had he never said anything? Why all the secrecy? All those days together, talking and eating and planning, and he'd never thought to say one word…even after they'd almost kissed? Had it all been some kind of game?

Quinn surged to her feet as she blinked back tears. She tucked away the copy Landon handed her. "Okay, thanks, Landon. I'll let you get back to your job."

"Sis, stay. Let's—"

She cut him off with an overly bright smile. "No, I'm good. I need to, uh…"

"If you're going back to the farmhouse to confront him, you shouldn't do it alone. I have an appointment in an hour, but I can go with you after that. Maybe Janet can work her magic on my schedule."

She smoothed out a wrinkle in her pants. "No, don't worry about it. I'm sure this is some weird fluke. Thanks for your help."

Quinn turned on her heel and fled her brother's office before she started sobbing. She felt stiff and her legs wooden as she walked down the sidewalk to the small parking area the businesses on ProRow shared. She almost lost her battle at beating back the tears when she spotted her reflection in the window of her truck. The skin across her neck and cheeks stretched tight. Her jaw jutted forward in an effort to keep her chin from wobbling. But it was her eyes, swimming in unshed tears, that really battered her resolve.

She leaned against the side of her truck, despite the farm dust and mud caked to the side. Quinn slowly dragged in breath after breath, holding the air in her lungs for a beat before exhaling. By the third inhale, she'd won the battle against any further waterworks. By the sixth, the muscles in her neck relaxed and she no longer had to worry she might whimper.

With a cool calm, she unlocked her truck and slid behind the wheel. She couldn't drive if she was a mess. Denial and betrayal warred within her as she drove the return route to the farm. Give him a chance. Let him explain.

But he'd had nearly a month to explain. How could he? How could he listen to her talk about her dreams? Watch her spend money she didn't have? Nearly kiss her after she'd told the story of Roland and Natalia, while all along knowing he owned the Hardwick Ornament Company? How could he spend an evening under the roof with dozens of Hardwicks, laugh and break bread the same week he filed to take their company away?

The timing struck her as weird. If he'd wanted the HOC, why not take her company long before now?

No, the HOC is his company. Remember that. The Hardwick Ornament Company isn't yours. It never was.

Anger began to bubble inside her only to be numbed by betrayal, hurt, and her unspoken feelings for Nolan. Feelings that were crushed now. But none of those emotions stopped her from charging toward the workshop.

Quinn shook her hands loose outside the door. No, cool was the answer here. She needed to chase away that spark of adrenaline. To drive back the shock and outrage now imbued in every thought and muscle and cell of her body.

The soft sounds of Nolan humming floated to her ears. Hours ago, she would've found that habit charming, and fresh anger surged through her that she could possibly find anything about him charming.

She braced her shoulder against the frame of the workshop door as she dragged several breaths in through her nose and deliberately out her mouth. Her once-racing heartbeat slowed down and Quinn knew she could face him. Finally.

Heat wafted against her skin the moment she stepped inside, and she felt her skin flush. Nolan had finally used the furnace without prodding from her. A furnace she'd paid for. For a company she no longer owned. Nope. Had never owned, and he'd known that and let her do it anyway.

Tension, confusion and betrayal hit her chest like

a punch, as if the pressure hadn't liked being tamed only minutes ago and opted now to punish her with a double dose of strain and anger. Cool and collected was overrated anyway.

Quinn felt so foolish. She might as well have given him everything with a pretty red bow. Her dreams. Her business. Her hea— No. *Don't go there.*

Nolan edged around the side of the kiln. His warm smile welcomed Quinn, like he was happy to see her. To share with her.

She sniffed away the first stage of crying. *Be strong.*

"Perfect timing," he told her. "I just put the ornament in the kiln to cool. I need a shower and some sleep, and maybe not in that order. But tonight, I want to take you out to dinner to celebrate."

Celebrate? Celebrate that everything she worked for and dreamed about, he owned?

Nolan reached for her hand and spun her in a circle, and the sunlight glinted off his father's ring as they revolved. Joy softened his lips, and his laugh would have been infectious. This morning she would have joined in his playfulness. "Stop," she said, her tone brittle and without a hint of uncertainty.

Nolan immediately straightened, and his hands fell to his sides. His smile faded as his golden eyes searched hers. "What's wrong?"

She tugged a folded piece of paper from her back pocket and handed him the copy of the business paperwork he'd filed. Quinn studied his face as he began to read, his eyes widening…in surprise? Yeah, sure.

"Quinn, I…" he began, and then his words trailed away.

"Why?"

His gaze bored into hers for the briefest of time and then dropped to the paper he still held. "I don't understand how this happened." Confusion punctuated his words.

Quinn crossed her arms against her chest and nodded toward the evidence of his cruelty. "You filed the paperwork."

"My sister must have."

"Did you tell her to?" Quinn needed him to confirm it. Hope still burned somewhere deep inside her. An errant kind of faith that he would tell her his name as owner of the Hardwick Ornament Company must be some kind of mistake. She needed him to kill that hope inside her.

"I did at first—"

Quinn turned on her heel and aimed toward the exit.

"Quinn, wait. Please."

The deep emotion coating the word please halted her steps.

She pivoted to confront him head on. Quinn examined his eyes and his face, searching for signs of the man she'd grown to trust. To care for. Only the man before her held himself tall and rigid.

"I need to understand what's going on. Why did

you never say anything this whole time? How could you watch me day after day, and not utter a word? Nolan, help me understand." Her last words were barely a whisper.

"When I first arrived, I didn't know you. Had zero concept of what the HOC meant to you. With my life on hold, I thought I'd come out here and check out the place. No one in my family had ever mentioned we owned it."

"But you saw how much money I'd spent. Celebrated with me when I got the loan. How could you do that?" she asked.

He raked his fingers through his hair. "I figured I would buy you out when my insurance money came through—no harm, no foul. But, Quinn, you gotta believe me, everything changed after I saw you come out of the bank. That afternoon, I called my sister and told her I didn't want her to file the paperwork for this place."

Quinn wanted to believe him, with everything inside her. But he'd let her believe a falsehood for too long. "Why did you never tell me any of this?"

"By the time I realized how deep in I was, it seemed too late. I thought we were building something here together." Although his arms still remained at his sides, his hands jerked in her direction. Beseeching, almost. "I didn't want the deed to the HOC to come between us."

"I thought we were building something too. You were constructing secrets. That deed would've never come between us if you'd told me about it."

He rubbed at his chin; that sign of frustration she'd once thought charming. Quinn had believed she'd known this man, but she'd been so wrong.

"I told myself there was never the right opportunity," he finally said. "But I knew that was just an excuse. I'd let it go on too long and I tried to avoid having you think of me the way you are now. The day you told me of the loan changed everything for me. The way you looked at me—no one has ever looked at me that way. I decided to try to fix it, because I didn't want you to *not* look at me that way again."

"Fix it? How?"

"I called my sister and asked her to pull any claim we had off the database. You know how awful cell connection is out here. My words must have been garbled or cut off when I talked to Kaylee. She's acting as my lawyer." He scrubbed a hand over the back of his neck. "I should have made the call in town. I should have double-checked how I wanted her to handle the paperwork. I should have… I should have done a lot of things."

Quinn wanted to believe him. She tugged her keys from her pocket. "Then let's drive into town now. You can call her and get this whole mess straightened out now."

"Kaylee's left for vacation. She won't be able to handle anything until after Christmas."

And like that… hope died once more. Quinn hadn't even realized it had flared up again. Of all the plagues tucked in mythological Pandora's box, hope proved to be the worst.

"Quinn, I never meant—"

She shook her head. The last few minutes had sapped the remaining strength from her body. Weariness drained her spirit, and she only wanted to walk away from Nolan as quickly as her legs would take her. "No. I don't want to hear another excuse or explanation from you. Except..."

"Except what? Anything, Quinn."

"Just answer two questions for me."

His Adam's apple bobbed in his throat, but he gave her a tight nod.

"When you emailed me, and I offered you a job here, you already knew the Hardwick Ornament Company belonged to you and not me."

His hands fisted at his sides, his shoulders tight. "Yes."

"And that night we took the sleigh ride together, you'd already told your sister about filing the company as yours?"

He nodded. "Yes, but not in the way you think."

She lifted a hand to interrupt his words. "Then I guess that's all you need to say."

Quinn rotated on her heel ready to leave. *Please don't let me break down in front of him.* She'd give him her company and her dreams, but she wouldn't give him her tears.

"Quinn, wait. Please."

Frustration swamped her. She'd reached the exit,

even had the handle in her hand, but she hadn't fully made her escape. "No," she said, her voice cracking, but she no longer cared if he witnessed her tears or heard her voice break. Let him know how much he'd hurt her. There was nothing wrong with dreams and caring about things and hurting when someone you trusted hurt you.

"No," she said again, her voice stronger, but Quinn still couldn't turn around. "According to the documents Landon found, this workshop, the company name and any original design concepts belong to you. Since you aren't likely to find anyplace so close to Christmas, you can stay at the Berry House until the twenty-sixth. I know you're waiting on the insurance money, but afterward, I expect you to pay me back for the furnace and kiln and the supplies in the workshop since I've sunk everything I own into that."

She slipped out of the workshop before he said anything. Her pace quickened with each step toward the farmhouse. Only a few more steps. She fumbled with the lock, but soon she stood inside the sanctuary of her home. She leaned a hand against the wall, drew in a shuddering breath and finally allowed the tears to freely fall.

Chapter Sixteen

It took every bit of Nolan's strength not to run after Quinn. Watching her leave without trying to explain further might have been the biggest mistake he'd ever made, but he'd never seen Quinn fragile before. She'd stood before him, her face splotchy and her eyes brimming with tears. It gutted him that he'd caused her so much pain, especially when he'd only ever wanted to make her happy. See her smile. Design and dream and work beside her.

Quinn's accusations rang true. He should never have kept the secret from her in the first place. He'd wanted nothing more than to draw her into his arms and comfort her. To tell her he was falling for her. No, he wasn't falling; he'd fallen. Nolan had been a goner since the night of the sleigh ride when she'd shared Roland and Natalia's story. He'd just completed a heart that represented their love. And his. For Quinn.

Losing his shop and his home had wrecked his plans, but watching Quinn walk away from him wrecked his life. Unlike the fire, this time he'd created the damage to himself. Each step she took away from him tore at his heart.

His sister must have filed the paperwork on his behalf before she'd left for her vacation. The awful cell connection must have garbled his words as he'd spoken. Nolan tried to remember what he'd said to his sister that afternoon. Yes, if even a few of his words dropped, she could have gotten the complete opposite of his intentions. He wanted to smack his own forehead. That important of a call should have been made in town. And afterward he should have double-checked how he wanted her to handle the paperwork. He should—

He should have done a lot of things. Nolan had tried to play the "none the wiser" game with Quinn and the deed but ended up making the situation worse. Maybe irreparable. He'd messed up by not being open and honest.

The same as Roland, and the real reason he hadn't chased after Quinn. She'd never believe anything he said now. Just as Natalia hadn't believed, words never meant much when actions didn't match. He was kidding himself if he thought his biggest mistake was in not going after her. No, he'd blown it from the beginning by not being fully open about his ownership of the company.

But how could he make her believe that almost from the moment he'd stepped onto Quinn's farm, he'd thought of the Hardwick Ornament Company as theirs, not his? How could he prove to Quinn, and the rest of the Hardwicks, that he'd not only grown to love Quinn, but felt like part of their close-knit family?

The sight of the bright Yule Moon, the sound of the sleigh bells around Maribelle and Lulubelle's necks, the taste of Quinn's cranberry bread. These memories were part of him now.

His gaze fell to Milos's heart mold. The patterns in the swirls were indistinguishable to him, but there had been a reason his great-great-grandfather had taken the time to add those details rather than fashioning the ornament with simple smooth glass. Meaning lay in the outlines. Something important to the man. His art, the creation he'd shared came from a place deep in his soul. But what was the importance Milos wanted to reveal?

Nolan drummed his fingers on the table, gazing out at the waning sun. He pushed his chair away and started to pace, stopping only when he'd come to the very spot his relative had once stood and left his initials on the wall. The man had left his mark. Nolan dug a permanent marker from his pocket and added his own initials on the wall. A vow to himself that he would fix his mistakes and work to rebuild the trust he'd lost.

He stared at the original initials and his newly added ones. *Added.* That was the key. Nolan shook his head as he realized he'd placed too much importance on the lost elements. The pattern had never been the lesson. Imbuing his own meaning into the ornament he designed now held the message. Inspiration burned through him. His fingers itched to draw.

Nolan rushed to the table, reached for his sketchpad and tore out a new page. Using Milos Vesser's original design for a starting point, Nolan added his own unique spin. Within an hour, he had a working heart design on the page.

The heart in the kiln was worthy of any tree, but not the design Quinn deserved. Despite the ache in his back from working almost the whole night through, Nolan grabbed another block of cherry wood.

Quinn hated sleeping on her brother's couch. Of course, there'd been no way she would have bunked at her parents' house. No, she should have kicked Nolan off the farm. She couldn't possibly sleep there with him also on the property. Although technically he owned the workshop.

For tonight she'd developed a simple plan: Try to fade into the auction and Christmas Eve Ball tonight and just as quickly fade out. The silk of her gown whispered as she parked the truck outside the rec center. How optimistic she had been when she'd selected this vintage dress in Utter Clutter. Now she felt ridiculous in the stunning black and white number, complete with long black gloves. More for style than function; she'd almost not bothered with the gloves, but right now they hid the nails she'd neglected since walking out on Nolan.

According to Emmaline, no man was worth a bad manicure. Her sister was right, of course, but rather than visiting the nail shop, she had instead pored over every piece of paperwork she and Landon could locate, searching for a loophole.

No escape clause existed.

Nolan tried to call, and even texted her when she wouldn't answer the phone. She began dreading her cell, clearing any messages and eventually blocking his number. Probably childish, but she felt too raw and exposed to speak with the man she'd very nearly given her heart to.

After Christmas. She'd tackle everything then. The business and her feelings for Nolan could all wait until after the twenty-fifth.

The evening chill began to bite in the cab of her truck, and Quinn knew she had to go inside. Laughter and music drifted toward her as she stepped out of the truck and smoothed down the layers of her skirt. She'd been dreading this event. Had tried every excuse she could think of to get out of attending the auction for the recreation center, but Gram would have none of it.

Tonight was supposed to be the special moment she and Nolan unveiled the first ornament that would launch the new Hardwick Ornament Company. Instead, she'd had to inform the organizers of the auction there'd be no entry.

She dodged a few puddles in the parking lot until she made it to the safety of the sidewalk. Once inside, Quinn spotted Landon first. Not one for parties, he focused his attention on some of the auction displays. But her big brother immediately came to her side the moment he noticed her, which made her heart swell. Reserved he may be, but Landon knew she'd need him to get through this auction and ball.

"Say the word, and we're out of here," he told her, and Quinn couldn't help but laugh.

"Gram would never let us hear the end of it if we didn't stay at least thirty minutes," she replied.

Landon played with something on his watch. "Thirty minutes it is."

"Did you just set a timer? Never mind. Deal."

In the distance, she spotted a familiar blond head. Nolan hadn't spotted her yet, and she drank him in unobserved. Why did she always have to notice him? Be drawn to him? In profile only, he looked amazing in a tux. Why had he come here tonight?

"I don't know," Landon said.

"Didn't realize I'd grumbled that out loud."

"Even if you hadn't, your body language would have given it away," her brother said, his tone dry. He aimed angry looks in Nolan's direction.

"Do I strike you as wound up?" she asked, a bit alarmed.

"Like a spring," he confirmed.

She chanced another glance in Nolan's direction, now noticing the tenseness of his shoulders and the way his fingers tightly curled around the auction program. Was he nervous? *Good.*

Quinn shook out her hands and willed the strain

from her shoulders. She plastered on a smile. "Better?" she asked, because the last way she wanted to appear before Nolan was anxious and on edge.

Landon chuckled. "Marginally."

"I hadn't spotted his Jeep outside the Berry House when I picked up my dress. I thought he'd left for good. Grr, I hoped I wouldn't be camping on your couch another night."

"He dropped off the key to the Berry House at my office this morning, so my guess is he's staying in a hotel. Quinn, I hate to be so blunt, but if he hasn't left town yet, he might intend to keep his claim. I know he told you he'd take care of the paperwork after Christmas, but you must prepare yourself that he won't."

The muscles in her cheek twitched, and she felt her fake smile wavering. The thought of seeing him in Bethany Springs…

"When someone hurts you, why doesn't it kill the feelings you have for them too?" she asked.

"Afraid it doesn't work that way. Gram's heading over here. Perk up."

She and Landon had decided not to tell the rest of the family about the transfer of ownership of HOC until after Christmas. No sense in ruining everyone's holiday. Just their new year.

"Landon, Quinn. How are my two favorite grandchildren?" Gram asked as she neared. Today's Christmas vest resembled something like a patchwork quilt, but her earrings stole the show. From one ear dangled a red tree light bulb, and from the other a green one. Both flashed, and not in sync.

Landon bent and kissed her cheek. "We can't all be your favorite."

"Of course you can. I have six grandchildren and each one of you is my favorite." Gram turned her attention to Quinn. "Honey, you look lovely, but it's a party. You need a little more bling. I had to buy two packs of these earrings. Can you believe they'll only sell them by the color? I've stashed the other two somewhere in my purse."

"Earrings come in packs?" Landon asked, trying to draw the focus away from Quinn.

Gram flashed him an exasperated glare, although she knew he teased her. "The good ones do. Be nice or I'll introduce you to Jennifer Wade's granddaughter when the dancing starts."

The color drained from Landon's face. Gram knew how to make good on a threat. Jenny Wade was nice enough, but he avoided anything that even sounded like a fix-up. Especially after Gram had "tricked" him into going to the town's first-ever speed dating night. Thirty "dates" in one evening had almost broken him.

"Found them." Gram gripped Quinn's arm and placed the earrings in her palm. "There's a little button on the back that makes them blink."

"Thanks, Gram."

"You can put them on as we walk to your booth. I love the color scheme you chose. So festive."

"Booth?"

"For your auction ornament."

"But there shouldn't be... I told them yesterday that..."

But Gram wasn't paying attention. She gripped Quinn by the hand and tugged, weaving a path through the crowd. She drew Quinn to an elegant table draped in a delicate mint fabric and surrounded by dozens and dozens of beautiful old-fashioned Christmas lights. She'd been positive she'd alerted the auction staff of her cancellation; she had very decisively marked a line through the task on her to-do list.

"I almost had a tear when I read that sign," Gram said, pointing to a small placard tucked in the folds of the fabric. "'Donated by the Hardwick Ornament Company' has a wonderful ring to it. Your grandpa would be so proud."

Seeing the joy in Gram's face, her pride... It felt like a dozen cuts to Quinn's heart.

"Hey, kiddo." Quinn turned to see her mom and dad. Both smiling, and clearly so pleased. She gave them both a quick hug. Any longer and she might begin to cry.

Barbara Hardwick kissed her temple then sized up the display. "I can't believe you and Nolan got the ornament done. I was a little dubious of Gram's plan, but she said the deadline would spur you on."

"And I was right," her grandmother proclaimed.

"It's good to see the name of our company sponsoring things again," her dad told her, beaming with pride.

Quinn's stomach clenched. Not their company anymore. Nolan's. How had this happened? Who had set up this display? Who wrote out that placard?

"Any chance I can get a peek under that cloth?" Gram asked.

Quinn spotted the drape covering a box she hadn't noticed earlier. Someone had donated something for the charity auction. But what? Who? Her family expected the unveiling of the latest Hardwick ornament. A new beginning for the next generation. They'd be so disappointed. Honestly, she didn't think this evening could get worse, and then it had.

She caught Landon's gaze and felt a small sense of relief. He must have given the organizers something from their personal stash of old Hardwick ornaments. She flashed him a grateful smile, but he only shrugged and shook his head. Her sister joined the small throng surrounding the booth, followed by Chloe, her aunt and uncle, Derrick, and a still-ringless Alara. Nolan happened to be right again.

Quinn had a lot of things to be irritated with Nolan about, but this moment, standing with her family while they awaited the "unveiling" of something new and special, was the worst.

Quinn took a step backwards. And another.

But why should she be the one fading into the background? She'd done nothing wrong. Come to think of it, why should she give up on her dream to create a new ornament company? So Nolan owned the Hardwick name—Quinn would create a new one. He owned the workshop—Bethany Springs offered plenty of warehouse space. Somewhere along the way, she'd forgotten something really important. All this—the booth, the ornament—all came to be here because *she'd* had the dream. *She'd* been the catalyst. *She'd* put everything in motion. So Nolan no longer factored in the equation. So what? She'd found him; she'd find another glass blower.

Quinn took a deep breath and straightened her back. She did have a lot to be proud of, and next year the auction would feature one of her designs from her new ornament company.

Mayor Kingston approached the Hardwick booth carrying a portable microphone and sporting a different Christmas tree bowtie from the one he'd worn to the Longest Night of Light celebration. The organizers had opted to conduct the auction by traveling from booth to booth in order for potential patrons to mingle. While it made for a tighter squeeze, next year she'd appreciate more eyes on her creations.

Mayor Kingston lifted his arm, and the crowd gathering around quieted. "Next up, the first ornament from the new Hardwick Ornament Company."

Quinn scrunched her eyes tight and dragged a deep breath to drown out the mayor's booming voice. The mayor's wife removed the drape with a flourish and the crowd gasped. "I present to you the Firelight Heart."

The roiling in her stomach stopped. Her muscles seized. She had studied decades of Hardwick Ornament catalogues, and there'd never been one called the Firelight Heart. Quinn blinked her eyes open, but the crowd standing between her place against the wall and booth blocked her view.

She stood on her tiptoes, but that didn't help. After taking a deep breath, she weaved her way through the gaps between patrons. The red of the ornament struck her first, but the color was subtle, like the hue of a ripe cranberry. Delicate raised ribs covered the entire ornament, adding to its beauty. Only as she peered closer at the glass did she spot the patterns tucked in the raised areas.

To anyone else, the ribbing would appear as simply swirls, a pretty addition to blown glass. But Quinn saw the outline of a Yule Moon. The shape of a jingle bell like the one around the necks of her horses on the night of their sleigh ride. She even found a smaller heart. A heart like the one from a story of a man trying to prove his love. The judges gathered around the ornament might never notice the patterns, but she knew Nolan had forged this heart with touches of their shared times together.

The mayor prepared to read off the description card. "'The Firelight Heart is inspired by the flames of love and the belief that everlasting happiness comes from work rather than luck.' Oh, we have Quinn Hardwick here, the young woman who has worked tirelessly to revitalize the Hardwick Ornament Company. Quinn, based on the reaction of the crowd, your first ornament is a hit."

The mayor directed the microphone toward her face. She spotted Nolan's familiar golden-brown eyes and sandy blond head. Her heart surged inside her chest. His eyes met hers, and a myriad of emotions flared in his gaze. Regret, sadness, and finally hope. He'd been the one to set up the booth and donate the ornament. The placard clearly said Hardwick, not Vesser. And that gorgeous, amazing ornament declared what meant most to him—his time with her.

"Quinn, tell us what inspired your first ornament?" Mayor Kingston asked.

"Love," she said, her gaze never leaving Nolan's.

Blinking back happy tears, Quinn watched as Nolan bolted toward the display. He extended his palm to her and she placed her hand in his. As her family began to advance, he sidestepped the group and led her to a more private area.

"Nolan. That ornament you created it's… incredible. So beautiful."

"*I* didn't create that. At least not alone. The Firelight Heart and what the ornament means and represents is something we created together." He gathered her hands in his. "I know I should have told you about the deed right from the beginning, and I'm sorry. I'll tell you 'sorry' every day, if that's what it takes. I want to go on creating ornaments, a company, and a life together. If you'll have me."

She gasped. "Nolan Vesser, did you propose to me in a crowded room surrounded by family?"

He appeared a little stunned, and lost his light grip

around her hands. "I guess I did," he said, his lips parted and his eyes dazed. But not one hint of regret burned in his gaze.

"Whatever happened to your favorite place?"

"Quinn, wherever you are, *that's* my favorite place."

She drew her hands to her chest, but remembered her earlier pain. "You know, you don't get off the hook that easily. No secrets between us. Ever."

"Never," he vowed, and she knew from his vehemence Nolan never would.

"I loved the color of the glass you chose. It's funny—in all the renditions of a Hardwick Heart, not one of them was ever red. That's cranberry glass, isn't it? But what did you use to make it?"

"I used my father's ring," he said.

Quinn gasped, and her gaze flew to the chain around Nolan's neck. It no longer hung there. A harsh bolt slammed through her body. "Nolan, how could… I know how important his ring was to you. It's one of the few things you had left of him."

Nolan shook his head. "No, I have something much more important from him. I have what he taught me. To blow glass. To create. To love." He gathered her hand in his. "I want to use all that to create a legacy. With you."

She blinked back tears. "I do too."

He flashed her a rueful smile. "Since we're not keeping secrets, Dad's ring made enough aqua regia for two ornaments. The one auctioned just now and this one. Merry Christmas, Quinn."

He presented her with a hand carved box, and when she lifted the lid another ornament, identical to the one auctioned away only a few moments ago, rested in a cushion of fabric. "This is *your* ornament." Made from the gold of his father's ring. His only connection to his mom and dad, melted to make a new tradition for them.

Quinn hugged the box tight to her chest. "Ours."

The clearing of a throat broke them apart. Derrick and Alara stood next to them, grinning ear to ear. "Guess we have to scratch this off as a place where I'll ask you to marry me," Derrick said.

"Now I know, Derrick Hamill, you weren't going to propose to me at the rec center."

"Why not? It's where we snuck our first kiss."

Alara rolled her eyes and the two of them walked away after offering them a quick congratulations.

"You ready for this?" Quinn asked, indicating her family.

"Always up to the challenge."

The Christmas morning snow fell in gentle flakes and Nolan wondered if his Southern California side would ever get used to the sight. Or the cold. He glanced over his shoulder where Quinn fiddled with a string of lights on the tree. She faced him and smiled. A smile only for him. His heart slammed in his chest. Now that was one thing he could get used to. For the rest of his life. He shuddered at how he'd almost lost it all.

"You finally satisfied?" he asked, as she stepped away from the tree and examined her work.

"Almost." She pulled from her pocket the red and green bulb earrings Gram had given her at the auction last night. She settled each one on a branch and pressed the buttons on the back so they'd flash. "Now it's perfect."

"Almost," he said echoing her from earlier. Nolan handed her the box where their first ornament rested. Working together, they placed the ornament on their first tree as a couple. He put his arm around her shoulders as they stared at the beginnings of what they'd build in the future.

Quinn crouched and retrieved a large, flat gift she'd left for him under the tree once she'd verified the paint had dried.

"I thought we weren't going to open gifts until tonight," he said.

She shifted her balance from foot to foot, her impatience clear. "I can't wait. And you'd better rip that paper off fast. I almost knocked on the Berry House at five this morning to wake you up so you could open it."

"Okay," he said, laughing. As instructed, he tore off the thick wrapping paper to discover a hand-painted sign for the Hardwick Vesser Ornament Company.

"I made that last night after the auction. I repurposed some wood from the old storefront. Past and present. Yours and mine," she said, her voice solemn and filled with wonder and promise.

"I love you," he told her.

Quinn, the woman who'd soon be his wife, lifted to her tiptoes. "I love you too," she said against his lips, and he kissed her.

The End

Cranberry-Walnut Bread with Orange Glaze

A Hallmark Original Recipe

In *At the Heart of Christmas*, Nolan stays up late one night designing a very special ornament. Quinn brings him freshly-baked cranberry bread, because she knows it's his favorite. It goes perfectly with either a cup of tea (Quinn's beverage of choice) or coffee (the drink Nolan can't live without.)

Yield: 1 loaf (12 servings)
Prep Time: 15 minutes
Bake Time: 75 minutes

INGREDIENTS

Cranberry-Walnut Bread:

- 1½ cups all-purpose flour
- 1 cup granulated sugar
- 1 teaspoon baking powder
- ½ teaspoon kosher salt
- 2 eggs, large
- ¾ cup buttermilk
- ½ cup vegetable oil
- 1 tablespoon fresh squeezed orange juice
- ½ teaspoon vanilla extract
- 1 cup fresh cranberries
- ½ cup walnut pieces, toasted
- zest of 1 orange

Orange Glaze:

- 1 cup confectioner's sugar
- 2 tablespoons milk
- zest of 1 orange

DIRECTIONS

1. To prepare cranberry-walnut bread: preheat oven to 350°F. Lightly grease an 8 ½ x 4 ½-inch loaf pan.

2. Whisk together flour, sugar, baking powder and salt in a large bowl.
3. In a medium-sized bowl, lightly whisk eggs; add buttermilk, oil, orange juice and vanilla extract; whisk to blend. Pour over dry ingredients and mix just until combined.
4. Fold in cranberries, walnuts and orange zest. Pour batter into prepared loaf pan.
5. Bake for 60 minutes; cover loosely with foil and bake an additional 10 to 15 minutes, or until a toothpick inserted in bread comes out clean. Transfer loaf pan to a rack and cool for 15 minutes. Carefully remove loaf from pan and cool completely on rack.
6. To prepare orange glaze: in a small bowl, combine confectioner's sugar and milk and whisk until smooth. Add orange zest and whisk to blend. Drizzle orange glaze over cooled cranberry-walnut bread.

About The Author

Jill Monroe is the international bestselling author of over fifteen novels and novellas. Her books are available across the globe and one has been adapted for the small screen. When not writing, Jill makes her home in Oklahoma with her husband, enjoys daily walks with her dog Zoey, texting with her two daughters who are away at college and collecting fabric for items she'll sew poorly.

Thanks so much for reading *At the Heart of Christmas*. We hope you enjoyed it!

You might like these other books
from Hallmark Publishing:

A Timeless Christmas
The Christmas Company
Christmas in Evergreen
A Christmas to Remember
A Heavenly Christmas
Love You Like Christmas
Christmas in Homestead
Journey Back to Christmas